A Darkly Shining Star

An Oxford Murder Mystery

Bridget Hart Book 5

M S MORRIS

Published by Landmark Media, a division of Landmark Internet Ltd.

msmorrisbooks.com

ISBN-13: 978-1-914537-08-0

CHAPTER 1

'Ladies and gentlemen! Are you brave? Are you fearless? Are you of stout heart and sound mind?'

Bridget tucked her hand in the crook of Jonathan's arm and pulled him close as the penetrating gaze of the ghost tour guide fell on her. For an unnerving moment she felt as if he was seeing into the darkest corner of her soul, not somewhere she cared to look herself too often. But then his gaze moved on and one by one he scanned the rest of the group, some of whom giggled nervously, and Bridget realised that he was just a good actor with the sort of stage presence that captivated an audience. The people on the tour nodded and confirmed that they were indeed brave and fearless. Everyone was in the mood to play along.

'What about you?' asked the guide, singling out a girl of about ten or eleven who was there with her parents and older brother.

'I'm not afraid of ghosts,' said the girl in a loud, clear voice that made everyone laugh.

'Splendid!' The guide clapped his hands together. 'Then I invite you all to come with me on a tour of

Oxford's darkest, creepiest, most haunted corners. Let us discover the murder, mayhem and madness that lies within this ancient city! Let us unearth ghouls, ghosts, wraiths and spectres!' And with a theatrical flourish of his black cloak he beckoned everyone to follow him into Turl Street.

Jonathan leaned close to whisper in Bridget's ear. 'Which cemetery has this guy sprung from? There must be a grave lying empty somewhere.'

'Behave yourself,' giggled Bridget. It was true though. The guide, who went by the unlikely name of Gordon Goole, did have a cadaverous look about him. Tall and angular, with hollow cheeks, hooded eyes and a prominent Roman nose, he was everyone's idea of a Victorian undertaker in his long, black cloak and top hat. His gaunt features were enhanced with a layer of pale make-up and, Bridget suspected, a touch of black eye-liner. 'Come on, we're being left behind.'

She and Jonathan had spent the afternoon at the Christmas Market on Broad Street, going from stall to stall examining carved wooden ornaments, scented candles, homemade pickles and handwoven scarves as the smells of cinnamon, roasting chestnuts and French crêpes vied for her attention. She chose some unusual handcrafted jewellery for her sister Vanessa and some natural skincare products for her daughter Chloe. For her niece and nephew, Florence and Toby, she found some traditional wooden puzzles and board games that she felt sure would meet with Vanessa's approval. To keep out the December chill they enjoyed a glass (or two) of tangy mulled cider, and Bridget wasn't able to resist the lure of freshly-fried churros dunked in thick hot chocolate. It wouldn't do her figure any good, but who cared? It was nearly Christmas, and over the next few days her calorie intake would go through the roof anyway, so one doughnut hardly mattered. Well, all right, two doughnuts.

It had been a spur of the moment decision to join the ghost tour which was about to set off from near the old-fashioned carousel. Bridget had been sorely tempted by the brightly-painted carousel but feared she would struggle to climb on and off the wooden horses and still maintain her dignity, so they'd chosen the tour instead. Despite living in or near Oxford all her life, she'd never before been on one of Oxford's famous ghost tours, and on a winter night with the first flakes of snow starting to fall through the crisp cold air it seemed like a fun and romantic way to round off the day. And a walk around the city would surely counter any fattening effects of the churros.

'Are you here visiting Oxford?' asked a grey-haired woman who looked to be in her early sixties. She was on the tour with her husband.

'No, we live here,' admitted Bridget.

'Oh, I do envy you,' said the woman in what Bridget recognised as a light American accent. 'Oxford is such a beautiful city. We don't have anything like this where I come from.'

'And where is that?'

'We live in Cambridge, Massachusetts now, although I'm originally from Seattle. But my husband is from Oxford. We're over for the holidays, visiting his mother and family.' The man accompanying her nodded and smiled at Bridget and Jonathan. 'I'm Cheryl, by the way, and my husband is Trevor.'

'Bridget and Jonathan,' said Bridget.

Cheryl gave the impression that she would like to continue chatting, but they had now arrived at Jesus College on Turl Street and the guide was ushering them through the college gates and gathering them into a tight-knit group next to the porters' lodge in readiness to begin his first story. Bridget followed Cheryl and Trevor through the entrance, where she joined the family of four, who were already peering at the façades of the college chapel, dining hall and other buildings arranged around the first quadrangle. Yellow lights behind a few of the leaded windows cast a warm glow over the old stonework, and a brightly-lit Christmas tree illuminated one corner of the quad, while other parts of the college remained steeped in shadow.

'Come closer,' said Goole, beckoning to them with outstretched arms. 'I do not want to lose any of you on this cold, dark night. Are we all still here, so far?'

Bridget cast her gaze around the assembled group. It was a rather small crowd to be honest, and she wondered how the guide managed to scrape a living from giving these tours. Apart from Cheryl and Trevor, and the family with the girl and her older brother, there were just three more people on the tour, a group of forty-something women, all sporting novelty headbands from the Christmas Market – one with a pair of flashing reindeer antlers on her head, the other two wearing sparkly snowmen and miniature Father Christmases. Bridget could hardly criticise their lack of taste however, as she herself was wearing a bright red woolly bobble hat and a Christmas scarf patterned with dancing snowmen that Chloe had bought her as a joke the previous year.

Whether it was their silly headgear or their general air of bonhomie, the three women gave the impression of being on a girls' weekend. Two of them laughed and giggled at everything the guide said (Bridget strongly suspected the influence of mulled cider), but Ms Reindeer Antlers seemed rather distracted, constantly checking her phone and paying little attention to the guide. The woman looked vaguely familiar but Bridget couldn't quite place her.

Then the final member of the group made his way through the college gates – a thin, pale-faced boy in his late teens, who had been loitering a little way behind the rest. Dressed in black jeans, a black shirt and a thin black jacket which hardly seemed adequate for the icy temperature, he pushed his way to the front and joined the family of four, standing between the brother and sister. The two boys were the same age, Bridget guessed, although there was no family resemblance. Perhaps they were friends. As Goole began to recount the tale of a college principal who saw two mysterious men digging in the first quadrangle late one night, the new arrival leaned forward, listening intently and frowning repeatedly at the guide's storytelling. The boy seemed incapable of standing still. He shuffled his feet and kept touching his nose and chin in a repetitive gesture.

'But on close inspection the next morning,' said Goole with a dramatic flourish of his hands, 'not a single trace could be found of any digging. However, a search of the college records revealed that the site was the location of a grave dug during the English Civil War.'

The boy in black thrust his hands into his pockets, and muttered to the other boy. It was clear that the two knew each other well, but switching her attention to the parents, Bridget got the distinct impression that the mother and father rather wished their son hadn't brought this oddball friend along.

'Fascinating,' murmured Cheryl when the guide had finished his story. 'Isn't this interesting, Trevor?'

'Gripping.' Trevor smiled indulgently at his wife. He yawned and stole a quick glance at his watch and Bridget wondered if he'd perhaps prefer to be at home in front of a roaring log fire with a good book.

'And now, follow closely,' said Goole. 'Our way grows darker. I beg you, beware of uneven paving, loose cobblestones, and of course... the supernatural.'

Leaving Jesus College, he led them now down Brasenose Lane, a suitably spooky passageway running between Exeter and Lincoln Colleges. The group fell silent as they traversed the narrow road which was lit only by widely-spaced lamps fixed high on the walls of the old buildings. It was snowing properly now, coming down in big soft flakes that tickled Bridget's nose. After a minute's walk, they emerged into the open space of Radcliffe Square.

'Oh my, isn't this just so beautiful!' breathed Cheryl as she took in the eighteenth-century domed Radcliffe Camera, flanked by the Gothic crenellations of All Souls College, Brasenose College, the medieval Bodleian Library and the soaring tower of the University Church of St Mary the Virgin, standing floodlit against the blackened sky. In the snowy night air, it was certainly a magical sight to behold, and one Bridget herself would never tire of. She could just make out the strains of the organ and the descant of *Hark the Herald Angels Sing* coming from the University Church where one of Oxford's many choirs was holding its Christmas carol service.

'Do you have family in Oxford?' asked Cheryl, resuming their conversation as they skirted round the cobbled square towards Catte Street.

'I have a daughter,' said Bridget. 'She's fifteen. She didn't want to come Christmas shopping with us today. She prefers to be with her friends.'

In fact Bridget had been rather disappointed that Chloe had declined to come along to the Christmas Market. It would have been a treat for them to spend some fun time together. But at fifteen Chloe was developing a mind of her own, with opinions that increasingly didn't coincide with Bridget's.

'That's teenagers for you,' said Cheryl. 'Still it's nice to have family at Christmas time.'

'Yes,' said Bridget to be polite. In fact, although she loved the idea of Christmas, she was rather dreading the day itself. Of course, there was no question of her hosting Christmas in her tiny cottage in Wolvercote. She'd have struggled to fit a turkey in the oven, never mind cram everyone around the kitchen table. As usual, Vanessa, who prided herself on being something of a domestic goddess, was organising Christmas lunch, although quite frankly from the fuss she was making, you'd have thought the baby Jesus himself was going to make an appearance. She'd started baking months ago, saying that the Christmas cake needed time to mature, and filling her freezer with homemade mince pies. If it had been down to Bridget, she'd have done a last-minute shop at Waitrose, but Vanessa made everything herself, even the cranberry sauce. This year there would be nine of them for lunch on Christmas Day. To Vanessa's family of four would be added Bridget, Jonathan and Chloe, plus Vanessa and Bridget's parents who had been persuaded to travel up from Lyme Regis for the festivities. And therein lay Bridget's biggest concern.

Her parents. Her relationship with them had been damaged irrevocably by the death of Abigail, the youngest of the three sisters. After Abigail was murdered at the age of sixteen, her parents had retreated into a hard shell of grief and never emerged. At a time when the family had needed to stick together more than ever, they had instead turned away, leaving Bridget and Vanessa to console each other. They had sold the family house and moved to the Dorset coast, barely even showing any interest when their grandchildren were born. They rarely left Lyme Regis, and it was quite an achievement for Vanessa to coax them to Oxford for Christmas. Yet Bridget was hardly looking forward to the occasion. The atmosphere over the turkey and Brussels sprouts was likely to be as icy as the weather outside.

'I just adore Christmas,' said Cheryl, 'especially the way you English do it, you know, with plum pudding and mince pies.'

Bridget smiled weakly.

After a brief stop outside the Bodleian Library to relate the tale of how King Charles I, who had been refused permission by the librarian in 1645 to borrow books from the library, had taken revenge and appeared in the years after his execution in the upper reading room, snatching books from shelves, apparently sometimes without his head, Goole set off again, the group following behind.

'Reading without your head on. Now that's a tricky act to pull off,' commented Cheryl to her husband.

'Several of my students seem to be able to manage it,' he remarked dryly. 'Judging from the quality of their essays.'

'You're an academic?' enquired Bridget.

'A lecturer at Harvard, yes.'

'Follow me now. Don't get lost!' said Goole, crossing

the road and leading them beneath the Bridge of Sighs – or Hertford Bridge, to give it its correct name – the Venetian-style covered walkway that linked the two halves of Hertford College, and down New College Lane, which was dark and deserted at this time of night. Pausing beneath a Victorian-style streetlight that cast an eerie glow into the darkened lane and accentuated the shadows on his gaunt features, Goole proceeded to tell them his next tale.

'Gather round, my friends, and cast yourselves back to the darkest days of the English Civil War. The King against Parliament. Cavalier against Roundhead. Families torn asunder, their loyalties divided. The year is 1646. The King has made Oxford his stronghold, but the city is now under siege from the Parliamentarians. Bloody battles are being fought throughout the country. Death and treachery are rife.' He made a dramatic gesture with the finger of his right hand as if slitting his own throat. 'And here in Oxford, in this very spot where you are now standing, Prince Rupert, a loyal and devoted member of the King's entourage, gathers volunteers for a raid on a Parliamentarian pay train. Good men. Brave men. Men with families and children. But alas!' – Goole drew a deep breath – 'the sortie is doomed to failure. Prince Rupert's men are slain in their prime. And to this day, if you walk down here alone, late at night, you may still hear the clattering of hooves and the clanking of armour.'

The group held its collective breath, as if straining to hear the clamour of horses and men, but the only sound came from the boy in black who seemed to be growing even more agitated. His feet shuffled repeatedly on the pavement as he rocked backwards and forwards. Bridget tried not to stare but he was very distracting. At last he was unable to contain himself. In a tense, high-pitched voice he blurted out, 'You should tell them how it works!' Suddenly all eyes were on him, although he himself immediately dropped his gaze to the ground. He began to touch his nose and chin compulsively, as if trying to ward off the attention.

Goole looked taken aback at the interruption. 'You have an explanation for these ghostly phenomena? Perhaps you'd care to share it with us, young man.'

'Or better not,' whispered one of the three women to her friends.

'My name's Dylan.'

'Go on, Dylan,' urged the other boy. 'Tell them.'

'For goodness' sake, Luke, don't encourage him,' muttered the boy's father.

Dylan shook his head dismissively. 'They probably wouldn't understand. All they want to hear is silly stories.'

'Tell them anyway,' said Luke encouragingly.

Dylan rocked back and forth a little more, then began to speak. 'Some people believe that ghosts are evil spirits of the dead, condemned to walk the earth forever in search of vengeance or justice.' He grew calmer as he delivered his explanation, and ceased his rocking and nose touching, although still not making eye contact with anyone. 'In fact, ghosts are place-memories – recordings of voices, images, thoughts, and feelings imprinted on physical objects like stones – that sensitive people can play back.'

It was the American woman, Cheryl, who broke the long silence that met Dylan's proclamation. 'Stones, like crystals?' she suggested. 'I have a friend in Boston who recommends the healing power of crystals.'

'I tried crystal therapy once after a particularly nasty break-up,' commented Ms Reindeer Antlers. Her two friends exchanged a weary glance that Bridget interpreted as "she's had a lot of break-ups". 'The instructor told me it would help to realign my chakras.'

'And did it?' enquired one of her friends – the one with the sparkly snowmen perched on her head.

'I don't know about that. But it certainly resulted in a healthy alignment between me and the course instructor.' Ms Antlers dissolved into a fit of giggles.

'I knew they wouldn't understand,' said Dylan to his friend, Luke. 'I don't have time to waste on this. I'm leaving!'

'Hey, mate, don't go,' said Luke, reaching out a hand to stop him, but Dylan jerked out of his grasp and stormed off down New College Lane, his black jacket flapping behind him.

'Leave him,' hissed Luke's mother, in a voice quite loud enough for everyone to hear. 'You're staying with your family tonight. Not with that idiot.'

'Lynda, please,' said her husband, laying a hand on her arm. 'Today was supposed to be about quality family time, remember?'

'I'm sorry, Geoff. But honestly…'

A mutinous expression appeared on Luke's face, but he stayed where he was, watching his friend stalk away. His parents were clearly mortified that this family row was playing out in front of an audience. Luke's younger sister looked as if she wished the ground would swallow her up.

Bridget studied each actor in turn, taking in the dynamics of this little family drama.

'I do apologise for the behaviour of my son's friend,' said the father, Geoff. 'We had no idea that Dylan would be joining us this evening. Please proceed with the tour, Mr Goole. We're enjoying it very much.'

'Thank you,' said Goole. 'We do have a number of other sites to visit.'

The group began to move on again and Bridget was relieved. The presence of Dylan had been putting her on edge. They had stopped beneath the streetlight for a while and her feet had nearly frozen. She stamped them in an effort to warm them up. Then she cast one last glance down New College Lane, but the boy, Dylan, had vanished into the night as if he were nothing more than a ghost himself.

'Happy families, eh?' whispered Jonathan to Bridget as they followed the group back under the Bridge of Sighs.

'Mmm,' said Bridget, musing on her own dysfunctional family. She hoped that by bringing three generations together under one roof for Christmas, her sister wasn't inadvertently setting up the occasion for a similar incendiary argument.

Goole resumed the tour and led them next to Wadham College where he recounted the mysterious late-night wanderings of a priest, dressed in white robes, who had been sighted by a head porter and two scouts walking between the chapel and the dining hall, this part of the college having been built on the site of an old Augustinian priory.

But Bridget felt he rather rushed the tale, as if his flow had been disrupted after the incident in New College Lane.

The tour continued on to several other colleges, including New College, Trinity and St John's, and ended back near where they had started outside the Sheldonian Theatre on Broad Street. The *Hallelujah Chorus* from Handel's *Messiah* was clearly audible through the open windows at the top of the building. Everyone gave Goole a round of applause.

'Of course this was just a brief introduction to the many and varied ghosts of Oxford,' concluded Goole. 'Many more are described in my book, *Ghosts and Hauntings of Oxford*, available from a few good booksellers at a very reasonable price. In fact, I have some copies with me.'

He produced a handful of books from beneath his swirling cloak, and offered them to his audience. Cheryl, the American woman dutifully purchased a copy, as did Jonathan. The group of three women and the family of four politely declined.

'Perhaps we could buy you a drink, Mr Goole?' suggested Trevor, Cheryl's husband. 'I believe the Turf Tavern is doing mulled wine for Christmas. On such a cold night I think we could all do with some warming up.'

The snow had stopped now, but if anything the temperature had dropped further. The clouds had parted, and bright stars were appearing against the black velvet sky. The idea of warming her fingers on a glass of spicy mulled wine was very appealing to Bridget, and the others seemed to be in general consensus, perhaps because they were feeling a little sorry for Goole. The awkwardness caused by Dylan's outburst had rather derailed the poor man and taken some of the sparkle out of his storytelling.

'That sounds like an excellent idea,' said Jonathan.

The Turf Tavern, one of Oxford's most famous pubs, dating back to the twelfth century, was not easy for the casual visitor to find. Once a venue for illicit gambling, the pub had been built just outside the jurisdiction of the medieval city authorities, and was still bounded on one side by a section of the original city wall. The Turf had played host to many famous personalities over the years, including Richard Burton and Elizabeth Taylor, Stephen Hawking and the cast and crew of the *Harry Potter* films. According to local legend, it was also the spot where Bill Clinton had, famously, not inhaled.

Tucked away amidst a jumble of buildings between New College Lane and Holywell Street, the Turf was approached via a maze of narrow passageways. Goole led the way back the short distance beneath the Bridge of Sighs and down St Helen's Passage, once known as Hell Passage, an alley no more than a few feet wide that ran between Hertford College on one side and an old redbrick house on the other. A sharp turn halfway along the passage brought them to the pub itself, a crooked, half-timbered building shoehorned into the gap next to New College cloisters and overlooked by the teetering shaft of the college bell tower.

'This is amazing!' said Cheryl, taking in the scene.

The interior of the pub was notoriously poky, consisting of two low-beamed rooms either side of a central bar. But the lack of indoor space was compensated for by a number of outdoor courtyards on different levels, shielded from the worst of the elements by an assortment of canopies, umbrellas and, very welcome to Bridget, outdoor heaters.

As usual, the Turf was heaving. Shoppers from the Christmas Market had retreated there with their purchases and there was nowhere to sit down, inside or out.

'What can I get you?' Jonathan asked the tour guide. 'A

beer? Mulled wine?'

'A beer would be perfect,' said Goole, looking grateful. 'All that talking makes me thirsty.'

'Mulled wine?' Jonathan asked Bridget.

She gave him a smile.

Whilst all the men in the party, except for Goole, went off to the bar to get the drinks, Cheryl began relating a story about the healing power of crystals to the three singletons and the tour guide. Bridget found herself standing with the mother, Lynda, and her young daughter. The girl reminded Bridget a bit of Chloe at that age – slightly awkward in the presence of so many adults. Young people hated being treated as children. The poor girl had looked dreadfully embarrassed by the exchange of words between her parents and brother back in New College Lane.

'Did you enjoy the tour?' Bridget asked her.

The girl nodded, smiling shyly at Bridget. It probably helped to put the child at ease that, at five foot two, Bridget was not much taller than an eleven-year-old girl herself.

'Which was your favourite story?'

'I liked the one about the archbishop.'

'At St John's College? Yes, I enjoyed that one too.'

According to Goole's flowery narration, an Archbishop of Canterbury by the name of William Laud, who had imposed a number of strict reforms on the Church of England was tried for popery, tyranny and treason. In the year 1645 he was taken to the Tower of London and beheaded. The body of Laud, who had been born in Oxford and was chancellor of St John's, was returned to Oxford and buried under the altar of the college chapel. His ghost had been seen there many times over the centuries, and had adopted the unruly habit of pulling his head from his shoulders and kicking it along the floor like a football.

'Oh, Lucy,' said her mother despairingly. 'That one was the most gruesome.'

'That's why I liked it,' said the girl, pursing her lips in

defiance.

'Well, I liked it too,' said Bridget.

'It wasn't even scary,' said the girl. 'I was hoping for some really scary stories.'

'Honestly, Lucy,' said her mother. 'I don't know where you get these ideas.' She looked at her watch. 'It's already getting late for you to be out. What on earth has happened to Geoff?'

'It's probably just very busy at the bar,' said Bridget, trying to smooth things over. 'And I'm sure that one late night won't do Lucy any harm.'

Lynda laid a protective hand on her daughter's shoulder. The gesture suggested that in her opinion, Bridget had very little idea how much harm one late night might do to a young child. 'Do you have children yourself?'

'A daughter. She's out with friends this evening. She's fifteen,' Bridget added, aware that in Lynda's eyes, the fact that Chloe was out on her own might mark Bridget out as a rather negligent parent.

'Is she indeed?' said Lynda.

Bridget was rather wishing she had joined the conversation on healing crystals which, from the gales of laughter coming from Cheryl and the three other women, sounded a whole lot more fun.

'So, how old is your son?' she asked, trying to move the conversation on to less troubled waters. Luke had somewhat reluctantly gone with his father to help fetch the drinks.

A glow of pride immediately entered Lynda's eyes. 'Luke's nineteen. He's studying Law at New College.'

Bridget tried not to let her surprise at this news show. Luke and his friend Dylan had looked too immature to be students, although that was probably just Bridget's own advanced age getting the better of her. After all, it had been twenty years since she'd been an undergraduate at Oxford herself. 'Didn't the university term end a couple of weeks ago?'

'Luke stayed on to finish off some work,' said Lynda,

looking anxiously over Bridget's shoulder for her husband. 'He's such a diligent student.'

Beside her, the daughter rolled her eyes in exaggerated fashion, leaving Bridget wondering once again about the mysterious undercurrents at play within this family.

'Ah, here comes Geoff at last,' said Lynda with obvious relief.

Bridget was also relieved, and turned to see Lynda's husband and son wending their way through the throng. Following in their wake was Jonathan, carrying two glasses of mulled wine and a bottle of beer. Bringing up the rear was Trevor, Cheryl's husband, who had gallantly offered to buy a round for the three women in the novelty headgear.

But all was not entirely well. Geoff and Luke, the father and son, appeared to be embroiled in some sort of disagreement, and Bridget took the opportunity to extract herself from the quarrelsome family and re-join Cheryl, who was much easier company.

'Cheers!' said Jonathan on his arrival, handing Bridget one of the glasses, and giving the beer to Mr Goole.

Whilst Jonathan proceeded to engage Mr Goole in a conversation about local history, and Trevor excused himself to go and take a call on his phone, Bridget, Cheryl and the group of three women huddled under one of the outdoor heaters, drinking mulled wine.

The trio, explained Ms Reindeer Antlers, whose real name turned out to be Julia, were all former students of the university and 'the best of friends', who now in their early forties had found themselves newly single and had decided to return to their old stomping ground to 'live it up a bit'. They were staying at Malmaison, the former prison which had now been turned into a stylish and upmarket hotel, and were looking forward to not having to 'spend the whole of Christmas cooking and washing up' for the first time in years.

Julia gave a theatrical sigh as if she'd spent her entire life doing domestic chores, a fact that Bridget seriously doubted, judging from her smooth hands and perfectly-manicured nails.

'I so envy you girls booking yourselves into a luxury hotel,' said Cheryl. 'There'll be twelve of us for dinner on Christmas Day, and much as I enjoy a big family get-together, we'll be cooking on Trevor's mother's ancient Aga. Her kitchen doesn't even have a dishwasher.'

'Oh, I'm sure that will be fun,' said Bridget.

'Of course,' said Cheryl, grinning. 'I actually love that kind of thing.'

'Well, I positively hate it,' declared Julia. 'You won't find me in the kitchen at Christmas. Not unless I'm fetching a bottle of wine out of the fridge.' She tipped back the rest of her drink and held up her empty glass. 'Time for another, I think.'

Her friends, who were called Liz and Deborah, vigorously concurred.

As Julia gamely pushed her way through the throng in the direction of the bar, Cheryl turned and looked around. 'I wonder where Trevor has got to?'

Bridget peered around the courtyard too, but there was no sign of Cheryl's husband who had not returned from his phone call.

It was the first time Bridget had seen any trace of anxiety on Cheryl's face. She'd seemed perfectly relaxed before, but now her forehead was creased with worry. 'I'm sure he can't have gone far,' Bridget told her. 'I expect he just went somewhere quieter to take his call.'

'Yes, I'm sure you're right,' said Cheryl, although the worry on her face didn't diminish.

Bridget's view of the crowds outside was somewhat hampered by her short stature. The outside space was even more packed now than when they'd first arrived, and as usual everyone else seemed to be taller than her by several inches. She could still see Jonathan talking to Mr Goole, although a large group of revellers had positioned themselves between the two men and Bridget. Julia had disappeared to the bar, and the "happy family" was nowhere to be seen. Excusing herself from Cheryl, Bridget made her way towards the toilets. After the cider she'd consumed at the Christmas Market, and now the mulled wine on top, she wasn't going to last much longer without a bathroom break. Maybe she would come across Trevor on her way.

She inched her way slowly through the crush towards the ladies, which were located in a courtyard on the other side of the two bars. She caught no sign of Trevor or Julia on her way, nor any of the family of four. But trying to find anyone here was like searching for a needle in a haystack. Inevitably, on her arrival she was met by a queue of women snaking its way around the courtyard. She stood in line, stomping her feet in an effort to keep warm.

Ten minutes later, she emerged from the toilets and checked her watch. It was already ten thirty, high time for her and Jonathan to be setting off. She could hardly insist on Chloe returning home at a reasonable hour if she was always late herself.

She was about to go and hunt down Jonathan when a sharp scream came from the direction of St Helen's Passage. Bridget's instinct and training as a police officer kicked in and immediately she was running. There was no need for her to think. Someone needed help.

The narrow alleyway was only a short distance away, but her path was blocked by drinkers who had drifted over to see what was happening.

'Let me through,' she shouted. 'I'm a police officer.'

The crowd parted reluctantly and she barged her way past. Arriving suddenly at the cause of the disturbance, she almost tripped over a figure lying prone in the darkened alley that connected the Turf to New College Lane.

A long black cloak hid the features of the man on the ground, but Bridget didn't need to see his gaunt face to know his identity. 'Mr Goole?' she gasped, kneeling at his side.

All around her the onlookers continued to jostle, offering no assistance but instead taking pictures on their phones and chattering to each other in a state of high excitement.

Ghouls, thought Bridget. 'Please stay back!' she shouted in annoyance, but her words had little effect. 'Someone call an ambulance!'

'Already done,' said a voice, but Bridget couldn't see who had spoken.

She drew the black cloak aside and her fingers came away red. A dark pool of blood was seeping from a wound in the man's abdomen. She leaned in close and placed her fingers to Goole's neck, feeling for a pulse, but there was nothing. The tour guide's glassy, unblinking eyes stared back at her, unseeing.

Bridget pressed the heel of her hand to his chest and began to administer CPR, pressing down rhythmically several times. Then she blew air into his mouth. There was still no sign of life.

She continued to apply first aid until the paramedics arrived. Finally, standing back to allow the professionals to take over, she noticed that the tour guide's black top hat had rolled off and was lying crushed in the gutter.

CHAPTER 2

There must be a grave lying empty somewhere. Jonathan's words from earlier that evening came back to Bridget now with sickening clarity. Jonathan had been joking of course. Nevertheless, in life the proprietor of *Goole's Ghost Tours* had already looked half dead. And now he really was dead, having met his demise in a manner quite as violent and grisly as in any of his tall tales.

Attempts to resuscitate him had failed, the lingering onlookers had been moved away, and the body of Gordon Goole – or David Smith as he turned out to be more prosaically called once his driving licence had been retrieved from his wallet – had been screened off from the public.

Medical examiner Dr Sarah Walker pronounced that he had been stabbed in the upper abdomen with a steak knife, although the cause of death had been obvious even to Bridget.

The landlord of the pub confirmed that they used steak knives just like the one that had been used to kill Goole. 'But so do lots of pubs and colleges in Oxford,' he added, clearly keen to distance his establishment from the unfortunate incident.

'He wasn't murdered in another pub, though, was he, sir?' Bridget remarked, although it wasn't the landlord's fault that the tour guide was dead. She was still angry at the way the crowds had milled about, showing a distinct lack of respect for the victim, and hindering her efforts to reach the scene. If she could have arrived sooner, perhaps she could have done something to help, although realistically the victim had lost so much blood, she probably wouldn't have been able to do anything for him.

'The knife went deep,' said Sarah. 'It pierced the heart and probably severed a major artery for good measure. Blood loss was very rapid. He wouldn't have suffered greatly.'

Bridget nodded, recognising that Sarah was trying to make her feel better.

'You couldn't have done anything to save him,' Sarah continued. 'He would have died before reaching hospital even if an ambulance had arrived immediately.' She stood up, took in the sight of Bridget's woolly bobble hat and Christmas-themed scarf which was now stained with blood, and raised one appraising eyebrow. This wasn't the first time Bridget had attended a crime scene dressed inappropriately for the occasion. 'I'm guessing that you weren't here on duty when you discovered the body.'

'No,' said Bridget. 'I was actually out enjoying myself. Getting into the Christmas spirit and all that.'

'I find it's really not worth the effort,' said Sarah dismissively. 'So much hype, and yet Christmas is probably the most disappointing day of the year. The way most families carry on, it's a wonder there aren't more murders at this time of year.'

'I suppose so,' said Bridget, mulling over her own mixed feelings about the big family get-together that Vanessa had planned for Christmas Day, but she couldn't help wondering if Sarah's words were a way of arming herself against loneliness at Christmas. As far as she knew,

Sarah was single and had no family. Bridget really ought to invite her out for a drink sometime, but Sarah never showed much desire to socialise with her colleagues. She was already turning away to supervise the removal of the body to the waiting ambulance parked in New College Lane.

Instead Bridget turned her focus back to the investigation. It was a member of the public who had dialled 999 to summon the emergency services. The man, a Mr Alan Marsh, explained to Bridget that he and his wife had practically tripped over the body on their way to the Turf Tavern for a quick drink. They'd been attending the performance of Handel's *Messiah* in the Sheldonian and had decided to round off the evening with a nice glass of mulled wine. It was Mrs Marsh who had screamed so loudly upon discovering the body, thus drawing the attention of nearby drinkers, Bridget herself included.

Bridget quizzed the couple briefly, but quickly established that they had witnessed nothing of the attack itself. Goole had already been lying in a pool of blood when they discovered him. Bridget thanked Mr Marsh for his prompt action and suggested that he and his wife go to the bar and order themselves a drink. An officer would be along shortly to take their statements.

She had given instructions that no one should be allowed to enter or leave the Turf Tavern until the names and addresses of everyone present had been taken. But it was likely that the killer had already fled by the time she'd arrived at Goole's body, and it was quite possible that in all the confusion after the murder, one or more witnesses might have left the premises too, especially given the fact that there were two ways in and out – through St Helen's Passage, and by a second passageway leading to Holywell Street on the opposite side of the courtyard.

After arranging for the SOCO team – the Scene of Crime Officers – to attend, Bridget next called her boss, Detective Chief Superintendent Alex Grayson, to let him know what had happened and to inform him that she was dealing with the situation. It might be Bridget's day off, but there was no way she was going to allow anyone else to take this case. A man had been stabbed to death almost under her nose, and she was determined to uncover who was responsible.

She dialled his number and braced herself for his usual brusque response.

'Grayson.' From the sound of voices and clinking cutlery in the background, Bridget deduced that the Chief Super and his wife were at a dinner party. When she explained the situation to him he sounded exasperated, as if Bridget had deliberately chosen her timing in order to disrupt his social life. 'A murder... right before Christmas?'

'I'm afraid so, sir.'

'And you just happened to be nearby?'

'Yes, sir.'

'Do you want me to put Baxter on it?'

'No need for that, sir.' Detective Inspector Greg Baxter was Bridget's arch-rival in the department, and he and Bridget had crossed swords before. She certainly wasn't going to allow him anywhere near this investigation. 'I'll do it.'

'Very good,' said Grayson, sounding relieved that she had volunteered for the job. No detective would want to be assigned to a murder investigation immediately before Christmas. Unless – like Bridget – they were secretly looking for an excuse to avoid spending time with their family.

Duty comes first, she told herself, seeking to position herself on the moral high ground.

'What are your initial thoughts?' asked Grayson. 'Perhaps a mugging gone wrong?'

'I don't think so, sir. Mr Goole – I mean Mr Smith – was still wearing his money belt with all the takings from the tour. And his wallet wasn't removed either.'

'Hmm, well, I'm sure it won't take long for you to find some leads. A murder can't have been carried out in one of the busiest places in Oxford without someone having seen what happened.'

'No, sir.' Although so far no one had come forward to say that they had seen the murder take place. The location of the crime wasn't even in the pub itself, or the surrounding courtyards, which were all thronged with people, but in a dark side passage, tucked out of sight of the revellers. What had Goole been doing in that lonely alley, anyway? St Helen's Passage led away from the tavern, back to New College Lane. He must have been drawn there by something – or someone – he'd seen.

'Well, I have every confidence in you,' concluded Grayson.

'Thank you, sir. I'll do my best.'

After speaking to her boss, Bridget called the two most trusted members of her team, Detective Sergeant Jake Derwent and Detective Constable Ffion Hughes. She would need their help to coordinate the uniformed officers from St Aldate's police station and to ensure that witness statements were taken from everyone in the pub.

The two detectives had been behaving rather oddly this last month. Bridget had surmised that Jake and Ffion's short-lived romance from earlier in the year was no more. On more than one occasion Bridget had noticed Jake hanging around the coffee machine looking morose. And although Ffion wasn't the sort of woman to let her feelings get in the way of her job, the Welsh DC had been even more curt and abrupt with her fellow colleagues than usual. Bridget felt some sympathy for the pair. She knew from personal experience how hard it could be to have a relationship when your job demanded so much of your time. Her own marriage to a fellow officer had long ago ended in divorce and acrimony.

But work was the best antidote to a broken heart, and as long as Jake and Ffion were still able to operate together as a team, there was no one else Bridget would rather have working alongside her.

Finally, having secured the crime scene, called in all the professionals and informed her boss, it was time for her to find Jonathan and break the bad news to him – that their weekend was over, and she would be tied up with the investigation for the foreseeable future. It would surely come as no great surprise to him. He was used to her putting work before her personal life. And she was grateful to him for his acceptance of that.

She found him in the courtyard with the other people from the ghost tour. His mulled wine was finished and he was now sipping a coffee. She kissed him quickly on the cheek.

He gave her a quick hug in return. 'Are you all right?'

'I'm fine.'

'And was it Mr Goole who was attacked?'

'Yes.' It still felt easier to think of the murdered man as Gordon Goole than as David Smith. Even though she had spent only a couple of hours in his company, she felt that she had an understanding of Goole the flamboyant tour guide. Smith, the real man, was as yet an enigma. 'He was stabbed to death.'

'Who would do such a thing?'

'Well, it's my job to find out,' said Bridget. 'You were talking to him when I went off to the ladies. That was only a matter of minutes before he was attacked. What happened during that time?'

'After you left, he asked me if I wanted another drink. He went off to the bar and never came back.'

The rest of the ghost tour participants had clustered anxiously around the nearest heater. News of the demise of their erstwhile guide had drawn them together, even though at the start of the evening they had all been strangers to each other. Trevor and Cheryl were nursing large whiskies. The young girl, Lucy, had clearly been crying and was being comforted by her mother, whilst her father, Geoff, looked on, grim-faced. Their son, Luke, was no longer with them, and Julia, she of the Reindeer Antlers, had disappeared. Her two friends were still present, although they had removed their novelty headgear, presumably out of respect for the dead tour guide.

'Can you tell us what's going on?' asked Geoff. 'It's late, and Lucy is tired and frightened. We need to get back to our hotel. You never said you were a detective inspector,' he added, as if Bridget had somehow deceived them by failing to mention this fact.

'This was supposed to be my day off.'

'Poor you,' said Cheryl sympathetically.

'I realise it's getting very late,' said Bridget. It was now half past eleven. She'd sent a quick message to Chloe to let her know where she was, but Chloe had been unconcerned. Bridget wasn't sure whether that should make her pleased or worried. 'We'll need to take statements from all of you, but we don't need to do that tonight. If you can give me your contact details, then I can come and speak to you tomorrow.'

'You don't think that one of us might be involved, do you?' asked Geoff, glancing around nervously at the other members of the group. 'I mean, it's just a coincidence that we were all on the tour and then Goole ended up getting attacked. We didn't know the man.'

Bridget was careful not to encourage or contradict Geoff's speculation. 'You're all key witnesses. David Smith – that was his real name – was with us until just before he died. Did any of you see anything you think might be significant? Did he meet someone on the way to the bar, for example?'

They all shook their heads. 'It was impossible to see anything in this crush,' said Trevor.

Bridget frowned, wondering exactly where Trevor had been while she had been chatting to his wife. Taking a phone call, he had said. She could pursue that in the morning.

There were two other unexplained absences now. 'Where is your son?' she asked Geoff.

'Luke?' Geoff's face darkened. 'He's here somewhere.'

The explanation seemed rather inadequate, but Bridget let it go for now. There seemed little to be gained from tracking the boy down. She would be able to speak to him tomorrow. 'Just let me know where you're staying and be sure not to leave Oxford before I can interview you.'

'We're staying at the Eastgate Hotel. But we can't hang around all day. We're supposed to check out by lunchtime.'

'Don't worry,' said Bridget. 'I'll be there well before then.' She turned to Cheryl who was writing something on a scrap of paper torn from her diary.

'We're at Trevor's mother's house,' said Cheryl. 'Here's the address.'

Bridget thanked her and then looked enquiringly at the remaining two women. 'What happened to your friend, Julia?' The last time Bridget had seen the reindeer antlers, they were on their way to the bar.

Liz and Deborah exchanged a look. 'It seems that she got a better offer,' said Liz.

'That tends to happen with Julia,' added Deborah.

'What kind of better offer?' asked Bridget.

'I think that it's safe to assume it was a man,' said Liz.

'No doubt we'll know more in the morning,' said Deborah. 'You can find us at the Malmaison. We're staying in Oxford for the whole week.'

'We don't have anywhere better to go,' added Liz with a sigh.

The fun-filled Christmas that the three women had planned was falling apart at the seams and it wasn't even Christmas Day yet.

'All right,' said Bridget. 'You can go.'

The crowd of drinkers was thinning now as the police took the contact details of witnesses and allowed them to leave. There must have been a hundred or more here tonight. One of them had surely seen something that would enable them to identify the killer.

Bridget waited behind with Jonathan while the other members of the ghost tour dispersed. Luke, it seemed, had been found by his parents skulking in a corner of the courtyard. He and his father exchanged more angry words as they walked away.

Bridget took Jonathan's hand. 'Sorry how the evening turned out,' she said, giving him a rueful smile.

'It wasn't your fault.'

'No, but still… perhaps you're starting to regret dating a police officer.'

'I could never regret meeting you.'

St Helen's Passage was now completely sealed off with crime scene tape so they walked together to the other exit on Holywell Street. The relaxing haze induced by the wine and cider had long since worn off. Bridget's head was now crystal clear and so was the sky. The flashing blue lights of the response cars in the street beyond leached any residual warmth away from the yellow Cotswold stone of the buildings, turning the scene an arctic hue. The temperature was dropping as night deepened, and the first frost was already forming where snow had fallen earlier. It crunched underfoot as they walked. At the exit to Holywell Street she stopped.

'Aren't you coming with me?' asked Jonathan.

'You go. I need to stay here until I know that everything's been done properly. I'll get one of the constables to give me a lift back later.'

'You should come home and get some rest,' he said, taking her in his arms and planting a kiss on the top of her head. 'You're going to have a busy day tomorrow. You don't have to run the investigation single-handedly, you know. You have a team.'

'Yes,' she said, 'but it's my responsibility. I won't be able to sleep until I know that nothing's been missed.'

CHAPTER 3

The incident room at Thames Valley Police Headquarters in Kidlington had been decorated – somewhat amateurishly and misguidedly, in Bridget's opinion – in an effort to spread festive cheer even to the murky world of serious crime investigation. The result was less winter wonderland and more a hotchpotch of bad taste. The loops of garish tinsel were already coming unstuck from the ceiling, and a rather spindly Christmas tree that leaned to one side was dropping its needles over the carpet tiles at an alarming rate. Before beginning her team meeting, Bridget removed the magnetic snowmen that had been scattered across the whiteboard and swapped them for their usual non-festive counterparts.

She had come in to the office extra early, unable to sleep properly after staying late at the Turf. When she had eventually dozed off, her dreams had been haunted by spooky apparitions lurking in darkened alleyways, and hooded phantoms carrying daggers dripping blood. She woke after a few hours of disturbed sleep with a creeping sense of dread and knew that the only way to shake it off was to go into work and make a start on the case. She'd left Chloe asleep in bed, leaving a note for her in the kitchen, before driving through the dark and deserted streets to the station. The days were so short at this time of year that even on a normal day she went to work in the dark and came home in the dark. It was really quite depressing and made her yearn for the long days of summer and the heat of sunny climes.

Two days before Christmas was not the best time to be opening a new murder enquiry. In the previous week there had been a general winding down in the office, a sense of relaxation as the year wound to a close. On the previous Friday, the department had raised money for charity with a "wear a Christmas jumper to work day" and the various members of her team had competed with each other to see who could wear the most ludicrous knitwear (DS Ryan Hooper had won by a country mile with a light-up Rudolf design). And at the Christmas party, even Chief Superintendent Grayson had let down what little remained of his greying hair by joining in a raucous rendition of some Christmas pop classics.

But now, whatever festivities might be going on in the background, and whatever plans her team members might have made for the holiday itself, Bridget needed everyone to be back on form and to treat this new case just as seriously as they would any other. If necessary, leave would have to be cancelled.

Detective Constable Ffion Hughes was the first to arrive after Bridget, striding into the office in her green motorcycle leathers just before eight o'clock. 'No one else here yet?' she asked in her melodic Welsh accent.

Bridget was pleased to see that Ffion, at least, was on top form, whatever difficulties she might be going through in her personal life. The young detective was perhaps the only member of the team who showed no signs of slowing down and hadn't mentioned any plans for Christmas.

'I expect they'll be here shortly,' Bridget said.

'I'll put the kettle on. Tea?' Ffion retrieved her Welsh dragon mug from her desk and selected one of her aromatic herbal infusions for herself.

'White with one sugar, please,' said Bridget. 'And make it strong.'

By the time Ffion returned bearing two steaming mugs, the other members of the team were starting to drift in. Jake arrived breakfasting on a bacon roll and a Mars bar. Ryan Hooper and Andy Cartwright had called in at Starbucks *en route* and the aroma of their coffees was battling against Ffion's ginger tea for dominance. DC Harry Johns was sipping an energy drink, no doubt to replenish himself after his early-morning run. Bridget wished she could have half the energy and self-discipline of the eager young constable.

'Right,' she said. 'If we're all ready, let's make a start.'

She turned to the board where she had pinned a photo, taken from the website of *Goole's Ghost Tours*, of the tour guide in his Victorian undertaker's regalia. She would have preferred a picture of him not in make-up and grinning like a malevolent pantomime villain, but for now this was all she had.

'This is David Smith, age forty-three, stage name Gordon Goole, who was stabbed last night in St Helen's Passageway.' She pointed out the location of the crime scene on a map that was also pinned to the board. 'St Helen's is the narrow alleyway that leads from New College Lane to the Turf Tavern. Smith had just finished conducting a ghost tour of Oxford, which I happened to be on. After the tour we'd gone to the pub to warm up with some mulled wine. The attack took place at approximately half past ten, which was when I was alerted. The victim was stabbed in the upper abdominal region' – she placed a hand just below her breastbone to demonstrate – 'with a steak knife, most likely taken from the pub, although it's a common design of knife that you'll find in many colleges and restaurants. The murder weapon has gone to forensics to see if we can lift any prints from it.'

'Was he mugged?' asked Ryan.

'I don't think so,' said Bridget. 'His wallet wasn't

missing and he was still wearing his money belt with the takings from the tour. So either the mugger was disturbed and didn't have time to steal anything, or else this killing was never about money in the first place.'

'Perhaps he got into an argument with one of the other pubgoers,' suggested Ffion. 'Spilled someone's pint, or looked at them in the wrong way. It's been known to happen.'

'At this stage we have to keep an open mind,' said Bridget. 'The fact is that despite the presence of more than a hundred potential witnesses, so far we have no concrete leads. But that's about to change,' she added.

There was an audible groan from Ryan. 'Let me guess,' he muttered. 'Witness statements.'

Bridget gave him a smile. 'Excellent deductive work, DS Hooper. In total, we have the names and contact details of one hundred and thirty-six people who were present in the Turf at the time of the attack. Every single one of them needs to be interviewed. I'm going to ask Grayson to provide us with some additional support, but even so we'll have our work cut out. The sooner we start, the less chance that I'll be forced to cancel Christmas leave.'

More loud groans greeted her pronouncement.

'There are a few other lines I want to follow up,' she continued. 'Jake, get onto St Aldate's police station and Oxford University security services and ask them to send us as much CCTV footage as they can for Broad Street and the area around New College Lane and Holywell Street. Then go into town and see what you can get from the Turf itself, the King's Arms and any of the nearby shops such as Blackwell's.'

'Will do, ma'am,' said Jake, scrunching up his chocolate bar wrapper and swigging back the last of his coffee.

'Ffion, you come with me. We're going to visit David Smith's house and see what we can find out about him. The rest of you, you know what you have to do. I realise it's only two days until Christmas, and that some of you are already mentally on holiday, but a man died last night and it's our job to catch his killer. Understood?'

'Yes, ma'am,' chorused the officers.

CHAPTER 4

When Jake arrived in Broad Street after leaving his Subaru parked on the equally wide thoroughfare of St Giles', the Oxford Christmas Market was already in full swing. An enormous Christmas tree stood in the middle of the road, and the stalls and shopfronts were a blaze of light and colour. A jolly Santa Claus was making his way between the stalls of the various traders, calling out greetings to children, and music from a carousel was playing in the background. Meanwhile, a brass band was setting up across the street, preparing to blast festive tunes over the hubbub.

Jake had visited the market the previous week in search of some interesting and unique gifts for his mum and dad but had ended up buying a slightly kitsch set of table mats and coasters featuring historical prints of Oxford from one of the tourist shops on Broad Street. Not the most original present ever, but useful and, he hoped, the sort of thing his parents would appreciate.

He was supposed to be travelling back home to Leeds the next day and had planned to get away early to beat the Christmas Eve traffic heading north on the M1, but now with this new case he was worried he might have to cancel his leave. His mum would be so disappointed if he didn't make it home for Christmas and, to tell the truth, so would he. He really needed a break from Oxford.

Only a couple of months earlier he'd thought he would be spending Christmas in the company of the gorgeous Ffion Hughes. He had even envisaged taking her up north and introducing her to his folks. He'd imagined his mates' eyes popping out of their heads when he walked into one of the pubs off Boar Lane, arm in arm with his beautiful new girlfriend. But none of that would happen now and he had no one to blame but himself.

Their tentative relationship, so slow to get off the ground, had crashed and burned after he'd become involved again with a previous girlfriend, right in the middle of a murder investigation. He'd been so stupid, and weak. He'd apologised repeatedly to Ffion, but it seemed that no amount of sorrow or regret could change her mind. She had rebuffed all his attempts to make amends, even going so far as to block his number on her phone. She had walked away from the relationship without as much as a backwards glance. Had he meant that little to her?

Now Jake was back to being single, and his rented flat above a launderette on the Cowley Road felt lonelier than ever. Alone in his cramped and somewhat dingy living room, munching – as he so often did after a day at work – on a takeaway curry or Chinese, he found his thoughts drifting increasingly to his family and friends in Leeds, wishing that he had never left them behind. The ties that bound him to Oxford were unravelling.

He hadn't said anything to anyone at the station, but in his spare time he'd been secretly browsing jobs in Yorkshire. There was an opening for a detective sergeant with his level of experience in Halifax, an industrial city near Leeds that would provide a complete contrast to the dreaming spires and dusty libraries of Oxford. Somewhere grittier and more down to earth, with none of Oxford's pretensions. He'd even be able to afford to buy himself a decent house in Halifax, whereas getting on the property ladder in Oxford seemed like an impossibility. Maybe it was time to cut his losses and move back up north.

'All right, mate?' A familiar voice cut through his doleful soul-searching, bringing him back to the task in hand. It was Stu, the homeless Big Issue seller he'd first got to know when investigating the murder of a student at Christ Church back in the summer. It was during that investigation that he'd first met Ffion too. Those sunny days felt like a very long time ago.

'Stu, how's it going?'

The overnight frost was beginning to melt under the influence of the morning sun, but it must have been bitterly cold sleeping rough last night. Still, Stu was his usual cheery self. Jake hoped he'd managed to find a place at the local homeless shelter.

'Can't complain.' Stu tapped the pile of magazines he held in his arms and gave Jake a gap-toothed grin. 'Folk are more generous at this time of year, I find.'

Jake took the hint and rummaged in his pocket for some pound coins which he handed over in return for a copy of the magazine. It would be something for him to read when he was back in his flat this evening.

'Cheers, mate,' said Stu. 'Got anything planned for Christmas?'

'Hoping to head back up north. How about you?'

'A couple of days off. Christmas isn't such a bad time at the shelter. Loads of do-gooders come scurrying out of the woodwork to volunteer, and we get a few extra treats. Plus, who wouldn't enjoy sitting down to watch a repeat of *White Christmas* after dinner?'

'No one, I'm sure,' said Jake, unable to tell whether Stu was being serious or if his dry sense of humour was at work. Behind him the piped organ music of the carousel started up a fresh round of its relentless melody.

'So what's up?' enquired Stu. 'Doing some last-minute Christmas shopping?'

'Working actually. Like you.' Jake had an idea. 'Stu,

you work this same spot every day, right?'

'Got to. Don't want to lose it, especially at this time of year.' He rubbed two fingers together. 'It's a goldmine when the market's here.'

'Do you know the bloke who runs the ghost tours? I think they start from Broad Street.'

'You mean Goole? Yeah, I've known him for years. Bit of an odd character, dressed up in his black cloak and everything. But he tells a good yarn, and he buys me a coffee sometimes too.'

'I'm sorry to have to tell you this, but he was stabbed last night in one of the alleyways leading to the Turf Tavern. He died at the scene.'

Stu whistled through the gaps in his teeth. 'Holy crap. That poor bugger. Who'd want to hurt Goole? Was it for his money?'

'That's what we're trying to establish. Did he have any enemies?'

'Not that I know of. Everyone liked old Goole.' A frown crinkled Stu's weathered face. 'Hold on. He did get into a bit of argy-bargy with Bill Tomlins the other day.'

'Who's Bill Tomlins?'

'That mean bastard running the carousel.'

Jake glanced over his shoulder at the shaven-headed man with the boxer's profile who was standing in the middle of the carousel whilst the brightly painted horses on poles danced round and round, up and down. The man's unfriendly expression was markedly at odds with the cheerful music blaring from the ride.

'What did they disagree about?' asked Jake.

'Nothing much. Just some stupid argument about where Goole was starting his tours. He always leaves from here, but Bill said he was getting in the way of the customers waiting for the carousel. He claimed Goole was spoiling his business.'

'I see,' said Jake. 'Not exactly peace on earth and goodwill to all men, then?'

Stu laughed at that. 'Bill's a nasty piece of work at the

best of times. I think that starting punch-ups must be his hobby.'

'So what was the outcome of this dispute?'

'I don't think they actually came to blows. Goole probably realised he couldn't win, what with Bill's carousel being stuck right where his tours were supposed to start. In the end, he moved his sign a few yards up the street and carried on as before. But I'm not sure Bill was happy even then.'

'Why was that?'

'He just never is.'

Jake turned again to study the man who was running the children's ride. He looked exactly the kind of man parents warned their children to stay away from. Bill Tomlins caught his eye and returned his stare, a malevolent sneer spreading over his face. Could this man have stabbed another man to death over a minor dispute? Jake couldn't rule it out.

'You've been very helpful,' he said to Stu, pulling a tenner out of his wallet. 'Treat yourself to something hot and tasty with that.'

'Cheers, mate,' said Stu. 'And a very merry Christmas to you.'

CHAPTER 5

Bridget was a little disappointed to discover that David Smith hadn't lived in a haunted house with a turret – the sort of property that she had imagined for his alter ego Gordon Goole – but rather a modest redbrick terrace in South Oxford, just off the Abingdon Road.

Lake Street was one of many narrow Victorian streets in this part of Oxford, crammed with cars parked half on and half off the pavement. Bridget squeezed her red Mini into a tight spot between a builder's van and a Volkswagen Golf outside the South Oxford Community Centre, then she and Ffion walked the short distance to Smith's anonymous little house.

She'd already established from the police database that the tour guide was unmarried and was an only child whose parents were both dead. It was possible that a distant cousin or uncle might yet be traced, but based on the information they had, the man had no living relatives.

The house's blue-painted front door gave directly onto the pavement, and Bridget rapped loudly on the knocker. When there was no answer she tried the key that had been retrieved from the victim's body. The door opened straight into a narrow hallway leading to a steep flight of stairs. She flicked on the light switch and a dull bulb in a mustard-coloured shade cast a reluctant glow over the rather dingy surroundings.

Two small rooms led off the downstairs hall. In many properties of this type they would have been knocked into one and given a lick of white paint to open up the space and create a modern, fresh feel. But here the original dividing wall between the rooms remained intact, giving the house a cramped, enclosed feel. The wood-chip wallpaper and heavily patterned carpets suggested that the place hadn't been decorated in decades. In estate agents' parlance it was "an opportunity to start again with a clean slate".

The furniture in the front room looked as if it had been salvaged from a junk shop: a brown, velour three-piece suite badly worn in places, a wooden coffee table marked with circular coffee stains, and an old-fashioned television of the kind that Bridget hadn't seen in ages.

The bookshelves either side of the fireplace were stacked with musty-smelling paperbacks, their spines cracked and yellowed. Classics of English literature and a well-thumbed set of the complete works of Shakespeare vied for space with popular thrillers and mystery stories from years gone by. Two shelves were devoted to a collection of books on the supernatural, ghost legends and the history of Oxford, and on the floor were piles of cardboard boxes, in which Bridget could see copies of Goole's own book, *Ghosts and Hauntings of Oxford*.

The only picture in the room, propped up on the mantelpiece, was a framed matriculation photograph taken at Pembroke College and dated twenty-five years ago. So, David Smith had been a student at the university. Bridget scanned the photograph and quickly spotted a much younger, but still recognisable David Smith, sitting on the front row in the obligatory *sub fusc* outfit of dark suit, academic gown and white bow tie that students were required to wear for matriculation, graduation and university exams. Bridget's own matriculation photo was hidden in a box somewhere in her attic. She preferred not to remind herself how slim she had been as an eighteen-year-old.

'No Christmas cards on display,' said Ffion.

'That's true.' Bridget's own house, which was probably even tinier than Smith's, was currently overflowing with cards. As usual, she hadn't got around to sending any in reply and had now missed the last posting date. Whereas Vanessa organised her cards on attractive display stands, Bridget's were scattered haphazardly on shelves, tables and worktops all over the living room and kitchen where they were constantly falling over and getting in the way. But here there wasn't a single card anywhere in sight. Did David Smith have no friends? Had he not kept in touch with anyone from his student days?

The back room, a dining room with an oval wooden table and a mis-matched sideboard, looked as if it was rarely used. At the rear of the house the narrow galley kitchen gave a few more clues to David Smith's solitary existence. A single mug, cereal bowl and spoon stood on the draining board. The cupboards were stocked with tins of Heinz soup, a packet of Cornflakes, and a few other essentials. The fridge contained a half-used pint of milk, some Cheddar cheese, a few slices of ham, and a couple of apples. It was spartan, even by Bridget's lackadaisical domestic standards – at least she always had an open bottle of wine on the go – and gave the impression of someone who didn't really care about what he ate.

They headed upstairs.

'Ugh,' said Ffion, wrinkling her nose in distaste at the avocado suite in the small bathroom. The sink, bath and toilet were all badly stained with limescale, and the wall under the window was spotted with mould. A single toothbrush stood in a Golden Jubilee mug on a shelf above the sink.

It was all making Bridget feel rather down, this solitary

existence of a man who had scratched a living by giving ghost tours and selling occasional copies of his book to tourists, and who now lay, dead and cold, in the mortuary refrigerator until Dr Roy Andrews could carry out the post-mortem. Who would attend his funeral? Smith appeared to have no personal relationships. Keen to get this over, she pressed on to the bedroom at the front of the house.

The bed was neatly made, with a pair of striped pyjamas folded tidily on the pillow. A dressing gown hung on the back of the door and a pair of tartan slippers were positioned on the floor beside the bed. A copy of Henry James's *The Turn of the Screw* lay on the bedside locker. It was the room of a man with simple, fastidious habits. The wardrobe contained a couple of dark suits, plain shirts, grey flannel trousers and a spare black cloak, as well as some more casual clothing, every item old and worn. It was all so plain and ordinary.

And yet Smith's stage persona of Gordon Goole had been so colourful and extraordinary. She couldn't help feeling desperately sorry for the guide who had completed his flamboyant tour each evening only to return to this lonely and dreary home. She wondered who the real man was – the dull and anonymous David Smith, or the animated and theatrical Gordon Goole. Closing the wardrobe door, she followed Ffion through to the last room of the house.

'Ma'am, you have to see this!' Ffion was peering through the open door to the back bedroom.

'What is it?'

'Come and see!'

As Bridget entered the room, the reason for the lack of care and attention given to the rest of the house, and the complete absence of any social or personal relationships in the owner's life, finally became clear.

The walls of the room were plastered from floor to ceiling in newspaper cuttings, photographs, police and coroner's reports, and yellow sticky notes covered in spidery handwriting. A shelf of box files, all neatly labelled, stood above a tidy desk with a stylish anglepoise lamp. The ceiling light, in contrast to the lighting in the rest of the house, was bright and modern. And the chair in front of the desk was a comfortable high-back ergonomic model. This was the place where David Smith spent his time, when he wasn't guiding tourists around the haunted corners of Oxford. And this project, whatever it was, was his true life's work.

David Smith, alias Gordon Goole, had been a man with an obsession.

CHAPTER 6

David Smith had simultaneously become much more interesting and yet even more of an enigma. Bridget began to scan the newspaper articles that covered the walls of the back bedroom almost like wallpaper. A few of the headlines jumped out at her: "Student Goes Missing" from the *Oxford Times*; "Rising Star Vanishes" from the *Oxford Mail*; "Hunt for Missing Oxford Student" from the *Daily Mail*. It appeared that David Smith had been conducting his own private investigation into the disappearance of a young woman from almost twenty-five years ago.

Bridget read a front-page article from the *Oxford Times* which accompanied a photo of a smiling young woman taken from a college matriculation photograph and another photo of the same woman dressed in Shakespearean costume:

Concerns are growing for the safety of nineteen-year-old Oxford university student Camilla Townsend who has not been seen since starring in a university production of *Twelfth Night* at the

Burton Taylor Studio at the Oxford Playhouse.
Camilla, who was playing Viola in Shakespeare's
romantic comedy of mistaken identity and gender
politics, disappeared at some point during the
party following the last performance on Saturday
night. 'We're all really worried about her,' said a
fellow student who was playing Viola's twin
brother, Sebastian. 'It's out of character for her
to just vanish like this.'
Camilla, originally from Godalming in Surrey, is
a student at Pembroke College, Oxford. Her
family have appealed for help in finding her.
Anyone with information should contact Thames
Valley Police at the St Aldate's station in Oxford.

The other articles filled in more of the details. The
production of *Twelfth Night* had been organised under the
auspices of the Oxford University Dramatic Society and
had starred students from a number of different colleges.
The director, an undergraduate at Worcester College, was
quoted in the *Oxford Mail* as being 'devastated' by
Camilla's disappearance. 'Camilla has such a magnetic
onstage presence, and a great acting career ahead of her.
Everyone in the cast loves her, and we just want to see her
again.' But judging from some of the later headlines,
Camilla's acting career was never to be realised, and the
young director's hopes of seeing her alive again would be
dashed.

'Could you fetch the matriculation photograph from
downstairs?' Bridget asked Ffion.

'Sure.' Thirty seconds later Ffion was back with the
photo. 'There she is,' she said, pointing to a young blonde
on the back row who was smiling confidently at the
camera. 'That's Camilla.'

Bridget nodded. The woman in the photograph
matched the close-up shots that appeared in the newspaper
articles. 'So David Smith and Camilla Townsend were
both students at Pembroke College in the same year. And

he seems to have devoted the past twenty-odd years to investigating her disappearance.'

'There's more,' said Ffion. 'Look at this.' She pointed to a newspaper article from the *Oxford Mail*. 'He wasn't just investigating her disappearance. He was her boyfriend and he was arrested for her murder.'

"Man Arrested on Suspicion of Murder," read the headline. Bridget read on.

Police have arrested Oxford University student David Smith on suspicion of the murder of fellow student Camilla Townsend. Camilla, who went missing three months ago following a performance of Shakespeare's *Twelfth Night*, has never been found and police now suspect her boyfriend of killing her and hiding the body. Smith, who denies the allegations, says he is as devastated as anyone by her unexplained disappearance.

The article was accompanied by the photograph of Smith taken from the college matriculation photo.

'Were they allowed to do that?' asked Ffion. 'I mean, just publish a photograph of a man who'd been arrested, and broadcast his name to the world.'

'Remember that this was a quarter of a century ago,' said Bridget. 'Data protection rules had barely been invented then. Was David Smith ever charged with her murder?'

Ffion scanned the wall. 'We'll have to study this in more detail, but I can't see anything about that. If no body was discovered, they would presumably have had to let him go for lack of evidence.'

'And he's spent a lifetime trying to discover the truth.'

Bridget had a lot of sympathy for someone who would do that. Her own sister's killer had never been caught. Not knowing the truth could eat away at you, and Bridget feared this was what had happened to her own parents. For

David Smith to have been arrested on suspicion of his girlfriend's murder must have been devastating for him. Having spent an evening in his company on the ghost tour, Bridget couldn't see the man as a killer, despite his obvious fascination with the dark side of life. Maybe he had even seen a parallel between Camilla's disappearance and the supernatural – both were unexplained mysteries.

'This is interesting,' said Ffion, rummaging through one of the box files on the shelf. 'There's a whole file devoted to the production of *Twelfth Night* after which Camilla went missing.' She fished out a programme and handed it to Bridget. 'There are notes on every member of the cast and crew, right down to the props manager. Smith seems to have tracked them all for years, following their careers, printing off their social media posts. He's basically been stalking them all this time.'

Bridget felt a shiver go down her spine. She had never encountered anything quite like this before. Smith's obsession went well beyond any normal, healthy interest. She stared at the photos and cuttings that filled the wall. 'He was basically trying to do the job that the police failed to do all those years ago, wasn't he?'

'It looks like it,' said Ffion. Then she asked the question that was already in Bridget's mind. 'Do you think there's a connection between Camilla's disappearance and what happened to David Smith last night?'

'It's impossible to say without more evidence,' said Bridget with her professional detective inspector's hat on. But her gut told her otherwise.

CHAPTER 7

Bridget's resources were already stretched, but on balance it seemed worthwhile assigning Ffion to the task of digging out the case file on Camilla Townsend and finding out what was known about the missing student. With no other definite leads to go on, she couldn't ignore the possibility that there was a connection between the historic case and Smith's murder.

'Sure,' said Ffion, looking pleased to have a job that would enable her to utilise her research and analytical skills. 'Is there any particular angle you want me to examine?'

'I'm assuming from the fact that David Smith was still actively engaged in trying to discover what happened to Camilla that her body was never found. Read through the file and see if anything obvious jumps out at you. And compare the known facts to what Smith himself managed to unearth. He may have uncovered a lead that the police didn't know about.'

'You're thinking that whoever abducted Camilla Townsend might have realised Smith was onto them and decided to silence him?'

'I'm not assuming anything right now. This is just an obvious line of enquiry to follow.' Bridget didn't want Ffion getting too wrapped up in this kind of speculation. It was clear that the eager young DC was already conjuring up all kinds of wild explanations for Smith's death. 'But I'd like to know what avenues Smith was working on recently. Had he been to visit someone, for example? Did he have a theory, perhaps about anyone in the cast of the play? The more we know, the sooner we'll be able to establish if this is worth following up.'

And, Bridget refrained from saying, keeping Ffion away from Jake might well be a wise course of action, given the tension between the two of them right now.

'Right, boss,' said Ffion. 'I mean, ma'am. I'll get on it straight away.'

Arriving back at Kidlington, Bridget took a moment to call Chloe. She would have a full day ahead of her running this investigation, and she didn't want her daughter to think that she'd been abandoned. She glanced quickly at the time. Ten thirty in the morning. Probably still way too early for her teenage daughter to be up and about, but Bridget was always optimistic.

To her surprise, her call was answered after a few rings. 'Mum? What is it? Is something wrong?'

'No I just wanted to make sure you were all right.'

'Of course I am,' said Chloe. 'Or at least I was, until you woke me up. Why are you calling so early?'

Bridget refrained from saying that she'd already been at work for several hours. She didn't begrudge her daughter a lie-in during the school holidays. This Christmas would be her last chance for a proper rest for some time. In January Chloe would be sitting her mocks, and then in June her GCSE exams. The exams would determine her future prospects, and Bridget was hoping Chloe would manage to fit in some revision time over the next two weeks. But she wasn't going to start nagging too hard until after Christmas was over.

'I called you now because I might not get another

chance for the rest of the day.'

'You're not at work, are you?' asked Chloe. 'It's nearly Christmas.'

'I know, but something came up. Look, there's probably not much food in the house, but I've left you some money on the kitchen table. Will you be okay on your own today?'

'Of course. No probs.'

Bridget nodded silently. Her daughter was well capable of fending for herself. With Bridget's demanding job, she had to be. 'So what are your plans for today?'

'Plans? Mum, give me a break. I'm on holiday, I don't need a plan.'

'I suppose not. Well, have a nice time whatever you decide to do.'

'Sure. Bye.'

Bridget imagined Chloe pulling the duvet over her head and going back to sleep. If only she could do the same. But the investigation was only just getting started and she needed to make sure it was progressing rapidly. With the Christmas holiday just two days away, time was very much not on her side.

Entering the station she was pleased to discover that the incident room was a hive of activity. Grayson had been good to his word and had drafted in detectives and uniformed officers from other teams to help interview the witnesses. Several phone conversations were underway as she entered, as officers made appointments to go and speak to the people who'd been present in the Turf last night. Ryan and Andy were coordinating the effort.

Jake was busy at his desk, his attention focussed on his computer screen. He looked up as she approached. 'So, I managed to round up all the CCTV footage I could find. The university security services are being a little slow to respond, but the council have just given me access to their Broad Street camera, and I'm also expecting to get some footage from Blackwell's book shop and a couple of the local pubs.'

'Anything showing St Helen's Passage itself?'

'No, unfortunately not.'

'We have to work with what we have,' said Bridget.

She called Andy over. 'Can you start working through the CCTV that Jake's acquired? Focus on the period between ten and eleven. I want to know if there was any suspicious activity during that time.'

'Certainly, ma'am.'

Andy was a diligent officer with a keen eye for detail. Bridget knew that he was the best man for the job. 'Do we have any other leads yet?' she asked.

'Just one,' said Jake. 'It might be something or nothing, but Stu, the homeless guy who sells the *Big Issue* on Broad Street, told me that David Smith got into an argument with the bloke running the carousel.'

Bridget recalled the brightly-painted horses and the piped organ music. The ride had been running right next to the spot from where the ghost tour started. 'What kind of argument?'

'They were treading on each other's patch apparently. Like I said, it could be nothing, but where money is concerned, feelings can run high.'

'Do you have a name for this carousel owner?' asked Bridget.

'Bill Tomlins.'

'Okay,' she said, 'we'll keep him in mind, but for now I want to focus on interviewing everyone who was in the pub at the time of the stabbing. What's the progress with that, Ryan?'

'So far nobody's claimed to have witnessed the attack itself, but we still have plenty more people to talk to. Then, once we start cross-referencing all the statements, we should be able to piece people's movements together more precisely.'

'Okay,' said Bridget.

It was this kind of painstaking detailed work that might throw up a discrepancy between witness accounts and lead to a suspect being identified. But there would be no time for that to be done before the Christmas closure. Bridget really wanted to move faster.

'I'd like to speak to the people who were on the ghost tour myself. They were with David Smith just before he was attacked, and as far as we know they are the only ones with any kind of personal connection to him. Plus, I got to know them myself a little, and I'd like to follow up. Some of them won't be in Oxford for much longer so I need to catch them before they leave. Jake, can you come with me?'

She watched him cast a quick glance across to the nearby desk, where Ffion was now sitting, a steaming mug of herbal tea cradled in her hands. Was that a look of relief on his face at the chance to get out of the office?

He grabbed his jacket and stood up. 'Sure thing.'

CHAPTER 8

The Eastgate Hotel was a seventeenth-century coaching inn built on the site of the city's former east gate. Fronting onto the High Street and Merton Street, the old stone building with its leaded windows was one of the most charming and centrally-located hotels in Oxford, and was popular with tourists and business travellers alike.

'Nice place to stay,' remarked Jake as Bridget parked her Mini in the hotel's car park. 'But not cheap, I imagine.'

'No.' It was evident that the Henderson family – the mother, father, son and daughter who Bridget had met on the ghost tour the previous evening – were not short of money.

When Bridget entered the hotel's reception, she found the father, mother and daughter sitting with their suitcases already packed in the adjacent lounge, next to a real Christmas tree tastefully decorated in silver baubles.

The father, Geoff, rose to his feet to meet her. He was dressed in an open-necked checked shirt and beige jacket over grey trousers. His wife, Lynda, was wearing the same coat as the previous evening, with a Hermès silk scarf knotted at the neck. They gave the impression that they were hoping not to be detained for very long. Lucy, the couple's daughter, was absorbed in her mobile phone and barely registered Bridget and Jake's arrival.

'Mr and Mrs Henderson, I'm sorry to have kept you waiting,' said Bridget. 'It's been a very busy morning. This is my sergeant, DS Jake Derwent.'

'We're in a bit of a hurry, I'm afraid,' said Geoff. 'We have to collect our son, Luke, from college. He's supposed to vacate his room by midday.' He glanced at his watch. 'Knowing Luke, he'll still be lying in bed. I bet he won't even have started packing yet.'

'Geoff,' scolded his wife gently, 'the inspector doesn't want to hear about Luke.'

It was clear that the tensions that existed within the family unit had not eased off since the previous night. It was also apparent that Geoff's opinion of Luke didn't exactly square up with the "diligent, hard-working student" that Lynda had described to Bridget.

'I promise not to take up any more of your time than we need,' said Bridget, seeking to soothe the couple's concerns. 'But I'm sure you understand that we need to take a detailed statement from you under the circumstances.'

'Yes, of course.' Geoff Henderson sat back down, but still looked anxious to be off.

'Luke is studying at New College, right?' asked Bridget, seeking to confirm what Lynda had told her about her son the previous evening.

'Yes, that's right.'

'And you mentioned that he's stayed on for two weeks after term to finish off some work.'

Geoff glanced sideways at his wife.

'That's right,' confirmed Lynda, fiddling with the rings on her finger. 'Some extra study he was keen to get involved in.'

'I see,' said Bridget. It was clear from the couple's discomfort that there was more to the matter than this, but she decided not to pursue it now. Their hackles were already raised, and she could quiz Luke directly when she went to speak to him. New College would be her next stop after the Eastgate.

Mrs Henderson rounded suddenly on her daughter. 'Lucy, will you please put that phone away. It's so rude when the detective inspector is talking to us.'

The girl scowled and slid the phone into her pocket. She leaned back in her chair, looking sullen.

Clearly Bridget's questioning had touched a raw nerve with Lynda.

'Let her be,' said Geoff to his wife. 'None of this conversation concerns Lucy. It doesn't matter if she plays with her phone.'

Lynda pursed her lips in obvious irritation at being over-ruled by her husband, but refrained from contradicting him. Beside her, Lucy pulled the phone out again and resumed her game.

'May I ask where you live?' asked Bridget, shifting to a less controversial question. Taking the conversation off-topic usually enabled people to relax and open up more, and a little background information could often be useful.

'We're from Beaconsfield,' said Geoff.

Beaconsfield was a small market town in the nearby county of Buckinghamshire, about an hour's drive away along the M40. Located in a very affluent part of the country, Bridget recalled reading in a Sunday newspaper that it had been named "Britain's richest town" by virtue of its house prices. The only other fact she knew about it was that it had been the home of Enid Blyton, who had written her stories of childhood adventure and idealised boarding school life from her mock-Tudor mansion called *Green Hedges*.

'And what do you both do for a living?'

'I'm a senior manager at an accountancy firm,' said Geoff.

'And I'm a full-time housewife and mother,' said Lynda rather smugly, 'obviously.'

There was no "obviously" about it, thought Bridget, who'd had no choice but to juggle a career with being a single mum. Mrs Henderson's comment seemed peculiarly outmoded, especially for a woman just in her forties. No doubt having a husband with a well-paid job made it easy to live on a single salary, even in a place as pricey as Beaconsfield, but in Bridget's experience many women with successful husbands followed similar high-powered career paths themselves. Then again, her sister Vanessa had chosen to abandon her own job after having children, and was now dedicated to being the perfect wife and mother. Bridget wasn't one to judge.

'I'd like to establish first whether you'd ever met Mr Goole before last night,' she said. 'You might have known him by his real name, David Smith.'

'No,' said Geoff. 'We'd never seen him before.'

'Mrs Henderson?' prompted Bridget.

'Definitely not.'

Lucy looked up from her screen briefly. 'I preferred it when he was called Gordon Goole. David Smith sounds much too boring for someone giving ghost tours.'

'I agree,' said Bridget. And no doubt so had David Smith himself, which was presumably why he'd created his larger-than-life alter ego.

Bridget switched her attention back to the girl's parents. 'Was there any particular reason why you decided to go on the ghost tour?'

'It was a last-minute decision,' said Lynda. 'We were having a family day, spending some time together.'

'Sounds lovely,' said Bridget. 'What else did you do during the day?'

'We went to a matinée performance of the pantomime at the Playhouse,' said Lynda. '*Jack and the Beanstalk*. Afterwards we stopped to have a look around the market and that was when we saw the ghost tour.'

'Then my main interest is pinning down your movements last night, between the end of the ghost tour, and the time of the murder. That would be between ten and ten thirty. It would also be helpful if you're able to recall the movements of any of the other people on the tour.'

Beside Bridget, Jake's hand was poised over his notebook, ready to record all the details.

'Shall I go first?' said Geoff. 'All right. The first thing I did when we arrived at the Turf was go inside to the bar. The place was heaving. It took me ages to get served.'

'Was Luke with you?'

'Yes. He came to help me carry the drinks.'

'How long did it take you to get served?' asked Bridget, recalling that she'd been stuck with Lynda and Lucy for quite some time before Geoff and Luke returned with the drinks.

'Ages,' moaned Geoff.

'As I recall you were arguing with Luke when you returned from the bar. Do you mind if I ask what that was about?'

Geoff frowned. 'We weren't really arguing. We were just discussing his friend, Dylan. You remember him, I presume?'

Bridget wasn't likely to forget the boy dressed all in black who had behaved so strangely during the first part of the tour, before getting into an argument with Goole and storming off into the night. 'You don't approve of Luke spending time with Dylan?'

'Well, no. He's hardly a good influence. That boy's probably the reason why –' He caught himself and stopped, looking embarrassed.

'The reason why what?' enquired Bridget.

'The reason Luke decided to stay on at college instead of coming home to his family.'

Bridget wondered if that was what he'd intended to say. She glanced at Jake and saw that he was making a note in his book.

'And what did you do after returning from the bar?'

'I stayed with my family.'

'For how long?' Bridget remembered that she had used

the return of Geoff and his son as an opportunity to extricate herself from Lynda and to join Cheryl and the three other women. But she had noticed first Luke and then Geoff vanishing into the crowd several minutes later. She waited to see if Geoff would elaborate.

'Luke went off on his own,' he conceded at last. 'He was still being grumpy after our discussion.'

'And?'

'And then Lynda sent me to look for him.'

Jake jotted it down. 'Did you find him?'

'Not immediately,' admitted Geoff. 'But I caught up with him later.'

Jake looked up. 'How much later would that be?'

'I really don't know.'

'Before or after Mr Goole was stabbed?'

'I honestly couldn't say,' said Geoff. 'I didn't even know that Goole had been attacked until sometime after the event.'

'You hadn't returned by the time I went to the ladies,' said Bridget.

'Well it was probably just after that then,' said Geoff. 'I wasn't really paying attention to the time.'

'So you can't say with any certainty where you were at the time of the murder?' said Jake.

Geoff was beginning to flail under the onslaught of the questioning. 'Well, no, but I certainly wasn't anywhere near it, if that's what you're insinuating.'

'I'm not insinuating anything, sir,' said Jake calmly. 'Just trying to establish the facts.'

'We'd really just like to establish everyone's movements and to find out what you might have seen,' said Bridget. 'Even a small detail might help us with our enquiries. She turned her attention to his wife. 'And what about you, Mrs Henderson?'

Lynda seemed surprised to have been asked. 'Me? Well, I was with you and Lucy while Geoff and Luke were at the bar. And then I was with them.'

'Until they went,' said Bridget.

'Yes, and then I stayed behind with Lucy.'

On mention of her name, the girl glanced up from her phone again. 'You left me with that American lady when you went to look for Dad and Luke. She was telling me all about her dog back home in America.'

'What's the dog's name?' asked Bridget.

'Charlie. He's a cocker spaniel.'

Bridget smiled at her. It was little details like that that often meant someone was telling the truth. Details that her parents seemed unwilling or unable to give about their own movements, and the movements of their son.

Lynda frowned at her daughter in irritation. 'Well, yes, when Luke and Geoff hadn't reappeared after about ten minutes I did just go and have a quick look around. I was beginning to wonder what had happened to them.'

'And did you find them?' inquired Bridget.

'I bumped into Geoff eventually. By the time we got back to Lucy, Luke had returned too.'

'Where had he been?'

'He'd been for a smoke,' said Lucy.

Lynda pursed her lips in obvious disapproval. 'It's a disgusting habit. I expect he picked it up from that boy, Dylan.'

'So in summary,' said Bridget to Geoff, 'both you and Luke were on your own for perhaps fifteen minutes, and your wife was absent for five or ten minutes?'

'It really wasn't that long at all.'

'Finally, Mr and Mrs Henderson, was there anything you recall about last night that strikes you as in any way suspicious?'

'No, nothing,' said Geoff. 'Like I said, the bar was absolutely heaving. There were far too many people there for any one of them to stick out in any way.'

Bridget thanked them for their time. 'I know you want to collect your son,' she said, 'but I'll need to speak to him before you do.'

'Is that really necessary, Inspector?' asked Lynda. 'We've already told you what happened, and he's just a boy.'

'He's nineteen,' said Bridget. 'And yes, I'm afraid that it is necessary.'

CHAPTER 9

So what did you make of the happy family?' Bridget asked Jake as they walked the short distance along Longwall Street to New College. It was no more than a five minute journey, and quicker to leave her Mini parked at the Eastgate than to brave Oxford's tortuous one-way system.

'Honestly, I was thinking I'm glad I don't have to spend Christmas with them,' said Jake.

'Funnily enough,' said Bridget, 'I was thinking exactly the same.' However bossy Vanessa might be, and however awkward Bridget might feel in her parents' company, the constant undercurrents of tension within the Henderson family would make Christmas a hell.

'I was also thinking that I barely believed half of what they said,' continued Jake, 'particularly with regard to their son, Luke. They were obviously covering up for him for some reason.'

'Then it seems we're in complete agreement,' said Bridget with a smile at her sergeant.

The hard frost that had set in overnight had melted away in the warmth of the morning sun, and the ghostly atmosphere that had cloaked the streets under cover of darkness had been banished. Yet as they turned the corner into Holywell Street, the looming presence of the college buildings once more cast a faintly sinister spell. Bridget glanced up, taking in the tall, stone façade of the so-called New Buildings. Rows of ill-tempered gargoyles and grotesques leered down at her from their stone perches, their snouts wrinkled, their teeth bared. The elaborately carved mullioned windows of the college gave the place the appearance of a medieval castle. A wide and pointed archway led into the belly of the building.

'So this is New College,' said Jake.

'One of the grandest colleges in Oxford,' said Bridget, who had attended many concerts in the splendour of the chapel. 'And one of the oldest, despite its name.'

Jake grinned. 'I'd pretty much gathered that, ma'am. I think I've been here long enough now to know that the word "new" means something different in Oxford.'

'So what are your plans for Christmas?' she enquired. She knew that Jake liked to visit his family and friends in Yorkshire whenever he took annual leave.

'I'll be heading up north, ma'am. There's nothing to keep me here.'

He sounded downbeat, and Bridget debated if she should say more, but at that moment her phone buzzed with an incoming message. When she saw it was from her sister, she ignored it and put the phone back in her pocket. Vanessa was forever fussing over the arrangements for Christmas Day. It probably wasn't anything important.

The college was largely deserted at this time of year, with Michaelmas term having been finished for two weeks. Following the porter's directions, they crossed the Great Quad, then on towards Luke's room in the Garden Quadrangle. It would be a beautiful place to spend your undergraduate years. The seventeenth-century rooms of the quad looked out across the college gardens, which were enclosed by the original city wall dating back to the thirteenth century. The sense of being inside a great medieval fortress was even stronger here. In the summer the flowerbeds would be a riot of colour. Now, in the depth of winter, the bare trees and evergreen shrubs held a serene and restrained beauty. Bridget had to remind herself that just a few hundred feet away, beyond the serenity of the college cloisters, a man had lost his life last night, stabbed and left bleeding to death.

They climbed the stairs to Luke's room and Bridget rapped loudly on the door.

It opened after a little while, and a somewhat dishevelled Luke stared at them in surprise. 'Oh! I thought it was my mum and dad.' He was dressed in a loose-fitting T-shirt and a pair of jogging pants, with bare feet. Not quite still in bed as his father had predicted, but not long out of it.

In his current state he looked even younger than he had the previous evening. His mother had been right when she'd said that he was little more than a boy. Bridget couldn't help reflect that her own daughter was just a few years younger. After GCSEs and A Levels, Chloe would be heading off to college or university herself. The idea made Bridget quite twitchy.

Luke frowned at her as if trying to place her. 'You were on that ghost tour last night,' he said eventually. He eyed Jake nervously. 'And who are you?'

'We're police officers,' said Bridget, showing him her warrant card. Luke hadn't been present when she'd revealed her occupation to the other members of the ghost tour group, and apparently his parents hadn't felt the need to inform him. 'I'm Detective Inspector Bridget Hart and this is my colleague Detective Sergeant Jake Derwent. May we come in?'

Luke seemed reluctant to allow them inside. 'Look if this is about… you know, then I thought that had all been sorted out by the college.'

Bridget sniffed the air. Beneath the surface stink of an unshowered male body and a term's worth of unwashed clothes, there was an unmistakable pungent aroma coming from the room. She could tell that Jake had noticed it too, and she immediately had a pretty good idea what might be making Luke nervous.

'I think that we'd better come in and you can tell us all about it,' she said.

'Er, yes, sure.' Luke retreated inside his room and sat down on his unmade bed. An open suitcase on the floor was overflowing with dirty laundry. Books and folders were piled chaotically on the room's only two chairs. Bridget and Jake remained standing.

Luke looked up at them in trepidation. 'Am I in trouble?'

'What kind of trouble do you think you might be in, Luke?'

'Is this a trick? Are you trying to get me to confess?'

'To possession of cannabis?' asked Bridget, because that was what she had smelled.

Luke nodded miserably.

'That's not why we're here. We've come to speak to you about the murder of Gordon Goole, the ghost tour guide, real name David Smith.'

'Oh, that,' said Luke. A look of sudden alarm flashed across his face. 'You don't think I had anything to do with it, do you?'

'Why don't we start at the beginning,' suggested Bridget, 'and you can tell us what you're really doing in Oxford two weeks after the end of term.'

'Right, yeah, sure. I don't suppose there's any point trying to hide it. The thing is, I got into some trouble with the college over smoking weed. It wasn't the first time, either. I'd already received a verbal warning from the police. I thought I was going to be sent down, but instead the dean offered me another chance if I agreed to stay on after term ended and do some work around the college.'

'Academic work?' asked Bridget.

Luke snorted with nervous laughter. 'No. Helping the maintenance staff. I've been doing some work on the sports fields. It's been quite good fun, actually. And it meant I could postpone returning home for another two weeks, so it's all good.'

'You don't get on with your family,' said Jake.

Luke pulled a face. 'Yesterday was bad enough. Playing at being happy families and spending "quality time" together.' He mimed a pair of quotes in the air with his fingers. 'Mum even insisted on taking us to that stupid pantomime, as if Lucy and I are still little kids. Honestly, I don't know how I'm going to survive Christmas cooped up with them.'

'Perhaps you could tell us about your movements last night?'

A cautious look immediately reappeared on his face. 'My movements?'

Jake consulted his notes. 'Your father has told us that you went to the bar with him to help carry the drinks back.'

'Oh, yeah, that's right,' said Luke. 'We brought them back to Mum and Lucy.'

'When you returned, you were engaged in some kind of argument with your father.'

'Right. That's basically our normal state of coexistence. Mum and Dad are always getting at me about something.'

'What was it this time?'

'Dad was giving me a hard time about Dylan.' He glanced at Bridget. 'You remember? My friend who joined us on the tour?'

'I remember.'

'Well, Mum and Dad think that Dylan's a bad influence on me. They just don't understand him, that's all. It's really unfair, actually. It's because he's a bit OCD, you know? Mum calls it a "mental health issue" – honestly! They just can't handle anyone who's different to them.'

'So your father was pressurising you to spend less time with Dylan?'

'They'd like me to shun him entirely. I told Dad that Dylan's my best friend, and that he should respect that. I mean, loyalty to your friend's a virtue, right? The problem is that Mum and Dad always want to control everything.

I'm only here because they wanted me to follow in their footsteps.'

'So it wasn't your choice to study at Oxford?'

Luke shook his head vigorously. 'No way, man. I wanted to go travelling and see the world, but they wouldn't hear of it. They said I needed to get a degree so that I could get a good job. But Dad's idea of a good job is putting a suit on each day and sitting in an office. I mean, what sort of life is that?'

'One that supports you financially?' suggested Jake.

Luke glared at him but said nothing.

'And what happened after the argument?' asked Bridget.

'What do you mean?'

'After you returned with the drinks you went somewhere again.'

'Well, yes. Dad and I were mad at each other, so I disappeared for a smoke.'

'On your own?'

'Sure.'

'And where did you go for this smoke, exactly?'

'I stayed in the grounds of the pub.'

'Did you see Gordon Goole, or anyone acting in any way suspiciously?'

'No. Is that everything now?' he asked. 'I'm supposed to be getting packed ready for Mum and Dad to pick me up.'

'Just one last thing, said Bridget. 'Why did your friend Dylan get so upset during the ghost tour?'

'He's really into the paranormal. It's his big thing, so he took offence at the way the tour guide was just telling ghost stories as a way to entertain the tourists.'

'It seemed rather an overreaction.'

'Maybe,' admitted Luke. 'But what you need to understand about Dylan is that he's had a really difficult time. His mother was a heroin addict and she died of an overdose when he was a kid, so he's lived in care or with foster parents most of his life. But the guy's a bloody genius. He's studying Physics but he knows a ton of stuff about everything. He's probably going to be as famous as Einstein one day.'

Bridget raised her eyebrows at this but didn't question Luke's assessment of his friend. He clearly received quite enough criticism from his family. His admiration for his maverick friend, and his frustration with his parents was obvious. But Bridget couldn't help feeling that he just didn't quite have the confidence to stand on his own two feet and make his own decisions. Perhaps the run-in with the college authorities, and his two-week period of atonement would prove to have a lasting and beneficial effect.

'And will Dylan also be going home today?'

'No, he's staying on in Oxford. He doesn't really have another home to go to so he lives in private rented accommodation in the city. He said I was welcome to stay with him but you can imagine what my parents said to that.'

'We'll need to take his address and phone number,' said Jake.

Luke scowled, but gave them an address in Union Street and a phone number. 'I hope you're not going to give him a hard time. Dylan really doesn't have anything to do with this at all. He wasn't even around when the murder took place.'

'Don't worry, we'll treat him fairly.'

'I'm sorry the ghost tour guy's dead,' said Luke. 'He was a good storyteller, even if Dylan didn't like him much.'

Bridget thanked him for his time and gave one last glance around the untidy room. 'We'll let you get on with your packing now. I expect your mum and dad will be here any minute.'

★

The files had been gathering dust in the police archives for years. Ffion blew hard and sent a thick grey cloud billowing across her desk.

'Hey, watch out!' cried DC Harry Johns.

'Sorry,' said Ffion. She set the pile of box files down in front of her computer and began to sort through them.

'What is all this lot, anyway?' asked Harry.

'Ancient history.' The missing person enquiry into Camilla Townsend had been closed over twenty years ago, with no body ever found and no one charged over her disappearance. And yet, for David Smith, the investigation into the missing student was anything but over. On an adjacent desk, Ffion had piled all the newspaper articles, photographs, and handwritten notes that had been recovered from Smith's house on Lake Street. He had amassed almost as much material as in the police files.

Where to begin? That was the question.

She decided to start with the police investigation, to ground herself in facts rather than speculation. Looking at the mound of paper spread over the other desk, it would be easy to lose yourself down a rabbit hole if you tried to follow Smith's own line of enquiry. The way that the newspaper articles had covered almost one entire wall of the spare room in his house pointed to obsession, and Ffion knew that obsession led quickly to delusion. Even if he'd stayed grounded, he was unlikely to have made any kind of breakthrough. While it was conceivable that Smith had turned up some new gem of information, it was more probable that he'd run into the same dead ends as the professionals.

The case file had been opened some twenty-five years ago, at the beginning of December, immediately after Camilla had been reported missing by her housemates. She'd failed to return to her house after appearing in the final performance of Shakespeare's *Twelfth Night*, and the last time anyone had seen her was at the after-show party which had taken place at a café-bar on Walton Street, called Freud's. Ffion knew the venue well. It was just a few streets away from her own house in Oxford's hip canal-side district of Jericho. In tune with the funky vibe of the area,

Freud's was situated within a converted neoclassical church that had been saved from demolition. With its stone Ionic columns, cavernous interior and stained-glass windows, the café-bar had a unique style and was a cool place to enjoy a coffee or a cocktail.

The police had interviewed everyone present at the party, which included the director, actors and other people involved in the theatre production, as well as various hangers-on, but had been unable to arrive at any definite conclusion. With little to go on, they'd taken the decision to interview David Smith under caution and then arrest him.

The victim's boyfriend was always the guy most likely to have committed the crime. Assuming that Camilla had actually been killed. David hadn't been present at the final-night party because he hadn't been in the cast, and he'd been unable to account satisfactorily for his whereabouts to the police. But with no firm evidence, they'd been forced to release him. It didn't seem to Ffion like they'd made much effort to identify any further suspects. A few more people had been interviewed, including Camilla's housemates, as well as her tutor at Pembroke College. But with nothing to go on, the investigation had been wound down and eventually closed. The files had sat in the archive, and no one had looked at them until Ffion had requested them that morning from the records officer.

She turned her attention next to David Smith's own investigation. The material here was surprisingly well organised. Smith had clearly been a diligent researcher, even though his techniques had been a little less orthodox than the official enquiry. Not only had Smith collected every article relating to the disappearance from both the local and national newspapers, he'd carried out his own interviews with the same people the police had spoken to, recording his notes in neat, handwritten reports that were as detailed and precise as any police investigation Ffion had ever seen.

She was impressed.

Among the various people Smith had collected information about, one stood out – the play's director. And in contrast to the police's conviction that David Smith was most likely responsible for the missing student's disappearance, Smith himself had been convinced that it was the director who had something to hide. It seemed that David had broken up with Camilla shortly before the theatre production began, with David accusing her of sleeping with the director in order to secure her role in the play. He had meticulously tracked the director's career ever since, from Oxford student to repertory theatre in the Midlands, to his big break at the National, and on to the height of success in the West End. The man appeared to have done everything from Samuel Beckett to Shakespeare to box-office-breaking musicals.

Yet despite all his research, Smith had uncovered nothing that could prove with any certainty what had happened to Camilla that night. In fact it was possible that she was still alive, and had left Oxford of her own volition for some unknown reason.

Whatever the truth of the matter, it seemed clear enough to Ffion after reading through David Smith's extensive notes that the ghost tour guide himself was innocent of any crime. Unless, of course, he had somehow deluded himself into believing his own story, and this was all some elaborate hoax designed to bolster his self-deception.

Finally she thumbed through a handful of photographs in a paper envelope. They appeared to be a selection of amateur photos taken at the last-night party at Freud's. Camilla appeared in many of the shots, her pretty young face and long blonde hair immediately recognisable. Also recognisable after sifting through so much material was the face of the play's director. He and Camilla often appeared together in the photos, although she was just as often pictured being equally friendly with other men. The remaining photos showed other men and women, presumably members of the cast or the production crew.

The final items at the bottom of the file were a poster and a programme from the production of *Twelfth Night*. As well as a synopsis of the plot, the programme contained thumbnail black-and-white photos of all the cast members, together with their names, colleges and a brief bio. The director's confident smile beamed out from the back page above a list of the stage crew – stagehands, prop manager, wardrobe manager and so on.

Ffion replaced everything in its original files and sat back to sip her peppermint tea. It had long since gone cold, but it was still refreshing and stimulating. She'd lost all track of time and become completely engrossed in her task. It was a habit she was well used to. Growing up bisexual, and holding ideas that the inhabitants of her tiny Welsh coal-mining village had considered bizarre, she'd used the twin disciplines of study and exercise to filter out the isolation that she'd experienced as a teenager. Even though Oxford was a hundred times more liberal than her childhood home, she still sometimes felt alienated from conventional society. Perhaps it was partly her own fault. She refused to make changes to accommodate other people's expectations. Her unconventional appearance – tall and slender, with a pixie haircut, and often clad in green biker's leather – tended to intimidate people. But she could no longer be certain whether people reacted against her because of her looks, or whether she presented herself that way in order to deliberately wrongfoot people.

No matter. She'd found her niche, working her dream job of police detective, and sharing a house with friends in Jericho. It was a shame that her two housemates would be away for Christmas, leaving her on her own. Claire had just flown back from a research trip to Johannesburg, and was now off to spend Christmas with her family. Judy was going away for a week with her boyfriend.

Ffion's thoughts drifted to Jake. They'd been a couple, briefly, and if things had turned out differently, she would have been spending Christmas with him. But she refused to dwell on what she'd lost. Self-pity was an act of self-harm.

Besides, she was used to being alone. She'd spent Christmas on her own before, and knew she could handle it. She began to wonder how she might enjoy her time. She'd probably keep to her usual weekend routine. An early-morning run, followed by a hot shower, then a leisurely breakfast at a nearby café, if any were open. Perhaps she'd take her Kawasaki out for a spin while the roads were quiet. Then there was a race meeting on Boxing Day in the grounds of a nearby country house. The problem would not be boredom, but finding enough time to pack everything in.

CHAPTER 10

Leaving Luke's room and making her way back through New College, Bridget began to worry that she was wasting her time interviewing the people who had been on the ghost tour last night. After all, the various groups had been strangers to each other before the tour began, and presumably strangers to David Smith too. But these people had been with him immediately before he died and it was just possible that one of them had seen or heard something that might prove critical.

'Do you think we ought to have confiscated his stash of weed, ma'am?' asked Jake as they headed towards the porters' lodge.

'To be honest, I think he's going to need it.' Bridget suspected that she herself would be relying quite heavily on alcohol to get her through the Christmas season.

As they set off along Holywell Street she checked her phone, which she'd set to silent for the interview with Luke. There was now a missed call from Vanessa, Bridget having failed to reply to her text from earlier. Well, Bridget didn't think that arrangements for Christmas were more important than a murder enquiry. Vanessa would just have to wait.

'Do you want to go and talk to this Dylan guy next?' asked Jake.

'It doesn't sound like he's going anywhere for the moment. No, our next stop is the prison.'

'Ma'am?'

'Malmaison.'

The Malmaison Oxford had once been a Victorian prison, but was now a luxury boutique hotel, located in the city's historic Castle Quarter. The original jail cells had been turned into well-appointed rooms, and the former solitary confinement wing was now a brasserie. The three-storey atrium retained the prison's original wrought-iron staircases and walkways, making a stunning centrepiece to the building, and on a cold but sunny day like this one, you could enjoy a hot drink in the old exercise yard if you were feeling brave. It would no doubt be a fun place for three women of a certain age to spend Christmas, and Bridget hoped that she would find Deborah, Liz and Julia there, making good use of its facilities.

'What do we know about these three women?' Jake asked her.

'Not much,' admitted Bridget. 'Divorcees in their early forties, in search of a good time. They were friends at university apparently, and have returned to make the most of their new-found freedom. One of them, Julia, left the Turf early, supposedly in the company of a man she'd just met.' Bridget shot her sergeant a mischievous glance. 'Watch out for her, Jake. I think she might be a bit of a maneater.'

Jake looked suddenly alarmed at the prospect of meeting the three older women.

Bridget gave him a wink. 'Don't worry. I'll come to your rescue if any of them try anything on.'

They found Liz and Deborah in the bar, lunching on a selection of chicken wings, deep fried squid and a bowl of French fries. Bridget's stomach rumbled in response to the smell of the food, reminding her that she hadn't eaten anything since a hastily cobbled together breakfast that morning.

The two women were seated at one of the low glass tables that dotted the room. With its dark panelled walls and stylish comfy chairs, the bar was the perfect place to while away a cold winter's afternoon. The two women gave the impression that they were here for the day. Liz was already perusing the cocktail menu, and Bridget wondered how long it would be before they were knocking back the margaritas and Bloody Marys. Not long she suspected.

'Oh, hello,' said Liz when she noticed Bridget. 'Come and join us.'

'And your friend, too,' said Deborah, raising a glass of white wine to her rouged lips and giving Jake a good look over. Bridget didn't need to study her sergeant herself to know that his ears would now be turning a shade of salmon. She pulled up a chair.

'Isn't Julia with you?' she asked. She'd really been hoping to speak to all three of them, and Julia in particular, in view of her sudden disappearance last night at close to the time of the murder.

'Julia, it seems, has decided to abandon us,' said Deborah, nursing her long-fluted wine glass in delicate fingers.

'For the man she met last night?' enquired Bridget.

'Precisely.' Liz jabbed the air with a chicken wing for emphasis. Bridget realised that the two of them had already been drinking for some while.

'It's really nothing unexpected,' continued Deborah. 'In fact, it's very much Julia's style.'

'Julia likes to think of herself as a free spirit,' said Liz. 'She's always going off on a whim, following her heart, trusting her instinct, whatever you want to call it. She's just been in Bali for a month *finding herself*. Well, she may have found herself, but I'm afraid she's lost us.' They both dissolved into a fit of giggles.

Bridget glanced at Jake, who had his notebook and pen at the ready, waiting to take notes. He'd written nothing yet, but Bridget guessed that the two women had plenty more they wanted to get off their chests about their absent friend. They were talking freely, and she decided to let them run. Who knew what they might reveal if given free rein to speak their mind?

Deborah took up the thread. 'When we were young we used to love this side of her, you know, the way she could just breeze in and out. We wished we could be as carefree as her, but now that she's in her mid-forties, it's growing a little tiresome. When people get older they ought to become more dependable, don't you think? Not husbands, obviously. But friends should remain loyal. I mean, we're only here together for a few days. But Julia likes to go where the wind takes her.'

'And where precisely has the wind taken her this time?' asked Bridget.

'The same place it always does. In search of true love,' said Liz. Bridget waited for her to elaborate. 'We went to the New Theatre on Saturday night to see *West Side Story*. It's the new production that recently transferred from the West End. It's got rave reviews.'

'I know the one you mean,' said Bridget. She'd tried to get tickets for herself, Jonathan and Chloe but it had sold out.

'We were looking through the programme before the show started,' said Liz, 'and Julia suddenly squealed. She'd just noticed that the director was none other than Guy Goodwin.'

'Who?'

'A blast from the past,' explained Liz. 'When Julia and Guy were students, they had a brief fling together. And although Julia hadn't seen him for years, as soon as she saw his name in the programme she just "knew" that fate had brought them back together. What was it she said, Deborah?'

'"*It's written in the stars, darlings,*"' said Deborah, affecting an overly theatrical voice. 'Once Julia gets an idea into her head, there's no talking her out of it. After the show she claimed she had a headache and was going back to the hotel, but afterwards we found out that she'd gone backstage and hooked up with Guy. That's why she was constantly checking her phone during the ghost tour last night. The two of them had arranged to meet up afterwards.'

'I see,' said Bridget.

'No, I don't think you do,' said Liz. 'What you need to understand is that we all agreed a no-man pact for the duration of our stay in Oxford. Just three girls together. Debs and I are recently divorced, and Julia has had a string of disastrous relationships over the years. We wanted to put all that behind us and forget our problems, just for a week.'

'We took a solemn vow,' said Deborah. 'An oath.'

'And then, on the very first night, Julia sneaked off to find Guy. She's a traitor, there's no other word for it.' Liz reached for her wine glass and found it empty. 'Waiter! Can we have... what are you having, Debs? Something with gin? How about a martini? Two martinis, please.' She switched her attention to Jake. 'Care to join us?'

It took only a moment before Jake's ears blazed with colour. 'Um... I'm on duty,' he mumbled.

'Quite right too,' said Liz. 'Very conscientious. I do feel safe with you around. What was your name again?'

'Jake. DS Jake Derwent.'

'Well, DS Jake Derwent, maybe you'd like to come back later when you're off duty? We wouldn't say no to having a nice tall policeman to look after us.'

So much for the no-man pact, thought Bridget. She stepped in quickly to rescue her flailing sergeant. 'So back to last night. Did Julia explain why she was leaving the Turf?'

'She didn't need to,' said Deborah. 'It may as well have been written in the stars. She slinked off to go and meet Guy again.'

'Have you heard from her since?'

'No. She's ignoring our calls. Too ashamed to face us.'

'So you haven't heard from her at all since last night?'

'She sent a text this morning to tell us not to worry,' said Liz. 'I texted back to say that we weren't *worried*, just *angry*. I didn't get a reply.'

'She'll be back,' declared Deborah, 'with her tail between her legs. And there'll be tears too. There are always tears.' She sighed. 'We should refuse to take her back, really. But it's hard to stay mad at Julia for long. We love her too much.'

The conversation had taken on a maudlin tone, and Bridget worried that tears might begin to flow sooner rather than later. 'What is it that Julia does for a living?' she asked. She was unable to shake off the idea that she recognised Julia's face.

'She's an actress,' supplied Liz. 'She started out in repertory theatre, then got a few bit parts in TV soaps. A few years ago she had a big break with a role in a TV crime drama. She played the wife of the murderer.'

'Carstairs,' said Bridget. 'Julia Carstairs.' That's why the face had been so familiar. Bridget had watched that crime drama herself. 'So what can you tell me about Guy Goodwin?'

'Guy? Well, like I said, he and Julia were together briefly in their student days. Now he's a theatre director in the West End. He made a name for himself in serious drama and then turned to musicals. I suppose that's where the big money is.'

'Did either of you know the man who was murdered last night?' Bridget asked. 'His real name was David Smith.'

The two women shook their heads. 'Such an entertaining tour guide,' said Deborah sadly. 'Why on earth would anyone want to kill him?'

The question seemed to hang over them, its weight pressing down on the two women's valiant attempts to enjoy themselves and to forget about their failed marriages. Bridget and Jake took their leave, leaving them to sip their martinis in silence.

CHAPTER 11

'Next stop Staverton Road,' said Bridget. She and Jake had dropped by a sandwich shop to grab a bite to eat before returning to the car. She watched in a mix of admiration and disgust as he devoured first an enormous sausage roll and then a bacon and egg butty, before turning his attention to an extra-large chocolate muffin.

'Hungry,' he explained, catching her sideways glance.

'Me too.' Bridget had been tempted by the array of pastries and cheese-filled paninis on offer, but had exerted every last ounce of her willpower and stuck to a low-fat chicken wrap, penance for the churros and hot chocolate consumed at the Christmas Market the day before. She really must try and show some restraint before Christmas Day itself.

That reminded her, Vanessa was still attempting to make contact, but she really had no time for her sister's trivia today. She consulted her notebook. 'Cheryl and Trevor Mansfield are over from the States visiting his elderly mother who lives in North Oxford. Cheryl's an American, originally from Seattle, although now they live in Cambridge, Massachusetts. Trevor's a lecturer at Harvard.'

Given half a chance, Cheryl would probably have revealed her entire life story to Bridget. Hopefully both she and her husband would be happy to talk about anything they might have seen or heard last night. Bridget was particularly keen to discover whether Trevor had seen something useful while he'd been away from the rest of the group taking his phone call.

'Harvard?' said Jake through a mouth still full of cake. 'That's the American equivalent of Oxford, I suppose.'

'That's right,' said Bridget, 'although perhaps there are still a few crusty Oxford academics who regard Harvard as a young upstart. After all, it's only a few hundred years old.'

The house on Staverton Road was a rambling redbrick Edwardian semi spread over three floors. It was unusual for such a house to still be a family home. These huge properties, once inhabited by successful businessmen and wealthy dons, sold for millions these days. Many had now been divided into apartments, or taken over by one of the colleges as student accommodation. Mature shrubs lined the path to the front door which was decorated with a magnificent holly wreath interwoven with ivy and mistletoe. Bridget rang the bell which chimed somewhere deep inside the house.

A minute later the door was opened by Trevor, dressed in a chunky, cable-knit sweater, beige slacks and slippers. 'Inspector, we've been expecting you. Do come in.'

He led them through to the lounge where a log fire crackled in the hearth, adding a mellow smokiness to the fresh, woody scent of pine from the Christmas tree prominently positioned in the wide bay window. The floor beneath the tree was stacked with a tantalising pile of presents in different shapes and sizes, all wrapped in brightly coloured paper. Family photographs adorned the mantelpiece and bookcases in the slightly cluttered but homely room. Bridget sensed that this was a happy family home, full of fond memories and shared experiences.

Cheryl was sitting in a comfortable armchair by the fire, a thick hardback on her lap. Next to her sat an elderly lady, presumably Trevor's mother. She was absorbed in a newspaper crossword, her reading glasses perched on her nose, a pencil in one hand. She looked up to study Bridget.

From upstairs came the sound of running feet and children's excited voices. 'My great-nieces and nephews,' explained Trevor, pointing towards the ceiling. 'My brother and sister and their families have just arrived and are settling in.'

'So there's going to be quite a crowd of you for Christmas,' said Bridget.

'The more the merrier,' said Cheryl, getting up from her chair to greet Bridget. 'Trevor and I don't have children of our own, so we love seeing the youngsters.'

The old lady by the fireside set aside her crossword and rose to offer her hand.

'This is my mother,' said Trevor.

'Pleased to meet you, Mrs Mansfield,' said Bridget.

The old woman seized Bridget's hand in her age-mottled fingers. Her grasp was surprisingly strong. Although she looked well into her nineties, her eyes were clear, giving the impression of a sharp mind behind them. The cryptic crossword in the newspaper was very nearly completed. 'Call me Margaret,' she said pleasantly. 'Trevor has told me all about what happened last night. How simply dreadful.'

She remained standing, and now Bridget noticed something else behind those bright blue eyes. A guardedness, perhaps.

'I realise you'll want to speak to Trevor and Cheryl in peace,' said Margaret after a moment, 'so I shall make myself scarce. Shall I put the kettle on?'

'That would be lovely, thanks,' said Bridget, never one to turn down an offer of food or drink.

'Milk and two sugars, please,' said Jake.

'I'll fetch some biscuits too,' said Margaret. 'I expect

you have a good appetite, a strapping young man like you.'

She isn't wrong there, thought Bridget.

The room was warm and the sofa inviting. Bridget positioned herself as far away as possible from the blaze of the fire, worried that if she made herself too comfortable she would likely be lulled into a contented drowsiness. Jake, she noted, chose to remain standing, his notebook and pencil in his hands. Trevor took a wing-backed chair near the tree, while Cheryl returned to her own fireside seat, laying her book aside.

'I understand that you're visiting Oxford from Harvard,' said Bridget to Trevor. 'What's your subject?'

'Social Studies,' said Trevor.

'Trevor was originally a tutor at Oxford,' supplied Cheryl, obviously keen to fill in all relevant details, 'but, luckily for me, he moved to the US some twenty years ago.'

Bridget thought she detected a slight shadow passing across Trevor's face at the mention of this unasked-for fact, but if it had ever existed it was quickly replaced with a broad smile. 'That's right. Best move I ever made,' said Trevor. 'And I'm not just talking about my career.'

Cheryl beamed at him from across the room.

'What made you leave Oxford?' asked Bridget.

Trevor was quick with his answer, as if he'd been asked the same question many times before and had his reply thoroughly rehearsed. 'I didn't want to become a fossilised don in an Oxford college. Oxford does that to people, you might have noticed. The politics of the senior common room, the dinners at high table, the ceremonies in Latin, the weight of hundreds of years of history pressing down on you. I didn't want to get stuck in a rut. When such a great opportunity came up across the pond, I took it. It's as simple as that.'

'And what is it that you do?' Bridget asked Cheryl.

'I'm a lecturer too. I teach MBA students at Harvard Business School.'

'Do you come to Oxford often?'

'Usually about twice a year. Christmas, and again in

July for Margaret's birthday. She'll be ninety-two next summer. It's a great opportunity to catch up with Trevor's family too. I love the idea that they all grew up in this big, old house, and keep coming back here.'

Another series of footsteps and shouts came from overhead. It was clear that the children were having a fantastic time. Bridget had also loved Christmas as a child. She had fond memories from the old house in Woodstock, the three girls growing up together with loving parents. All that had been cruelly shattered when Abigail died, and Christmas had never been the same again.

The door opened and Margaret reappeared bearing a tray set with a china teapot, cups, saucers, a jug of milk, a bowl of sugar and a plate of shortbread biscuits. Trevor jumped up to help her set the tray down on the coffee table.

Bridget waited patiently while the ritual of pouring the tea, milk first, and handing the biscuits around was performed with true English civility. Once Margaret had withdrawn again from the room, she picked up the thread of the conversation.

'Trevor, I'd like you to tell me as much as you can recall about what happened last night at the pub. You went to buy drinks at the bar when we arrived?'

'That's right. You know what the Turf can be like. Two tiny bars, a huge crush of people. It took me a good while to get served. Then I brought the drinks over to where Cheryl was chatting to those other three women.'

'They were such fun,' interrupted Cheryl. 'Despite going through some rather nasty break-ups, they were determined to put the past behind them and have a good time.'

'Quite,' said Bridget, although *desperate* might have been a better word than *determined*. She turned back to Trevor. 'And then what?'

'I had to take a phone call.'

Bridget waited to see if he would volunteer any further information.

'It was from Harvard,' he said after a pause. 'That's the

problem with the time difference when I'm over here. For them it was only late afternoon.'

'Where did you go to take the call?'

'I walked back out to New College Lane. You know, by the Bridge of Sighs. It was far too noisy to have a conversation in the Turf.'

'And how long did the call last?'

'I'd say about twenty minutes, give or take.'

'That's right,' confirmed Cheryl with a nod of her head.

Bridget did a quick calculation. That would have put Trevor in a prime position to have witnessed anyone entering or leaving the Turf just before or immediately after the murder. 'Can you tell me what you saw during that time?'

'I'm sorry. I was so wrapped up in my phone conversation, I really didn't pay any attention to what was happening nearby. Except that just as I was finishing my call, an ambulance arrived and the paramedics rushed into the pub. I tried to follow them inside to find out what was going on, but there was a crowd of people blocking St Helen's Passage, and then the police arrived and closed the entrance. I had to walk all the way around and return to the Turf from the other entrance in Holywell Street.'

'So you saw nothing?' said Bridget with dismay. 'Please think carefully. Did you see anyone enter or leave the pub during the time you were on the phone?'

Trevor balanced his cup and saucer on his knee and looked embarrassed. 'I'm really sorry, Inspector. I knew you'd ask me, and I've been racking my brains all morning, but I just don't know.'

Bridget turned instead to Cheryl. 'You spoke to the tour guide in the pub courtyard. How did he seem?'

'In good spirits. He was regaling us with various tales. He was a very amusing raconteur.'

'Did he say anything that might have indicated that he was worried or nervous?'

'No, he seemed quite relaxed to me.'

Cheryl's judgement confirmed Bridget's own

impression. Jonathan, too, had noticed nothing strange about the guide's behaviour. If he'd had any suspicion that he was in danger, he hadn't shown it.

'When he left you, where did he say he was going?'

'I left him with your, um, boyfriend, Jonathan, so I don't know for sure where he was going, but he headed in the direction of the bar. I think that Jonathan must have been the last person in our group to speak to him before...' she trailed off awkwardly.

Cheryl's account tallied with what Jonathan had told Bridget. So far no one had seen where David Smith had gone after telling Jonathan that he was going to the bar to get more drinks. She tried a different tack. 'I understand that Julia Carstairs left the Turf at some time that evening?'

'Yes,' said Cheryl. 'I was chatting to Julia, Deborah and Liz, but Julia seemed very distracted. She kept checking her phone as if she was expecting a message. Then, very abruptly, she suggested another drink, disappeared off to the bar, and never came back. It was quite mysterious, really. Liz and Deborah thought she'd gone off on some kind of romantic liaison. They seemed very put out. Liz tried phoning her, but Julia didn't answer. She just vanished.' She turned to Trevor. 'Julia's a famous actress, apparently, in a British TV show.'

'One last thing before I go,' said Bridget. 'Can I ask, did either of you know the murdered man? Although he went by the name of Gordon Goole for his ghost tours, his real name was David Smith.'

Both Cheryl and Trevor shook their heads. 'We've been to Oxford many times,' said Cheryl, 'but that was the first time we've ever been on a ghost tour.'

'I'm sorry,' said Trevor. 'The name doesn't ring any bells. I wish we could have been more helpful.'

'Never mind,' said Bridget. 'She put her cup and saucer back on the tray and stood up. 'If you do remember anything that you think may be relevant, please give me a call at any time.'

As they left the lounge, four small children came

hurtling down the stairs. They halted before Bridget and Jake, then turned and ran down the hallway towards the back of the house.

'Teatime,' explained Margaret, appearing at the kitchen doorway with an indulgent smile on her face. 'I do love having all the great-grandchildren here at Christmas.'

'Sounds like they enjoy being here too,' said Bridget. 'Thank you very much for the tea and shortbread.'

Outside, it was already growing dark and gloomy and Bridget was acutely aware of how much time had passed without any firm leads. So far all she'd managed to unearth was two missing actresses – one from twenty-five years ago, and one from last night. She hoped that the rest of the team was having more luck.

A light, wintry rain was beginning to fall as night drew in. It shone in the light of the nearest street lamp. Bridget buttoned her coat up to her chin and headed back to the car, with Jake at her side.

CHAPTER 12

Apart from the elusive Julia Carstairs, who was presumably still busy chasing after her theatre director idol, the only remaining person from the ghost tour that Bridget hadn't spoken to was Dylan, the so-called physics genius with the paranormal obsession. Although the young student had left the tour well before they had arrived at the Turf, the way he'd stormed off so angrily after getting into an argument with Goole bothered her. His untimely departure had been the only event to mar the evening, apart from the murder itself, of course.

She and Jake were returning to the car when Bridget's phone rang again. She debated with herself whether she could dismiss Vanessa for a third time, but decided that would be too rude, even for her.

'You ignored my other call,' accused Vanessa, sounding aggrieved. 'And my text message too.'

'Did I?' said Bridget innocently. 'Sorry, I didn't see them.' It wasn't completely a fib. She'd seen Vanessa's message, she just hadn't bothered to read it.

'Well, I need your help. Can you come round?'

'What, now? What's the problem?'

'The Christmas lights at the front of the house have fused.'

Bridget could tell from Jake's expression that he could hear every word of this conversation. He averted his gaze graciously.

'Can't James fix the lights?' Bridget asked.

'No, he's gone out. He's taken the Range Rover, so I'm stuck.'

'I'm sorry Vanessa, I'm working today.'

Her sister's voice expressed indignation. 'You're still working the day before Christmas Eve? Shouldn't you have finished by now?'

'I've just started a new investigation.'

'Oh, Bridget, promise me that you're not going to let work disrupt everything. It's Christmas! I've been planning this for months!'

'I promise. Look, don't worry about the Christmas lights. I'm sure that James can deal with them when he gets back. I wouldn't know how to fix them anyway.'

'Huh, well, thanks for your help,' said Vanessa gruffly. 'I'll sort them out myself.' She rang off.

'Don't say a word,' Bridget warned her sergeant.

'I wouldn't dream of it, ma'am. Union Street next?'

'Yes. Let's see what Dylan's got to say for himself before we head back to base.'

Union Street was a narrow Victorian terrace, located just off the Cowley Road. Like much of the accommodation occupied by students, Dylan's house had seen better days. The front gate was hanging off its hinges, and the cracked paving stones that led to the front door were overgrown with weeds. Several bicycles, one with a missing wheel, were chained to the fence. It reminded Bridget of the place she'd lived in during her second year at college.

She made her way up the uneven path, dodging around the rubbish bins that had been left on one side. There were no lights on in the house, and when ringing the doorbell produced no response, she knocked instead. She was considering whether to try around the back when a floorboard creaked from inside and a faint light flickered on.

A young man's voice came from the other side of the door. 'Who is it?'

'Police. Please open the door.'

After a brief hesitation, a bolt slid aside and the door opened a few inches on a brass chain. The occupant of the house peered warily through the crack. The only light came from a flashlight on his mobile phone and it was too dark for Bridget to make out his features. 'Dylan?' she ventured. 'I'm Detective Inspector Bridget Hart. I was on the ghost tour with you last night.'

'Show me your ID.'

She and Jake held up their warrant cards and Dylan swept the light across them. The door closed again, then reopened cautiously. He stood in the darkened hallway, dressed as before all in black. His pale face seemed to glow in the gloom. He avoided her gaze, keeping his eyes on the floor between them. 'What do you want?'

'May we come in, please, Dylan? We'd like to ask you a few questions.'

'I'm not sure,' he said. 'I have citizens' rights. Do I have to let you in?'

'You don't have to,' Bridget acknowledged. 'We can stay here if you prefer.'

'But it would be much nicer to have a chat inside, mate,' said Jake from behind, 'rather than out in the freezing cold.'

Dylan glanced up briefly at the tall sergeant, sweeping his flashlight across his face, then returned his gaze to the floor. He seemed oblivious to the cold himself, and was wearing just a pair of skinny jeans and a tight T-shirt. His feet were bare on the wooden floorboards. 'If I let you in, are you going to arrest me?'

'No, mate,' said Jake, rubbing his hands together. 'We just want a chat. In the warm.'

'All right.'

Dylan stepped back from the door, allowing Bridget and Jake to enter. The house wasn't much warmer inside than out. Bridget put her hand against the hall radiator, but it was stone cold. All the lights were switched off too. 'Is there a problem with the heating?' she asked. 'Or the electricity?'

'No,' said Dylan. 'I'm trying to save money.'

'I see. Are you here alone for Christmas?'

He nodded. 'The others have all gone home. But I've got work to do. Important stuff. What is it you want to talk to me about?'

'We'd like to speak to you about what happened on the ghost tour last night.'

Dylan began to touch his nose and chin in the compulsive manner Bridget had noticed last night. 'You mean that stupid argument? It's not a crime to disagree with someone. Especially if they're telling lies.'

'We know that, mate,' said Jake pleasantly. 'You're not in any kind of trouble.'

'You promise?'

'We promise. But perhaps we could go to your room?'

'Okay.' He turned and led them along the hallway to a room at the back of the house, using the light from the phone to guide him. To Bridget's relief, when he reached it, he switched on the main ceiling light.

It was a typical student room, with a narrow bed, a desk and chair, and a battered-looking wardrobe. A sink was fixed to one wall, with a mirror above. The place may not have been furnished to high standards, but it was very tidy. Pens, pencils and pads of paper were neatly arranged across the desk. Dylan reached out to straighten one of the pencils as he entered, aligning it perfectly with the others. He sat on the bed and indicated the chair by the desk. 'I've only got one chair.'

'No worries,' said Bridget. 'We'll stand.'

'So what do you want to know?' asked Dylan. 'Have you come here to discuss ghost stories? Half of them aren't real, you know. He makes that stuff up to entertain the tourists. He's not interested in proper scientific explanations. If he –'

'We're not here to talk about ghosts,' interrupted Bridget.

A scowl crept over Dylan's face and he touched his nose. 'What then? I already told you I have loads of work to do.' He began to rock back and forth on the bed.

Bridget wondered how best to put him at ease and win him over. If he remained this agitated, they'd get nothing out of him.

'Do you believe in ghosts, Dylan?' enquired Jake casually.

The boy's hand paused mid-way between chin and nose and he ceased his rocking. 'Yes, I do.' He lowered his hand to his side. His face became animated and he lifted his gaze to Jake's level. 'One day, everyone will believe.'

'Why's that, then?'

'Because they'll know the truth. Science will prove that ghosts are real.'

'How will science do that?'

Dylan nodded to himself, as if for confirmation. 'Stone tape theory.'

Jake glanced sideways at Bridget to confirm whether he should continue. She nodded. Dylan had visibly relaxed and was speaking freely.

'I've never heard of that,' said Jake. 'Can you explain it? To someone who's not a scientist?'

Dylan nodded eagerly. 'According to stone tape theory, crystalline rock like quartz, marble or granite can record audio-visual imprints of events, just like magnetic tape can record sound, or silicon chips store data. Smells, tastes and temperature can be recorded under the right conditions. Memories, too. Even emotions.' He leaned forward. 'Then, if someone with the right sensitivity to the phenomenon comes into contact with the stones, they can experience the sensations that are recorded.'

'I see,' said Jake. 'And are you one of these sensitive people?'

'I'm not really that sensitive,' said Dylan. 'Not like some people. It's all about resonant frequencies. But I want to find a way to detect the recordings, and amplify them, so that anyone can experience them. That's what I'm working on in my spare time.' He sprang from the bed and went over to his desk, where he grabbed one of the notepads. He began turning pages, showing Jake and Bridget his drawings and notes. 'This is the apparatus I'm constructing. It's almost ready to test.'

'That's all very interesting,' said Jake. 'Now I wonder if you could tell us where you went after leaving the ghost tour last night?'

Dylan's face fell. 'You're not really interested in ghosts. I knew it. All right, then. I went back to college for a bit and then came home.'

'You're studying at New College, is that right?' asked Bridget, glad to be back on firmer ground.

'Yeah. Same as Luke.'

'And you're studying Physics?'

'That's right.'

'Can you tell us how long you spent at the college last night?'

Dylan shrugged. 'I don't wear a watch.'

'Then perhaps you can tell us which exit you used. Did you leave the college via Holywell Street or New College Lane?'

Dylan peered at her suspiciously. 'New College Lane.'

'So you must have gone past the entrance to the Turf Tavern.'

'Yes.'

'Did you go inside?'

'I was on my bike. I didn't stop.'

'What did you see when you cycled past?'

'People. Cyclists. A car. What's all this about?' He was growing more agitated. One hand went again to his nose and chin.

'Dylan,' said Jake gently. 'Do you know what happened to David Smith last night?'

'Who?'

'The tour guide,' explained Bridget. 'He called himself Gordon Goole.'

'Why did he do that?'

'It was his stage name.'

Dylan shrugged as if that meant nothing to him.

'Sometime between a quarter past ten and half past ten Mr Goole was attacked in St Helen's Passage.'

A look of alarm flashed across Dylan's face. 'I didn't see anything. I wasn't there.' He began rearranging the pens and pencils on his desk, pausing after each one to touch his nose and chin. 'I don't want to talk to you anymore.'

'Hey, don't worry,' said Jake soothingly. 'No one's accusing you of anything. We just thought you might have noticed something, that's all. An observant lad like you.'

Jake's soft, northern tones seemed to have a calming effect on Dylan. The nose-to-chin movement slowed and he left the pencils in peace. Eventually he returned to his bed. 'What happened to David Smith? Was he killed?' The question was asked without emotion, as if he was asking what the weather was like.

'Yes, he was,' said Bridget. 'This is a murder enquiry.'

'That's why it's really important for you to tell us exactly what you saw,' said Jake.

Dylan seemed to be thinking it over. 'I didn't see anything, because I wasn't there,' he said at last. 'I don't think I can help you.'

Bridget exchanged a glance with Jake. This interview was getting them nowhere. She couldn't be sure whether Dylan was being straight with them. In all likelihood, he'd seen nothing of relevance, and even if he had, extracting the information from him would take more time than they had right now. She placed her card on his desk. 'If you think of anything, however insignificant you think it might be, please give me a call.'

He reached out immediately and turned the card so that its edges were parallel with his notebooks. As Bridget and Jake went to leave, he called after them. 'You should ask the stones. Go to the scene of the murder and listen carefully. The ghost of David Smith may tell you what happened.'

CHAPTER 13

What Detective Sergeant Ryan Hooper needed now was caffeine. The real stuff, not instant from the staff kitchen, nor that disgusting dishwater produced by the machine in the corridor. He scanned the incident room for Detective Constable Harry Johns but couldn't see him anywhere. Where had the young DC skived off to? If Harry didn't appear in the next five minutes, he might just have to make the trip to Starbucks himself.

The boss had given him the job of coordinating interviews with everyone who was at the Turf at the time of the murder – some one hundred and thirty-six potential witnesses. Ryan was glad he didn't have to conduct all the interviews himself. He'd be in need of more than a shot of coffee if that was the case. He was also relieved that Bridget had assigned the task of watching the CCTV footage to Andy. That was an even worse job, even with a team of DCs helping out. Central Oxford had been flooded with Christmas shoppers, concertgoers and late-night drinkers, and each frame had to be studied in case it contained an image of the killer in their midst. They had cameras in

Broad Street, Catte Street, New College Lane... the problem wasn't that they lacked material – it was that they had far too much to get through. It was Christmas Eve tomorrow, and Ryan had plans.

At a nearby desk, Ffion was engrossed in the files relating to the cold missing person case the murder victim had been pursuing.

'Hey, Ffion,' he called. 'Got any plans for Christmas? Must be a danger of getting snowed up in those valleys in the winter.' He conjured up an image of being snowed in with the svelte Welshwoman. It would be necessary to snuggle up for warmth, he supposed. The prospect was appealing and terrifying in equal measures.

She looked up and gave him a cool stare with her bright, green eyes. 'I'm not going back to Wales for Christmas. Not that it's any of your business.'

'You're not? What are you up to then? Jetting off somewhere hot and sunny instead?'

'I'm planning to stay in Oxford, actually.'

'On your own?'

'Why not?'

He hesitated before saying any more. He'd been roasted once before by the fiery breath of the Welsh dragon. But now that Jake had been burned off... 'No need for you to be alone at Christmas. You could come and spend the day with me and my folks in Abingdon. There's always space for one more. Mum wouldn't mind, she'd be delighted in fact.' He omitted to mention the politically incorrect comments his dad always came out with after a glass or two of wine and the way his grandmother would fall asleep and start snoring during the Queen's speech. Or the obligatory games of Monopoly with nieces and nephews. 'How about it, then?'

Ffion looked as if she'd rather spend Christmas camping on a hillside in the Brecon Beacons. She returned to her work without a reply.

'Suit yourself,' said Ryan. He searched the room for Harry again, but he was still nowhere to be seen. Outside, it had grown dark, and rain was spattering against the window. It was too horrible to venture out to Starbucks. He'd just have to manage without.

He got up and wandered over to where Andy was stuck in front of some grainy footage of a man in a black cloak and top hat crossing over the road by the Sheldonian Theatre, followed by a small group clustering around him.

'This is the end of the ghost tour just before ten o'clock,' said Andy. 'There's Bridget.'

Ryan leaned in and spotted the boss muffled up against the cold in a ridiculous bobble hat and scarf, arm in arm with a man in a winter coat, also with a thick scarf wrapped around his neck. Her new boyfriend, Jonathan, no doubt. There were three women wearing novelty headgear, an older couple, and a family with a boy and daughter.

'You reckon one of them's the killer?'

Andy snorted. 'Not likely.'

The group gave the guide a round of applause and then, after a brief discussion, they all trooped off in the direction of the Turf Tavern.

'Maybe someone followed them in,' said Andy.

They continued watching, but there was no obvious sign of them being followed. Then a few minutes after ten o'clock the doors to the Sheldonian opened and concertgoers started to stream out, followed a little later by the orchestral players carrying their instruments, and the singers dressed in black tie for the men and long black skirts for the women. Most of them headed in the opposite direction to the Turf, although a few drifted that way, or into the White Horse on Broad Street. 'Catching a cheeky beer before closing time,' remarked Ryan.

'Well, none of them look like they're about to go and commit a murder,' said Andy.

Then another figure appeared, striding purposefully down Broad Street, obviously not a concertgoer or a musician. Ryan pointed a finger at the screen. 'Pause the tape!'

Andy stopped the video, catching the man in his tracks.

'What is it?'

'Step it forward one frame at a time.' Ryan peered closely at the man on the screen. He was broad-shouldered, his hands thrust deep into the pockets of his denim jacket, bowed slightly with a cap pulled down over his head. As he prepared to cross the road, he looked up. 'There,' said Ryan. 'Freeze it!'

'You recognise him?'

'Yep. Just wait a second.' Ryan returned to his desk and grabbed some printouts. 'The guy that Jake reported earlier, the one who'd got into an argument with David Smith at the Christmas Market.'

'The carousel owner?'

'That's the one. His name is Bill Tomlins. I ran a background check on him earlier, and he's got previous. Assault occasioning actual bodily harm in Chester two years back. He got into a fight with another stallholder after an argument and a few drinks down the pub. Slashed his arm with a knife.'

'Sounds familiar. Have you got a picture of him?' asked Andy.

'Here you go.'

They stared at the mug shot of a bald, heavy-set man glowering at the camera. There was no need to confirm what they could both see with their own eyes.

Andy checked the time on the screen. 'Twenty-six minutes past ten.' He pressed play again, and they watched as the carousel owner crossed the road, continuing to make his way in the direction of the Turf. A few seconds later he passed out of view. 'Blow me down!' said Andy. 'It's him!'

★

Bridget had dealt with Vanessa but she was more concerned by the fact that she hadn't yet spoken to Chloe since the morning. On the last big case Bridget had worked on, Vanessa had, quite rightly, berated her for not paying more attention to what her daughter was getting up to, so when she got back to the station, her first priority was to give Chloe a ring. Her daughter's mobile rang and rang, and Bridget was on the point of giving up when a slightly breathless Chloe answered.

'Hi Mum.'

'Where are you?' asked Bridget.

'Nowhere. Just out.'

It was the sort of non-answer Bridget had become accustomed to lately when speaking to Chloe. She waited to see if any further detail would be forthcoming.

'I'm at Olivia's house,' Chloe volunteered eventually.

Bridget should have guessed. Chloe spent half her life with her best friend, Olivia. But at least that meant she was keeping out of trouble. Probably. Bridget recalled that recently the two girls had sneaked off to a late-night party together and drunk vodka. But Bridget was doing her very best these days not to nag her daughter. The slightest criticism could result in an argument followed by a stand-off, and a row was the last thing she needed right now. 'Well just as long as you're all right.'

'Yeah, Mum, I'm fine. Did you want anything else?'

Just to make sure you're still alive and haven't been run over by a bus or abducted by a serial killer, thought Bridget. Aloud she said, 'No, just wanted to check you're okay.'

'Yeah, I'm good. Bye then.'

'Bye.'

Bridget ended the call and put the phone on her desk. She ought to be glad that everything was fine with Chloe, but the brief conversation left her feeling somewhat down. There was something missing these days from her relationship with her daughter. A lack of trust. They didn't talk properly anymore. It was hard to pin down precisely when the gulf had started to open between them, but she couldn't remember the last time Chloe had really confided in her. Did Chloe reveal more to Vanessa, she wondered. Or her father Ben and his girlfriend Tamsin? For a moment Bridget felt a stab of jealousy, then told herself she was being silly. Chloe was just being a teenager, finding her feet and growing in independence.

Yet she dreaded the idea that Chloe might become cold and distant, mimicking Bridget's broken relationship with her own parents. Abigail's death had been the catalyst for that, creating invisible barriers that could not be torn down. She wanted better for herself and Chloe, but was at a loss as to how to achieve it.

'Ma'am?' Ryan was standing by her desk, an uncharacteristic look of concern on his face.

She wondered how long he'd been watching her sunk in her own gloomy thoughts. She couldn't afford to lose focus now. She needed to give the case her undivided attention. 'Yes? What is it?'

'I think we might have found something. That guy who runs the carousel at the market, the one who was reported getting into an argument with the tour guide, well we've caught him on CCTV heading towards the Turf just before half past ten. And he looks like he's spoiling for a fight.'

'Show me,' said Bridget. A breakthrough on the case was just the tonic she needed.

'What's more, he's got previous. A conviction for a knife attack.'

Andy played her the video. Even though the quality of the image was poor, there could be no doubting that the man in the video matched the photograph that Ryan had found on the criminal records database.

'What's his name?'

'Bill Tomlins.'

'Good work,' said Bridget. 'I think it's time we paid Mr Tomlins and his horses a visit.'

★

With only two days to go until Christmas, the market was busier than ever as people went about their last-minute shopping and enjoyed the festive atmosphere and attractions. They were all wrapped up against the cold. Outside Balliol College, a group of carol singers were gamely belting out all the verses to *Good King Wenceslas* in harmony, splitting into male and female voices for the roles of the kindly king and his doughty page as they tramped through the snow in their quest to deliver wine and pine logs. When they reached the last verse a couple of brave sopranos even tackled the descant. It was Bridget's favourite carol for its sheer heartiness and if she wasn't about to go and question a murder suspect, she would have loved nothing more than to join in.

She'd brought Jake with her, even though Ryan had clearly been disappointed not to have been asked. The fact was, Bridget would need Jake's six-foot-five-inch frame to act as an incentive for Bill Tomlins to cooperate with them. Although she would never admit it to anyone, in situations where she wasn't sitting safely behind a desk, her petite stature put her at a disadvantage. And Bill Tomlins sounded like just the kind of man who would use whatever advantage he could against her.

The carousel had just started up when they arrived, the incessant organ music blaring above the cries of children. Youngsters on horseback waved gleefully at proud parents and grandparents taking photographs on their phones. A queue of people, mainly parents with their excited offspring, waited their turn. The owner of the ride was certainly doing a roaring trade this evening. He wasn't going to take kindly to them interrupting his business.

Bill Tomlins was standing on the central platform, leaning against the mirrored pillar as the painted horses circled around him. He was instantly recognisable from his photo, but was if anything bigger and uglier in the flesh, with a bald head, boxer's nose and a cold, supercilious look of disdain. Bridget found it hard to imagine a less suitable-looking man to have the job of entertaining young children.

The carousel eventually stopped turning and the riders clambered off their horses. Bill made his way to the line of people waiting to pay, his leather satchel ready to accept payments, but Bridget jumped to the front of the queue, earning her a loud 'tut' from a mother waiting with her young son.

'Bill Tomlins? I'm Detective Inspector Bridget Hart of Thames Valley Police. Could I have a quick word, please?'

He glared at her. 'Can't it wait? I'm working if you hadn't noticed.' He turned his back on her and addressed the woman at the front of the queue. 'Is that one adult and one child, love?'

'Yes, please,' said the woman, giving Bridget an unfriendly stare.

'That'll be seven quid,' said Bill. Bridget was tempted to arrest him there and then for daylight robbery. But the woman was happy to hand over her money and the next person in the queue shuffled forward.

Jake stepped in front of them and held up a hand. 'Hey, mate,' he said to the carousel owner. 'We only want five minutes of your precious time. But if you won't talk to us here, we'll have to ask you to accompany us back to the station.'

Bill sized the sergeant up, as if considering which one of them would come off better in a punch up. It didn't take him long to reach a decision. 'Yeah, all right. No need to get shirty. Just let me get the carousel going. We don't want to disappoint the punters, do we?'

Bridget nodded. It was a concession she was willing to make if it meant that Bill Tomlins talked. She was glad she'd brought Jake along, but frustrated that bullies like Tomlins needed to be forced into cooperation. It only made her more determined to get to the bottom of his involvement.

When every horse on the carousel had a rider, and Bill had set the roundabout in motion, he grudgingly came over to talk to them. 'All right. What is it you want to know?'

'We're investigating the fatal stabbing of David Smith, otherwise known as Gordon Goole of *Goole's Ghost Tours*,' said Bridget, getting straight to the point.

'How does that concern me?'

'We understand that you got into an argument with

him recently about his tour getting in the way of your carousel customers.'

'Who told you that?'

'A reliable source,' said Jake.

Bill's face darkened and he crossed his arms in front of his burly chest. 'So what if I did? The bloke was getting in the way of my ride. I asked him to move, but he wouldn't budge. I told him, I can hardly pick up the carousel and stick it somewhere else, can I?'

'Did you threaten him?' asked Jake.

Bill shrugged. 'You might call it that. Just to get my point across, like. Look, I argue with people every day, doesn't mean I go round killing the buggers.' He glanced over his shoulder at the carousel. The ride was still going, the music blasting, the kids crying out in excitement.

'You were spotted heading in the direction of the Turf Tavern shortly before the stabbing took place,' said Bridget.

'So what? I like a drink in the evening. No law against that, is there? It's hard work standing here all day running this thing. A bloke gets thirsty.'

'So you're not denying that you were at the Turf Tavern on the night of the murder?'

He looked momentarily annoyed with himself for having given too much away. He clearly wasn't the sharpest knife in the cutlery drawer. 'Yeah, I was there.'

'But you were already gone when police arrived shortly after the attack. A list of everyone present was taken at the time.'

'Guess I didn't hang around.'

'Did you meet anyone you knew in the pub?' asked Jake.

'No. Can't say I did. Reckon that's why I didn't stop for a beer.'

'Did you see David Smith there?'

'No.'

'And yet he was stabbed in St Helen's Passage just a minute or two after you arrived there,' said Bridget, taking a gamble that her time estimate wasn't too far off. 'And, you have a previous conviction for stabbing a man after an argument in a pub. Do you believe in coincidences, Bill? I'm not sure that a jury would.'

He glared at her with undisguised loathing and she knew that she'd hit her target. She waited patiently for him to reply. He glanced at the queue of people that was forming, then turned his back against them. Leaning forward, he lowered his voice so that it was difficult to hear him above the organ music from the carousel and the competing carol singers who had now moved on to *God Rest Ye Merry Gentlemen*.

'Listen, I admit I went to the Turf that night, and I'll even admit that I stumbled over Goole's damn body, all right? But I didn't touch him, I swear. He was dead as a dodo when I got there. I didn't see who did it. I just turned and ran.'

Bridget stared at him coldly. 'You saw David Smith after he'd been stabbed? And you didn't try to help him, or even to call the police?'

'Like I said, he was dead. Or, at least, he looked dead enough to me. And I didn't call the police because I knew you lot would put two and two together and make five bloody thousand.'

Bridget continued to stare at him until he dropped his gaze to the ground. Perhaps even a man like Bill Tomlins was capable of feeling shame. 'There was nothing I could do for him,' he muttered. 'I didn't want to get involved.'

'We could arrest you for obstructing a police enquiry,' said Jake.

That wasn't strictly true, but it had the desired effect. Bill lifted his chin defiantly, a flash of anger in his dark eyes. 'I'm not the one you want to be arresting,' he said. 'You want to go after that bloke I saw running out of the alleyway just before I arrived.'

'What bloke?' asked Bridget suspiciously. 'You didn't mention anyone before.'

'He was a youngster, like a student. Pale as milk, thin

as a stick, dressed head to toe in black. He couldn't get out of that place fast enough.'

Bridget glanced sideways at Jake. She could tell what he was thinking. *Dylan Collins.* 'Can you remember anything else about him?'

'There was something wrong with his face, I think. He kept touching his nose and chin, like they were on fire or something.'

'And he was leaving the pub as you arrived?'

'Yeah. Came charging down the alleyway pushing a bike, nearly knocked me over. I yelled at him, but he was gone.'

'Which way did he go?'

'Left.'

'Down New College Lane?'

'If that's what it's called. I'm not from around these parts, am I?' The carousel music came to an end and the horses slowed gracefully to a halt. 'Will that be all, *Inspector*?' He gave the word an ironic twist, as if he found the idea of Bridget being a detective inspector ridiculous.

'That will be all for now, Mr Tomlins,' said Bridget, 'but an officer will be back to take a written statement from you later.' She spoke with exaggerated politeness to stop herself telling him what she really thought of him. 'Don't leave Oxford until we say you can.'

*

Bill's description of the young man he'd seen running down St Helen's Passage was too detailed and specific to leave any doubt in Bridget's mind. Dylan Collins, the physics student who'd claimed to have gone directly home after leaving New College. What had he been doing in the Turf, and why had he fled the scene of the crime?

Jake was clearly on the same page as her. 'We're going to pick him up?' he asked.

'You bet.'

They pushed their way through the crowds to the Mini

and soon they were crossing the Plain roundabout on their way to Union Street.

Jake rapped loudly on the door but there was no answer. All was dark and silent. Bridget opened the letterbox and called inside, but no lights appeared and no floorboards creaked. She tried his mobile number and was surprised when he picked up.

'Yeah? Who is it?'

'Dylan, it's Detective Inspector Bridget Hart here. I need to speak to you. Where are you?'

'At the Clarendon.'

'Where?'

'The physics laboratory,' he said impatiently. 'I can't see you now. I'm working.'

'I'm afraid that we have to speak to you as a matter of urgency. We can come and see you at the lab if you like.'

'Okay,' he conceded. 'Call me when you arrive and I'll let you in.'

They took the car back into town, retracing the route along Longwall Street that they'd walked earlier that day. The traffic was thick and slow, and heavy drops of rain pattered against the car windscreen. Christmas lighting ran overhead from streetlamp to streetlamp, but the red glow of traffic lights and the brake lights of the cars in front dominated Bridget's view of the road. She thumped the steering wheel in frustration as yet another light turned red just before she could slip through the gap. Oxford was such a compact city, and yet when driving around it, distance and time seemed to expand exponentially. Maybe a physicist like Dylan would be able to explain how that happened.

She parked the car at the edge of the university science area next to the university parks. The Clarendon Laboratory was a large Victorian building of red brick and stone. In front of it stood an uncompromisingly modern construction of glass and bronze that Bridget recalled having been completed just recently. If she remembered correctly, the new building, called the Beecroft Building, had been opened by Sir Tim Berners-Lee, inventor of the world wide web and now a professor at Oxford.

She phoned Dylan to let him know they'd arrived.

'Okay. I'll come upstairs and let you in.' He appeared a minute later, looking irritated by the interruption. 'Come inside, we can talk while I work.'

Bridget was happy enough to go along with that, if it encouraged him to be more open. She and Jake followed him into the large open-plan entrance atrium. The place was like a maze built on many levels, with a wide wooden staircase leading up. Inclining her head, she could see that the stairs meandered upwards following an irregular pattern, branching and winding around the outside walls of the building in a kind of Escher-like spiral of impossibility. It was as if the physicists who occupied this place had used their knowledge of the hidden workings of the universe to break the spacetime continuum. It made her dizzy just to look and she dropped her gaze back to focus on where she was putting her feet.

There was no one else around, and the building's silence felt vaguely sinister. Though some of the lights were on, other parts of the interior were shrouded in darkness. It would be creepy to work here all alone on a dark winter's night.

Something Dylan had said was puzzling her. 'When you answered the phone, you said you'd come *up* to meet us.'

A faint look of amusement crept across the student's face. He pointed up. 'What you can see here is just a part of the building. Most of it is below ground.'

'Below?'

'The Beecroft Building has the deepest basement in Oxford. Most of the labs are below ground. It's to reduce the amount of background noise and vibration. A lot of the work done here is at the atomic scale. Even a vibration as large as a few atoms would ruin an experiment.'

'I see.'

They followed him down a series of staircases, which

were all thankfully straight, until they reached the lowest level. Dylan led them along a white-painted corridor that smelled strongly of furniture polish. He opened a door at the end. 'This is my lab.'

The lab was a medium-sized room, whose walls, floor and ceiling were all white. Benches ranged around the edges, carrying an array of complicated-looking scientific equipment. Dylan went to the far wall and leaned over some apparatus, making tweaks and adjustments. He bent down and ran his eye along a long glass tube that protruded from the device. He seemed already to have forgotten that Bridget and Jake were present.

'What's that you're working on?' Bridget asked.

He answered her without turning around. 'It's a device for measuring paranormal residue.'

'And this is part of your Physics course?'

He laughed. 'No, of course not! Nobody here believes in ghosts. But I'm going to prove them wrong. If I can make this work, I'll be able to carry out a set of experiments that will demonstrate conclusively that stone tape theory is true.'

While Dylan was absorbed in his work there was none of the compulsive nose-to-chin touching he'd exhibited earlier. Instead he was relaxed and articulate, revealing a hint of the genius that his friend, Luke, had described. Bridget began to wonder whether there might even be something to his strange theories after all. But she hadn't come here to debate the existence of ghosts.

'Last time we spoke to you, Dylan, you told us that after leaving New College you cycled past the Turf but didn't go in. We've just come from the Christmas Market and we spoke to a man who says he saw you running out of St Helen's Passage. Did you go to the Turf that night, Dylan? It's important that you tell us the truth this time.'

'Uh-huh,' said Dylan, continuing to make adjustments to his machine.

'Is that a yes?' asked Bridget. 'Were you at the Turf?'

'Only for a minute.'

'A minute's quite a long time,' said Jake. 'But I guess you'd know that as a physicist.'

'Sixty seconds,' said Dylan, without looking up. 'Sixty million microseconds. Sixty billion nanoseconds. Long enough for a beam of light to travel to the moon and back twenty-three times. Long enough for the early universe to cool sufficiently for the first atomic nuclei to form after the Big Bang.'

'Quite,' said Bridget, her head spinning with the numbers. Physics had always been her least favourite subject at school. 'A lot can happen in a minute. For example, a man can lose his life. Did you kill David Smith, Dylan?'

'No.' His back was still to them as he worked. He was so skinny, and his T-shirt so tight that she could see his shoulder blades move beneath the black cotton.

'Then do you know who did?'

'No.' His right hand strayed briefly to his nose, but he grasped it with his other hand and clamped it to the edge of the desk.

'Can you tell us why you went to the pub?' cajoled Jake.

'To see Luke.'

'Why didn't you tell us that before?'

'I didn't want to cause him any problems. He's been in a lot of trouble already.'

'Because of possession of cannabis?'

'Yes.' Dylan turned round to face them. 'I didn't want to get myself into any trouble, either.'

'Over drugs?'

He nodded.

'Let's just get this straight,' said Jake. 'Are you saying that you gave some cannabis to Luke that night?'

'Yes. I buy it for him.'

'You know that's called supplying drugs, Dylan? You can get into a lot of trouble over that.'

Dylan's hand went to his nose, despite his efforts to control it. 'That's why I didn't mention it. But I wasn't selling it to him. I'm not a drugs dealer.' He laughed lightly to himself. 'You can't arrest me for passing some joints to a friend, can you?'

The boy stared at them beseechingly. It was tempting to believe that he was just an innocent caught up in something he didn't really understand. But Bridget had to remind herself that he was an Oxford undergraduate and clearly extremely intelligent. This all might be an act.

'Dylan,' she said gently, 'You need to understand that supplying drugs is a very serious offence, and that you could go to prison.'

His face fell, and he began to touch his face repeatedly.

'But we don't want to arrest you,' she continued. 'We just want to get at the truth. And that means that you have to tell us everything you did and saw that night. You mustn't leave anything out. Can you do that for us?'

He nodded. 'Okay. Now?'

'Now.'

He dropped his gaze to the floor once more. 'Luke needs the joints because he finds it so stressful being with his family. His Christmas would be a nightmare without them. His mum and dad are always nagging him, you see? They disapprove of him, because he doesn't want to be at Oxford at all.'

'Okay,' said Bridget.

'So I picked up the herbs while I was in college, then called back into the Turf to give them to him and say goodbye.'

'How did you know where to find him?'

'He messaged me on my phone.'

'And you handed him the cannabis?'

'Yeah. I stayed with him a while to have a chat. Then, when I was leaving the pub... when I was leaving...' He couldn't control himself any longer. His hand was in motion again, darting between nose and chin at lightning speed.

'Take a deep breath, mate,' said Jake.

Dylan stopped and filled his lungs with air. He breathed out again slowly. 'I saw him,' he continued. 'David Smith.

He was lying on the ground. I think he'd been stabbed.'

'What did you do then? Did you try to help him?'

An emphatic shake of the head. 'I ran away.'

'Why did you do that, Dylan?'

His right hand went to his nose and chin six times before he spoke. 'I was frightened. I don't like touching people, and I didn't want Luke to get into trouble. I already told you that. You should listen to what I say.'

Bridget contemplated the young man standing before her. She could arrest him on a charge of possession or even supply of a controlled drug, but that wouldn't get her closer to finding David Smith's killer. It wouldn't do anything positive for Dylan's mental health either. For now she was inclined to believe what he had told her.

'Did you notice anyone as you left the pub?' she asked. 'Anyone who you can describe to us?'

He nodded. 'I'm good at remembering. There was a bald man on his way down St Helen's Passage as I was leaving. I pushed my bike straight past him and he shouted at me. But I didn't see anyone else.'

Bill Tomlins, thought Bridget. Dylan's version of events confirmed what the carousel owner had told them. And from the CCTV images, they'd be able to pin down exactly when Tomlins had arrived at the Turf. That would help to narrow the window of uncertainty about the time of death. But it didn't look like they'd be able to get any more out of Dylan.

He flicked his gaze up to her briefly, before returning it to the floor. 'You're trying to find the truth, I get that. It's what I do too. We're not so different, you and me.'

'Perhaps,' said Bridget. 'Except that you're hunting for ghosts, whereas the person I'm searching for is very much alive.'

CHAPTER 14

It was late when Bridget and Jake returned to Kidlington. It had been a long day and they'd spoken to a lot of people, but so far their enquiries had led nowhere. But nothing more could be done that evening. Bridget sent her team home, before leaving the office herself.

On her way back to the car she called Chloe to let her know that she was on her way. It would be helpful if her daughter could switch the oven on so that they could have a couple of frozen pizzas.

'I'm actually at Olivia's house,' said Chloe.

'Still?'

'Is that a problem?'

Bridget bit back her reply. *Don't get confrontational*, she told herself. *Stay calm*. 'No, no problem. When do you think you'll be back?'

'Hang on.' There were some indistinct murmurings on the other end of the line. 'In about an hour?'

'I'm just getting into the car now,' said Bridget. 'Why don't I come and pick you up?'

'No, don't do that,' said Chloe. 'We're just finishing a

film. I'll be fine on the bus.'

But it's late and it's dark, Bridget wanted to say. She took a deep breath. 'All right, but don't be late.'

'I won't. Promise.' Chloe ended the call.

Were they drifting apart? Bridget supposed it was only natural that, at fifteen and a half, Chloe was starting to exert her independence. And that was a good thing, right? But it made Bridget nervous.

★

The following day was Christmas Eve and Bridget decided to leave Chloe sleeping in. Her daughter had eventually come home far later than promised claiming that she'd missed one bus and had to wait ages for the next one.

'You should have called me,' Bridget told her. 'I could have come and picked you up.'

'It was fine, Mum. I didn't want to put you to any trouble.'

'It wouldn't have been a problem.' At least not compared to what Bridget had endured, sitting at home alone, imagining rapists and muggers lurking at the bus stop and agonising over whether or not to phone Chloe again. A huge weight had lifted from her heart when she'd eventually heard Chloe's key in the lock just after ten o'clock.

Still, tomorrow they would be spending Christmas Day at Vanessa's house. It would give them an opportunity to spend some time together. Thankfully, Ben, Chloe's father, and his girlfriend Tamsin had swanned off to the Maldives for a family-free, stress-free, sun-soaked Christmas and New Year and that meant there was no risk of Chloe being tempted to visit them in London. Small mercies.

The car park at the station was quiet, with some of the police and support staff already on Christmas leave. They would be travelling the length and breadth of the country, visiting relatives and loved ones. By the end of the day, only a skeleton staff would remain on duty at police headquarters to deal with emergencies. Bridget knew that Jake would have a long drive ahead of him to travel north to his folks in Leeds. But she couldn't afford to let him slip away too early. Time was against her, and she needed all the help she could get.

As soon as everyone was in and armed with their favourite hot beverage, she mustered them for a quick team meeting. Her numbers were down, with some of the additional staff Grayson had allocated to her the previous day already gone. She sensed that her control of the situation was beginning to slip away.

'All right, listen up!' she called, bringing the assembled detectives to a hush. 'We've got one day – probably less – to make some headway on this investigation before all of you go home for Christmas. When that happens, we'll lose momentum. Witnesses will begin to forget what they saw. Evidence will be harder to gather. The investigation will drift. I don't want that to happen, and I'm sure none of you do either, so let's push on and get as much done as we can today. Okay?'

Her pep-talk resulted in a half-hearted murmur of agreement, but she knew that she'd placed a flag in the sand and sent out a clear message: this was a work day, and there was to be no slacking. She briefly summarised the conversations she'd had with Bill Tomlins, the carousel owner, and Dylan Collins, the physics student. 'So both of them saw the body, but preferred to look the other way,' she concluded.

'Do you trust this Dylan Collins?' asked Andy. 'Is there anyone who can verify his account of what happened?'

'We need to see if anyone can corroborate his story. Ryan, you're in charge of witness statements. I want you to identify anyone who was in the vicinity of St Helen's Passage immediately before the stabbing took place, and show them a photograph of Dylan. Find out if they remember seeing him.'

'Will do, ma'am.'

'And someone needs to go and speak to Luke Henderson again at his home in Beaconsfield. Tell him we know that he was lying about his account of his movements in the Turf and see what he says. Let's see if we can pin down exactly what happened in the moments leading up to the murder.'

'I can do that,' volunteered Ffion.

'Okay,' said Bridget. The task was well-suited to Ffion's skill set. If the boy had been lying to cover up his activities, a no-nonsense direct approach would be needed, and Ffion could never be accused of being unduly sympathetic. Her keen powers of observation would also be perfect for getting to the truth.

She listened next to Ryan's summary of the various witness statements, but it was clear that although more than a hundred people had been present in the pub that night, none of them had seen the attack on David Smith, or noticed anything that would lead directly to identifying the culprit. Bridget could hardly complain. She herself had been one of those potential witnesses, and had seen and heard precisely nothing.

'Andy, what about CCTV?'

'Well, we've got hold of everything that the university and the town council were able to provide, as well as a few private sources. We've pinned down the time that Bill Tomlins arrived at the pub to 10:26, so the stabbing must have taken place before that. Now we're working to ID everyone approaching or leaving the area around the pub.'

'Good work, Andy. Keep going.' Bridget was hungry for quicker results, but she fought back her impatience. Andy had already succeeded in spotting the arrival of the carousel owner, which in turn had led to the discovery that both he and Dylan Collins had been the first to see the murdered man. A chain of events was beginning to emerge, and the meticulous police work needed to add more links to the chain could not be rushed. Bridget knew that if anything more could be gleaned from the cameras, Andy was the one to find it.

She turned finally to Ffion. 'What about the missing person case that Smith was investigating? What did you discover?'

Ffion clasped her steaming Welsh dragon mug with both hands. The young DC never referred to notes but always seemed to have perfect recall of whatever she'd been working on. 'So, Camilla Townsend was a second-year student at Pembroke College. She went missing at the end of Michaelmas term twenty-five years ago, after the final performance of *Twelfth Night* at the Burton Taylor Studio at the Playhouse. She'd been playing the part of Viola. David Smith was her boyfriend at the time, and a student at the same college. He was arrested on suspicion of her murder but released after a day in custody. No body has ever been found and it's still officially a missing person case.'

'What's your feeling?' Bridget asked. 'Do you think this is worth following up?' With resources stretched, she was reluctant to commit Ffion to further investigation of an apparently unrelated historical case that might turn out to be a complete distraction.

'I did a bit of digging on Smith. I managed to track down his old tutor from Pembroke College, Dr Penn. He's well into his eighties now and lives in a retirement home in Abingdon, but he's as bright as a button and remembers David very well. Dr Penn told me that David was a promising student and also a very talented actor. But after his arrest for Camilla's murder, he dropped out of university. Even though no charges were ever brought, he suffered a mental breakdown and was unable to carry on with his studies.'

It was a cautionary tale, thought Bridget, how a life could be turned upside down so suddenly by a single event. What might David Smith have become if this tragedy had not befallen him all those years ago?

'But David didn't return to his family home,' continued Ffion. 'He stayed on in Oxford, making ends meet by giving ghost tours. And in his spare time he continued to investigate Camilla's disappearance. The main focus of his investigation seems to have been the student who directed the production of *Twelfth Night*.'

'Did Smith's investigations have any substance to them? Do you think he had reasonable grounds for suspecting the director of this play?' asked Bridget.

'It's hard to say. The police investigation at the time didn't seriously consider the director as a suspect. David's investigation seems to have been motivated partly by personal animosity between the two men. His theory was that Guy and Camilla had been sleeping together and –'

'Wait, did you say Guy?'

'That's right. The director's name was Guy Goodwin. After leaving university, he went on to become a successful theatre director. In fact, he's currently back in Oxford with a production of –'

'*West Side Story*,' concluded Bridget, the hairs on the back of her neck beginning to rise.

So, the student who had directed that ill-fated production of *Twelfth Night* all those years ago was back in Oxford, and was the very man that Julia Carstairs had abandoned her friends to go and meet on the night of the murder. Coincidence? Or was it – as Julia Carstairs had proclaimed – fate? The tangle of events seemed to be stretching chance to breaking point.

'All right,' said Bridget. 'I think it's time we tracked down Julia Carstairs, and also this director, Guy Goodwin. Jake, you can come with me. I'd like to find out what Julia's movements were around the time of the murder, and exactly where Guy Goodwin was that night.'

*

There were few things in life that could match the thrill of riding a high-performance bike on the open road. Ffion was glad to leave the dreary environs of the office behind and set out alone on her beloved Kawasaki Ninja H2. The neon green bike added a welcome splash of colour and excitement to the winter's day. Although the traffic on the M40 was heavy, the slow drizzle that had set in the previous day was gone, and the air was crisp and clear. It was the perfect weather for a ride. The rush of the wind and the shrill roar of the bike's supercharged engine made her feel alive and free. 'Blowing all the cobwebs away,' her grandmother would have called it.

The previous evening she'd enjoyed a final meal and a drink with her housemates, Claire and Judy, before bidding them farewell. She'd have the house in Jericho to herself for the whole week between Christmas and New Year, and was looking forward to peace and quiet. It would be a chance to fit in some meditation and reflect on the year past and the year to come. A lot had happened in twelve months – her transfer from Reading to Oxford, some high-profile murder cases, the short-lived romantic entanglement with Jake – but now it was time to make plans for the New Year and beyond.

Ffion always liked to look forward, never back. It was a habit formed during her teenage years – a by-product of never fitting in with her family or community. The tiny village in the South Wales valleys had not been a tolerant place for a shy, bisexual girl to grow up, and she had been glad to leave it far behind and move on to a new phase of her life. And yet, sometimes the past refused to let her go. Just the previous evening, after saying goodnight to Claire and Judy, she'd received an unexpected phone call from her sister, Siân.

Siân was five years older than Ffion, and her polar opposite. Full-figured, sociable and easy-going, after leaving school Siân had trained as a hairdresser and now ran her own salon in the village where she and Ffion had grown up. She'd married her school sweetheart, had two children in quick succession, and lived in a modest terraced house just a few streets away from their parents' house. In short, she was everything that their parents had wanted from a daughter. Unlike Ffion, the black sheep of the family.

'Ffion, love, how're you doing?'

Despite everything, it was always nice to hear her sister's cheery voice. 'Good, thanks. And you?'

'Yeah, great. The kids are so looking forward to Christmas. It'll be the first year that Owain's really old enough to understand what it's all about. He's dead excited about Santa coming down the chimney. And of course he and Arwen are desperately hoping for snow. Looking at the forecast, we might even have a sprinkling.'

It was easy to see why Siân was so popular with her clients at the salon. Words flowed so effortlessly from her smiling mouth. She seemed to move through life easily, in a way that Ffion had always struggled to match.

After a moment's hesitation, Siân asked, 'So, what are your plans for Christmas?'

Here was the question, then. It hadn't taken her long to get straight to the point. Like Ffion, Siân wasn't one for beating about the bush.

'I'll be staying here in Oxford. As usual.'

'With friends?'

'That's right.'

'You have some good friends in Oxford, then, Fi?' Her sister's voice was tinged with concern. Not concern exactly; more like worry laced with pity. She knew how hard it had been for Ffion to make friends back in Wales.

Ffion injected as much seasonal good cheer into her reply as she could muster. 'Yeah, loads. I've been fighting off the invitations.'

'Good. I'm glad to hear it. You know that Mam misses you? Dad too.'

'Sure, I know.'

A pregnant pause on the line. 'You couldn't change your plans just this once, could you? Come and see us for a change. After all, Christmas is for family, isn't it?'

Just for a second, Ffion was tempted by the prospect. It would be nice to catch up with her sister again, and to see her niece and nephew, who she hadn't seen since their christening. But the moment passed quickly. 'I don't think

I can, Siân. I'll be working all day Christmas Eve. There won't be time.'

'You're sure? It wouldn't matter if you only came for a short while. It would make Mam's day.'

The mention of her mother closed Ffion's heart and made her glad she'd refused the invitation. Her Mam may miss her, but it was her own disapproval of her daughter's sexual orientation that had helped to drive Ffion away. 'I'm sure she'll have plenty going on with you and the kids.'

'Well, all right. Then maybe you could pop down for a day or two at New Year instead?'

'Maybe,' she said, but they both knew she meant no.

'Take care, then, Fi.'

'You too, sis.'

A sudden rush of bitterness came to Ffion as she replayed the phone call in her head. She pulled the Kawasaki's throttle and felt the bike leap forward, like a caged beast being let loose. Her sister meant well, but she had stirred up unwelcome emotions that Ffion normally kept in check. Memories of home and childhood were painful and upsetting, and the only way she could deal with them was to lock them away. Ffion had never been the daughter that her mother had wanted, and never could be. So, no, she would not be heading back to Wales for Christmas or the New Year.

The sign for the Beaconsfield turn-off appeared up ahead, and Ffion signalled to pull off the motorway. It was time to consign any negative thoughts to the waste bin where they belonged, and to focus on the interview ahead.

Look forward, never back. That was the only way to live. It was the only way to survive.

CHAPTER 15

Oxford's New Theatre occupied a prominent position on George Street, close to the junction with Broad Street and the Christmas Market. It was a bustling part of the city, packed with cafes, restaurants and bars. Bridget and Jake skirted around a large gathering of people who were blocking the narrow pavement with their shopping bags, and made for the building's entrance.

She herself was a regular patron of the large, art deco theatre, having enjoyed a number of opera performances there over the years. Always with one eye on their commercial interests, the management staged everything from opera and ballet to hit musicals and stand-up comedians who had already hit the big time and would sell out the almost two-thousand seat auditorium. As a student she had only been able to afford the vertigo-inducing seats in the balcony with limited visibility of the stage. Nowadays when she attended a performance she treated herself to a more comfortable seat in the circle, preferably after a dish of pasta and a glass or two of Pinot Noir from one of the many Italian eateries that thronged George

Street. She'd hoped to go and see a performance of Puccini's *La Bohème* with Jonathan, but that trip had been cancelled at the last moment. Perhaps they would be able to go and see something in the New Year.

The box office was manned by a young man with a hipster beard and gravity-defying quiff, flicking through a copy of *Time Out*.

He glanced up from his reading as Bridget and Jake entered. 'Sorry, but we're sold out for tonight's performance,' he said before Bridget had a chance to say anything.

She showed him her warrant card. 'I'm not here for tickets. I was hoping to meet the director, Guy Goodwin. Is he around?'

As well as the famed director himself, Bridget anticipated that she would also find the elusive Julia Carstairs, bit-part actress in TV dramas, within his orbit. It was high time she accounted for her whereabouts on the night of the murder.

The young man stroked his beard apprehensively. 'Mr Goodwin's extremely busy right now getting everyone ready for this afternoon's matinée. I don't think he'll be able to speak to you. Maybe if you left a message and asked him to call you?'

'I think he'll find time to see us,' said Bridget. 'Where is he? Through there?' She pointed to the doors that led to the auditorium.

'Um, yeah, but...'

Bridget didn't wait for the cashier to finish but pushed open the doors that led into the stalls and made her entrance.

With the house lights turned up full and no audience in the seats, the space felt cavernous. She and Jake walked down the aisle towards the stage where a small group of actors stood in front of some rather precarious-looking scaffolding. A young woman was perched atop a ladder, while a man gazed up at her from below.

At the front of house, a man paced up and down

between the front row of the stalls and the stage, waving a sheaf of papers in the air with one hand whilst gesticulating wildly with the other. 'You're supposed to be in love with each other! Give me some emotion, give me some passion. Make me weep! I want to feel it here' – he beat his chest with his fist – 'when you reach those high notes.'

From the photos Bridget had seen on his website, Bridget recognised the good-looking but somewhat vain features of Guy Goodwin. He was significantly older than he appeared in his publicity material, and the smiling face that he liked to present to the public had been replaced by a darkened and scowling countenance. He wasn't conventionally handsome. His nose was too broad, his forehead too high, his eyebrows too bushy. His hair was wild and looked like it hadn't seen a comb in a long time. But there was an undeniable attractiveness to him. It was his eyes, Bridget decided. They had an intensity that was almost frightening. They flashed now as he turned them on the orchestral conductor in the pit with a look of barely-concealed fury. 'Let's take it from the top and try to get it right this time, shall we?'

As the orchestra struck up the well-known tune, Bridget spotted Julia Carstairs, minus her reindeer antlers, seated on the front row of the stalls. Her eyes were no longer glued to her phone, but instead followed Guy Goodwin as he continued to bark instructions even as the hapless actors sang their love duet.

'Miss Carstairs?'

Startled from her rapt attention to the proceedings onstage, the actress turned to Bridget with some irritation, but her fleeting glower was quickly replaced by a broad smile showing whitened, well-ordered teeth. 'Yes? What is it? Would you like my autograph?'

'No,' said Bridget, revealing her warrant card in return.

The dazzling smile vanished as quickly as it had appeared, and was replaced by a frown on Julia's delicate brow. 'Do I know you from somewhere?'

'I was on the ghost tour with you the night before last.'

'Were you?' Julia continued to look mystified. 'Ah yes,' she said at last, her face clearing. 'You were with that rather nice-looking man in the tortoiseshell glasses.'

It told Bridget something that Julia remembered Jonathan so much better than her, but she was secretly flattered that a woman like Julia would describe Jonathan as "nice-looking".

With her sculpted cheekbones and generous mouth that was perhaps slightly too wide for her narrow face, Julia herself was certainly a very attractive woman – at least when she had a smile fixed to her lips instead of a scowl – even though her best days were clearly behind her. Nevertheless, she looked good for her age. In her mid-forties, she could have passed at first glance for a woman ten years younger. A few tell-tale lines around the eyes gave a clue to her real age and her blonde hair had maybe been bleached once too often, giving it a dried-out appearance. She brushed it aside with one hand, perhaps conscious that it might betray her years.

'I'd like to speak to you about David Smith,' said Bridget, 'also known as Gordon Goole.'

But she had already lost Julia's attention. Her gaze drifted away from Bridget back to what was happening on stage. 'Poor Guy,' she mused. 'He's having such a hard time of it. His leading lady has just gone down with laryngitis and he's having to make do with her understudy. But as you can see, she's woefully unprepared. She claims she doesn't feel safe standing up on that scaffolding. The matinée is starting in a few hours, and I think it's going to be a disaster.'

The music stopped abruptly as Guy Goodwin's voice blasted out. 'No! No! No! You have to make me believe that you're floating on air, not about to fall off the ladder!'

'Between you and me, I think she's afraid of heights,' said Julia with a sigh.

'Perhaps there's somewhere quieter we could go to have a chat,' suggested Jake.

Julia looked up, appearing to notice him for the first

time. Her expression immediately changed from irritation to anticipation as she took in his height and appearance. 'A chat. That does sound cosy.' She offered him her hand and rose gracefully to her feet. 'And your name is?'

'Jake Derwent,' he muttered. 'Detective Sergeant.'

Bridget didn't even need to look to know that the back of Jake's neck would already be flushing pink.

'Well, Jake Derwent, Detective Sergeant,' said Julia, 'Come with me. I'm sure Ralph won't mind if we use the bar.' She swept her coat over one arm and strode back out to the box office. She clearly felt very much at home in the theatre, even though, as far as Bridget could make out, she wasn't involved in the production in any way.

Leaning over the counter, Julia addressed the young cashier who had been so reluctant to let Bridget enter. 'Ralph, dearest, you couldn't be a darling and bring a pot of Earl Grey up to the bar, could you? The detectives here just want a quick word with me about... a private matter.'

'No problem, Miss Carstairs.' Ralph was obviously eager to please the actress and no doubt desperately curious as to the nature of the private matter. Just as Julia had no doubt intended. Bridget had to hand it to her – the actress had a talent for creating drama even when she was off the stage.

They followed her through to the empty bar and took seats around a small circular table.

Julia tossed her coat casually over the back of a nearby chair. 'You're here about the murder, then. I heard about it on the news. How ghastly. Of course, if I'd been around when it happened, I'd have called you at once and told you everything. As it is, I didn't see a thing.' She sounded disappointed.

'We'd like to go through the events of that evening carefully and find out exactly what you did see,' said Bridget.

'All right, then,' said Julia. 'How did you track me down, anyway?'

'We spoke to your friends Liz and Deborah at the

Malmaison. They told us you'd probably be with Guy.'

'Ah, of course. I should have guessed. You can always count on your best friends to betray you, can't you?'

'Your friends seemed to think that you were the one who'd let them down by leaving them to go off with Guy.'

'Well, that's so typical of Liz and Debs to put the blame on me. But I suppose I mustn't be too harsh on them. They're both very emotionally fragile at the moment. Divorce,' she added in a hushed voice to Jake. 'I tell them, they ought to feel glad they've thrown off the shackles. There's nothing like being single again. Make the most of it, I say.' She winked at Jake and added, 'I certainly intend to.'

The sergeant bowed his head, his pencil poised over a sheet of his notebook, as yet still blank.

'I understand from what Liz and Deborah told us that the three of you are staying in Oxford over Christmas,' prompted Bridget.

'That's right. Drowning our sorrows in shared sisterhood. Girl power, that kind of thing.'

The shared sisterhood didn't seem to have survived the arrival on the scene of the handsome Guy Goodwin. 'Perhaps you could explain why you left them on their own at the Turf, and account for your movements between ten and ten-thirty on the night of the ghost tour.'

Julia raised her eyebrows. 'Isn't that obvious? I was waiting for a message from Guy to let me know that the show had finished and that he was free to see me. As soon as I heard from him, I went to meet him.'

'You met him here?'

'No, in his hotel room at the Randolph.'

'And what time exactly did you leave the Turf?'

'It must have been about a quarter past ten.'

'Your friends seemed annoyed that you left without telling them.'

'Well, I'm sure they'll get over it. They've known me for years and they understand what I'm like. I follow my heart – life's far too short not to.'

'As you were leaving the Turf, did you see David Smith on his own or with anyone else?'

'You mean Gordon Goole? No.'

'Did you see or hear anything suspicious in St Helen's Passage?'

'No, nothing at all.' She turned her head. 'Oh, look, here's Ralph with the tea. Such a sweetie!'

Bridget waited patiently whilst the young man set down a tray with three cups and a pot of tea. 'Anything else I can get for you, Miss Carstairs?' he asked.

'No, that's perfect,' said Julia. 'Mustn't distract you from your duties!' She gave him a gleaming smile and picked up the pot as if playing the part of a society hostess in a costume drama. 'How do you take your Earl Grey, Jake? With a slice of lemon?'

'Milk and two sugars, please.'

Julia looked briefly astonished by his reply, then grinned with pleasure. 'Well, how authentically working-class. I do like a real man. One who's not afraid to defy convention.'

Jake added the milk and sugar in bemusement, then retreated to the safety of his notebook.

'Perhaps you could tell us how you know Guy,' prompted Bridget, once the tea-pouring ritual was complete.

'Oh, Guy and I go way back,' said Julia. 'I first met Guy when we were students here at the university. I could see straight away that he was a talent to watch. He has an instinctive feel for what works in the theatre. He has a gift for drawing the best out of people.'

Bridget recalled the director bellowing at his somewhat browbeaten stars, and kept her own counsel.

'After university, we went our separate ways, Guy into theatre, and me into television. I had my first breakthrough with a small part in *Casualty*. I played a coma patient. The role didn't give me much scope for displaying my talent, but it got me in with the right crowd, you know? People began to perceive me as an actress with real potential.'

'I can imagine.'

'From there, it's been onwards and upwards. You've probably seen me on TV yourself?'

'I don't think so.' Bridget was reluctant to feed Julia's craving and admit that she had indeed seen her in a recent detective series.

'No?' said Julia with ill-disguised dismay. 'Perhaps you don't watch much TV. I expect you're far too busy. I've had a number of roles in crime dramas. But don't worry – I never play the villain!' She laughed at her own joke, then sipped her tea.

'I'd like to return to your relationship with Guy, if you don't mind,' said Bridget. 'In particular, when you were students together at Oxford. How did you meet each other? Were you at the same college?'

Julia seemed more than happy to talk about the subject. 'We were at different colleges, but at Oxford, theatre productions are organised at a university level. That's how we first got to know each other. Oxford's a small place. We both knew friends involved in the world of theatre, and it wasn't very long before we were introduced.' She tossed her blonde hair back, her eyes gleaming as she relived the memory. 'But there was more than just acting that drew us together. We both felt a strong physical attraction right from the start. At one point I thought we'd be together forever.' She gave a melodramatic sigh. 'But it's notoriously difficult to maintain relationships in our line of work. We were star-crossed lovers, I suppose you could say.'

The *Romeo and Juliet* reference didn't escape Bridget, even with her rather patchy knowledge of English literature. 'Guy directed a performance of *Twelfth Night* at the Burton Taylor Studio theatre. Were you involved with that?'

Julia sipped her tea before responding. 'I may have been.'

'You don't sound sure?'

'I did so much acting at university, and it was all such

a long time ago.'

'I would have thought that it would be very easy to remember one of your formative acting experiences, especially since Guy Goodwin was directing the play.'

'Ah, yes. Now you mention it, I do remember *Twelfth Night*. I played the part of Olivia, the wealthy noblewoman.'

'Was that the lead role?'

The hint of a shadow passed across Julia's face but she mastered it quickly. 'It was a good role, but not quite the leading lady. Not the *star* of the play. That would be Viola.'

'And who played the part of Viola?'

'A girl called Camilla Townsend. Why?'

'What can you tell me about Camilla Townsend?'

'Not much. I didn't know her well at all, we were at different colleges, you see.'

'I thought you said that wasn't important.'

'Well, I...' For once Julia seemed at a loss for words. 'Why are you asking me about Camilla?' she demanded.

Bridget regarded her coolly. 'Because Camilla Townsend went missing after the final performance of the play and was never seen again. But surely you already knew that, Miss Carstairs?'

CHAPTER 16

The Henderson family lived in a substantial 1930s detached house on a quiet tree-lined street in Beaconsfield. Regimentally-trimmed hedges; neat lawn and borders; a real Christmas tree prominently displayed in the window of the front room. Tasteful. Understated. Ffion took in all these little details as she left her bike behind the charcoal-grey BMW parked on the brick driveway.

She rang the doorbell and continued to study the house while she waited for an answer. The tree was a Norway spruce, she noted. Notorious for shedding pine needles all over the carpet. Mrs Henderson either employed an efficient and hardworking cleaner, or was highly proficient with a vacuum cleaner herself.

The door was opened by an aproned woman in her mid-forties, dusting her hands on a linen tea towel. The comforting smell of baking wafted from inside the house.

'Mrs Lynda Henderson?'

'Yes?' The woman regarded Ffion's green leather outfit with some surprise.

Ffion looked her up and down in return. The matriarch

of the Henderson family was immaculately turned out. Beneath her apron she wore an expensive cashmere sweater and black trousers. Her hair was salon styled, and she was evidently the kind of woman who felt it necessary to wear make-up even while baking a few last-minute mince pies. Ffion presented her warrant card, aware that her unexpected arrival would no doubt ruin Mrs Henderson's perfect day. 'DC Ffion Hughes. I wonder if I could have a word with your son, Luke.'

'Luke? What's this about?'

'Is he in?'

'Yes, but –'

'It won't take long,' said Ffion. *Unless you keep me waiting out here on the doorstep*, she felt like adding.

The woman's husband appeared behind her then, laying a protective hand on her shoulder. He was dressed in an accountant's idea of casual – beige chinos and a cotton shirt with silver cufflinks. 'What's going on, Lynda?'

'It's the police. They want to speak to Luke.'

'Is it about –'

'It's a police matter,' said Ffion, as if that explained anything. There was no need to give any information away. She'd learned that it was always best to keep your cards close to your chest. You never knew what people might volunteer if they didn't know why they were being questioned.

'If it's about the murder of that tour guide,' said Mr Henderson, 'then we've already told you everything we know.'

Ffion turned her sharp gaze on him. 'We have some further questions we'd like to ask Luke.'

Now Mr Henderson's day was ruined too. His face seemed to pale before Ffion's eyes. She had a pretty shrewd idea what was making him so anxious. Drugs. Despite the Hendersons' best efforts to keep their son's misdemeanours under wraps, a police constable had now turned up on their doorstep on Christmas Eve. She must be their worst nightmare.

'So, if I could come inside?' she prompted. 'No point staying out here and letting all the neighbours get a good look, is there?'

Her words had the desired effect. Mrs Henderson ushered her inside and showed her into the front room. 'I'll bring Luke down to see you.'

The room was furnished in coordinating shades of taupe, cream and walnut. Ffion declined the offer of a seat on the leather sofa and positioned herself next to the tree in order to have a good nose around.

The room was spotlessly clean with nothing out of place. The books on the shelves were arranged by colour and height. The only picture on the wall was of a calm seascape, and the handful of ornaments on the mantelpiece were arranged with mathematical symmetry. During her brief relationship with Jake, Ffion had often complained about the mess in his flat – the unwashed dishes piled in the sink, the pizza boxes stacked by the kitchen bin, the dust bunnies under the bed – and she'd done her best to instil order and cleanliness. This house, at the other extreme of the scale, should have been her idea of heaven, but it was too choreographed even for her tastes. Could it be that some of Jake's relaxed slovenliness had rubbed off on her?

The Hendersons appeared once more, this time with Luke in tow. His father pushed him gently into the room and they followed him inside, closing the door behind them. 'You don't mind if we stay, do you?' asked Mr Henderson.

'Suit yourself,' said Ffion. 'As long as Luke doesn't mind.'

Luke took a seat on the sofa, flanked by his parents. He appeared terrified.

'So, we spoke to your friend Dylan Collins yesterday,' said Ffion, not missing the small sound of disapproval that Mrs Henderson made in the back of her throat at the mention of Luke's friend. 'His version of events seems to contradict the statement that you gave to us.'

'In what way?' asked Luke's father.

Ffion addressed herself to Luke. 'According to Dylan, after the ghost tour, he came to meet you in the Turf Tavern.'

Luke's mother took a sharp intake of breath. 'Oh Luke, after everything we said!'

'Is it true?' demanded Mr Henderson angrily.

Luke seemed abashed. 'Yeah,' he admitted. 'The thing is, I got a message from Dylan saying he was going to be swinging by the pub on his way back from college, so I went to meet him. I just wanted to check he was all right after what happened on the ghost tour.'

'And was he?' asked Ffion.

'Oh, yeah, sure. He was fine.'

'According to your parents' version of events, you were away from them for at least twenty minutes.'

'I was chatting to Dylan. It was my last chance to see him before leaving Oxford.'

'You told my colleagues that you'd gone for a smoke.'

Luke's neck began to colour. 'Um…'

'Would it be a fair assumption that you and Dylan were smoking cannabis together?'

'Oh, Luke, how could you?' This from Mrs Henderson, who looked appalled. 'I thought you'd learnt your lesson after what happened last time…' She stopped herself as if realising that she might have said too much.

Luke's father was furious. 'You're in a whole heap of trouble now. If the police want to press charges, I won't stand in their way.'

'We just need to know exactly what happened that night,' said Ffion, cutting across the hysteria. It would have been much easier to do this interview without the interference of Luke's parents.

'Okay,' continued Luke. Now that he was talking openly, he no longer seemed too worried about what his parents thought of him. Perhaps getting everything out in the open at last had liberated him. 'Dylan was bringing me some joints to bring home for the Christmas vacation. I told him I honestly didn't know how I'd get through it otherwise.' He kept his gaze fixed firmly on Ffion, ignoring his mother's gasp of indignation. 'So we stopped to share one that night.'

'And how long did you spend with him?'

'I don't really know. But when I got back, everyone was talking about a stabbing and I realised that it was the ghost tour guy who'd been attacked. I didn't find out that he was dead until later.'

'Tell me everything you know about Dylan's movements that night,' said Ffion.

'Oh, come on. You don't think he had anything to do with this?'

'Please just tell me exactly where you met him and where you last saw him.'

'Well, all right. He sent me a message to say he was on his way, and I met him in the courtyard at the front of the pub.'

'Is that the one closest to St Helen's Passage?'

'Yes. We met there and then went round the back out of the way to have a smoke. And then afterwards I went back to my parents, like I said.'

'And where did Dylan go?'

'He just left to collect his bike and to cycle back to his house.'

'Where did he leave his bike?'

'I think he chained it to a drainpipe in St Helen's Passage.'

'But you didn't see him leave?'

'No.'

'Thank you.' She had established that Dylan's story was consistent with Luke's, even though he couldn't vouch for what his friend had done after leaving him.

'Is that everything?' asked Luke, looking relieved.

'Almost,' said Ffion. 'Just one final thing. Where is the cannabis now?'

Luke looked crestfallen. 'In my room. It's not like I've had a chance to smoke it or anything.'

'I think you'd better fetch it.'

After Luke had sloped from the room, Mrs Henderson vented her anger. 'That boy, Dylan, it's all his fault. Luke had never been in any kind of trouble before he met him. I've a good mind to report him to the university authorities myself. He ought to be sent down.'

'Hush,' said her husband, putting an arm around her shoulder. 'Luke has to take his share of the responsibility here.'

Luke reappeared then and handed over a plastic bag containing a dozen joints.

'Thank you,' said Ffion. 'I'll take these. But as this is your third offence I'm issuing you with an on-the-spot fine of ninety pounds, and a warning that possession can carry a sentence of up to five years.'

Mrs Henderson let out a small cry of dismay at the news, and her husband reached grimly for his wallet to deal with the fine. 'You can pay me back later,' he growled at Luke.

When it was done, he showed Ffion to the front door. 'Listen,' he said, pulling the door closed behind him. 'I won't deny that Luke's had a few problems, but we're working through them and sorting them out. This has been a huge strain on my wife in particular. She's been so worried, she hasn't been able to sleep. The doctor has prescribed Valium for her.'

Ffion nodded, but said nothing. The Hendersons' problems were no business of hers.

'Luke's not a bad boy,' he continued, 'he's just a little wild sometimes. It's his age. He needs to learn better self-control.'

Ffion wondered if that was what her own Mam had believed when she'd found out that her daughter had a crush on girls. A problem, to be fixed, through better self-control. 'Children need to be given their freedom,' she told Mr Henderson. 'If you try to mould them in your own image, they rebel. Luke's just trying to find his own feet. He needs your support, not condemnation.'

He looked at her, his head on one side, considering her words carefully. 'I'm sure you're right,' he said at last. 'What you did just now, well hopefully it will teach him a lesson. One small mistake shouldn't ruin someone's life.'

Ffion said nothing. She wanted to believe what he said, but so often it seemed that a single mistake certainly could ruin someone's life.

Her own Mam had made an unforgiveable error of judgement and had lost one of her daughters forever as a result. And her relationship with Jake had been brought to a bitter end by his moment of weakness. Mistakes were easy to make, but it was far harder to repair the damage they caused. She turned and climbed back onto her bike, kicking the engine into life. As she headed back to Oxford, it began to rain.

CHAPTER 17

Julia Carstairs leaned back in her chair, her arms folded tightly across her chest. 'If you think that I had anything to do with the disappearance of Camilla Townsend, you couldn't be further from the truth.'

'Actually,' said Bridget, 'I was wondering if Guy Goodwin might have been involved.'

'Guy? Why on earth would you think that?'

'David Smith thought there might have been a connection.'

Julia looked baffled. 'David who?'

Bridget wished that Julia would pay closer attention. 'The ghost tour guide,' she reminded her. 'Gordon Goole was his stage name.'

'But why would he know anything about Guy? Or Camilla, for that matter?'

Bridget wondered whether Julia was bluffing or if she really had no idea who David Smith was. 'David Smith was a student at Pembroke College,' she explained. 'He was Camilla Townsend's boyfriend, and he was arrested for her murder.'

Julia's hand flew to her mouth. 'That was Gordon

Goole? Of course I remember David. But I would never have recognised him. I hadn't seen him since my university days. He looked so different.'

Bridget recalled the photograph of the youthful fresher in Smith's house. The years had certainly not been as kind to him as they had to Julia. It was conceivable that she really hadn't recognised him as the young actor from her student days.

Julia still seemed puzzled by the revelation. 'But why did David think that Guy was to blame for Camilla going missing? It was David who the police suspected.'

'I was hoping you might be able to shed some light on the matter. Was Guy very close to Camilla?'

'No!' Julia's denial seemed to have been wrenched from deep within her. 'Of course not.' She glared at Bridget with fiery anger in her eyes.

'I imagine,' continued Bridget, 'that it would be inevitable for a director and a leading actor to become close. And as you said yourself, Guy gave the starring role to Camilla, not you. There must have been something between them.'

The observation seemed to have touched a raw nerve. 'Guy's a professional,' Julia protested. 'He would never allow personal feelings to get mixed up with a working relationship.'

Bridget raised one eyebrow. 'It was hardly a working relationship, was it? You were all just students at the time. Wouldn't it be natural for two young people to become fond of each other?'

Julia reacted angrily. 'When we started rehearsing the play, Guy and I were already a couple. So there was no question of him sleeping with Camilla!'

'I didn't suggest that she and Guy may have been sleeping together. I just asked if they were close.' Bridget waited for Julia to realise how much she'd given away by her reaction, then asked innocently, 'So do you know why Camilla was given the lead role?'

Julia studied her manicured nails. 'Some people said

unkind things about her and Guy, but it was just malicious gossip. I admit that I was hoping to get the part of Viola, and I'd rather assumed that Guy would give it to me. But one can't always get the part one hopes for. She was quite good in the part. I won't deny it.'

'Camilla went missing after the party to celebrate the final night of the play, is that right?'

'Yes.'

'Guy was at that party too?'

'Yes, with me.' She smiled victoriously. 'And that's why Guy couldn't possibly have had anything to do with Camilla's disappearance. You see, I was with him all night and I went back to his room in college after the party. So whatever happened to poor Camilla, it was nothing to do with Guy.'

Bridget glanced sideways at Jake, who was busily writing down everything that Julia had said, or at least the parts that seemed remotely relevant. She guessed they'd extracted as much information out of Julia as they could, at least for now. 'Well, thanks for your time,' she said. 'I'd like to speak to Guy next.'

Julia laughed. 'You'll be lucky. When Guy's rehearsing, he won't let anything come in his way. And there's only a couple of hours until the matinée begins.'

'That's all very well,' said Bridget, 'but this is a murder enquiry.'

Yet when they left the bar and returned to the front of house, Bridget was dismayed to find it in darkness. The director, actors and orchestra had all gone.

'Where's Guy?' squealed Julia. 'He can't have left without me!' She wheeled about and returned to the box office, where Ralph was leaning against the desk, looking bored. He straightened up as Julia burst in.

'What's happened to Guy?' she demanded. 'Where has he gone?'

'I'm sorry, Miss Carstairs. He and the others left about ten minutes ago.'

'But didn't he ask where I was? You should have told

him I was in the bar.'

Ralph fidgeted nervously. 'Mr Goodwin left in a hurry. He looked quite angry. I'm afraid that he didn't ask about you.'

Julia whirled around, fixing Bridget with a furious glare, as if it were her fault that she'd been deserted. 'Well, I hope you're satisfied, Inspector. Thanks to your fruitless attempt to rake up dirt from the past, you've taken me away from Guy's side just when he needed me most.'

'Thank you for your time, Miss Carstairs.' Bridget turned to Ralph, who averted his gaze in embarrassment. 'When Mr Goodwin returns, please inform him that I'll be returning to speak to him later.'

★

Back in the car, Bridget noticed that Jake seemed unusually quiet. He'd hardly said a word during the interview with Julia Carstairs, and it was perhaps unsurprising, given the way that she'd embarrassed him.

'What is it with these older women?' he said at last. 'I wish they'd act their age. I can't understand why they're all so desperate.'

'I think you'll find that they're lonely,' she said. 'It must be hard to reach a point where the best of your life seems to be behind you, and you find yourself alone, especially at Christmas.'

'But they're not alone, are they? Julia's with Guy, and Liz and Deborah have each other for company.'

'Perhaps those relationships are a little fragile. After all, Julia had no qualms about dumping her two friends, and now Guy appears to have gone off without her. I can't help feeling sorry for them all.'

'I suppose so.'

'What about you, Jake?' she asked brightly. 'Are you looking forward to spending Christmas with your friends and family?'

'If I can get away on time,' he said. 'It's a three hour

drive up to Leeds, even on a good day, and with the Christmas traffic, it's bound to take much longer.'

'All right,' said Bridget. 'Point made. You can head off as soon as we get back to Kidlington.'

'Really, ma'am? Thanks.'

Bridget wanted to ask him what was happening between him and Ffion, but she knew better than to pry. It was none of her business, and if either of them wanted some advice from her, they could surely ask. Her thoughts turned inevitably back to the investigation.

Her conversation with Julia Carstairs hadn't really gone anywhere. Julia seemed to have been genuinely ignorant of Gordon Goole's true identity, and had gone out of her way to defend Guy Goodwin, even providing him with an alibi, both for the time of David Smith's murder, and also for the night decades earlier when Camilla Townsend had gone missing. The chances were that there was nothing of substance to David Smith's conviction that the theatre director was somehow responsible for Camilla's disappearance. Without a body, the likelihood was that she had simply run away from Oxford for reasons unknown, and was still alive today. She could be out there now, living a new life, preparing for Christmas herself. Bridget certainly hoped so.

Returning to Kidlington, she was aware that there was now little more she could do before Christmas. But she fetched herself a coffee, and was pleasantly surprised when she returned to her desk to find a brown envelope waiting for her. It was the report from the mortuary.

The post-mortem confirmed what she already knew, that David Smith had died from a stab wound, the steak knife having punctured the heart and severed the aorta, the main artery carrying blood from the heart to the rest of the body. The senior pathologist, Dr Roy Andrews, had pulled off a small miracle in performing the post-mortem at such short notice in the run-up to Christmas. It seemed only right to pick up the phone and thank him.

'Inspector Hart,' said Roy in his Scottish burr, 'you're

not still at work on Christmas Eve, I hope?'

'Just wrapping up,' said Bridget. 'But I could say the same about you, since you're still at the mortuary.'

'Ah, well, you know me.'

Bridget reflected on just how well she did know the pathologist. They had known each other for several years, but only at a professional level. Bridget knew little of his personal life, except that he was a bachelor and a workaholic, and wondered what plans he had, if any, for the festive season. 'You're not heading north of the border?' she asked. Roy had left it rather late if he was planning to go all the way up to Scotland.

'Ach, no! Just spending a couple of quiet days at home. I relish the chance to catch up on my reading.'

Bridget wondered what kind of reading Roy might get up to. Not medical textbooks, she hoped. She often wished she had more time to read herself, but she felt rather sorry for Roy. His claim that he was looking forward to spending Christmas alone with a pile of books wasn't easy to swallow. How many others would be alone for Christmas, with nothing more than a book or the TV for company?

'Unless,' he said, 'I can persuade someone to spend a little time in my somewhat morose company and sample my home cooking, which, even though I say so myself, is competent, if unexceptional.'

Bridget must have paused a little too long before responding, because he added tetchily, 'Don't worry, DI Hart. I didn't mean you. I had someone else in mind.'

Who could he mean? Roy never usually discussed his personal life. 'Well, enjoy yourself, Roy'

'Aye, I intend to do just that. And have a merry Christmas yourself!'

Bridget put the phone down not sure what to make of Roy's comments. Was his claim that he hoped to spend Christmas with a mysterious friend merely bravado? She hoped for his sake that it wasn't.

Ffion had returned from Beaconsfield, and Bridget listened to her report of what Luke Henderson had said under questioning. It seemed that Dylan's story matched what Luke had said, although of course she couldn't rule out the possibility that the two students had communicated by phone to make sure that their accounts tallied. But if they were hiding something, Bridget couldn't guess what it might be. Dylan Collins might be a disturbed young man, but he didn't seem like a vicious killer. Besides, what reason could he possibly have had for stabbing a tour guide to death?

Her pensive mood was shattered by the booming voice of Chief Superintendent Grayson. 'Still here, Inspector? Surely you've got better things to be doing on Christmas Eve than sitting at your desk.'

'I still have a few jobs to wrap up, then I'll be on my way, sir,' she told him. It was unlike Grayson not to be demanding an update on the investigation. It was also unlike him to be looking so cheerful. Perhaps the Christmas spirit had penetrated even his hardened shell. Or maybe he'd enjoyed a glass or two of another kind of spirit at lunchtime.

'Don't leave it too late,' he told her. 'Then go home to your family.'

The office was emptying rapidly, as detectives finished their work and slunk out of the door before Bridget could stop them. It seemed futile to hold anyone back, with the lack of leads to follow up. It seemed that Bridget's fears of running up against the clock had been proven true. 'You may as well go home,' she said to Ffion. 'There's nothing more you can do before Christmas. Have a good break. Just come back ready to catch a killer.'

★

Jake locked his things away in his desk drawer and switched off his computer. Glancing at the window he could see that it was already dark outside, and a few snowflakes were drifting up against the glass and melting. He'd really hoped to leave a lot earlier in the day. What with the mad Christmas traffic and the inclement weather, there was likely to be a string of hold-ups on the M1. But it couldn't be helped. Murder was murder, even at Christmas. He was just relieved that Bridget had allowed him to get away for a few days. He'd been worried that she might have asked him to cancel his plans. If there was any time he needed to get away from Oxford, it was now. The more miles he could put between himself and Ffion the better.

But before he left, he wanted to make one further attempt at reconciliation. So far, all his apologies had been greeted by stony silence. Ffion was as immovable as the mountains of her homeland. But Jake was unwilling to leave it at that. He knew he'd blown it on the romantic front, but he wanted the two of them to be on speaking terms. They still had to work together, at least until he'd found another job to go to. In a last effort to put things on an even keel, he'd nipped into the Christmas Market and bought a small gift for her.

He'd debated with himself whether or not to give her anything. He didn't want her to think he was trying to buy his way back into her affections. In the end he'd chosen a bar of handmade soap and some scented candles. Nothing too pricey, just a token gift. He didn't know how she'd react. Ffion was always so unpredictable and could be incredibly spiky at times. But if she didn't like them, that was her problem. At least he could tell himself he'd tried.

He pushed the wrapped box into his coat pocket and went over to where she was busy typing away at her keyboard, a freshly brewed mug of tea steaming fiercely on her desktop, even though most of the other people were getting ready to leave. He thought he could smell lemon, or perhaps lemongrass. Was lemongrass tea a thing? He had no idea.

'Hi,' she said, without looking up.

Since their break-up, Jake had become acutely self-conscious every time he found himself in close proximity to Ffion. That blonde spiky hair. Those chiselled cheekbones. Those long legs wrapped in skin-tight leather trousers. Everything about her seemed simultaneously attractive yet designed to keep him at bay.

'I'm just off,' he said. 'I wanted to say goodbye.'

He wondered if she would rebuff him with a dismissive farewell, but she said, 'So you're going back to Leeds?' She kept her eyes on her computer screen, her long fingers continuing to strike the keys.

'Yeah. To see my mum and dad. What about you?'

'What about me?'

'Going anywhere for Christmas?'

'No.'

That seemed to be the end of that avenue of conversation. He wondered why she wasn't going away anywhere, but knew better than to ask. She'd never talked much about her family, even when things were good between them. He'd sensed that there was some unspoken anguish that Ffion preferred to keep to herself.

Still, at least she'd spoken to him without biting his head off. That was a good sign. He produced the present and laid it on her desk. 'Just a token,' he said quickly. 'Nothing expensive. No worries if you haven't got anything for me in return.'

She stopped typing and glanced at the box with her almond-shaped eyes. 'That's good. Because I haven't.'

'Well, like I said, I wasn't expecting anything.'

He tried to think of something else he could safely say. He was tempted to open up to her and tell her about the job he was thinking of applying for. He'd like to see her reaction. Would she tell him to go for it, or ask him to stay in Oxford? Actually, on second thoughts, he wasn't sure he wanted to hear her response. And he hadn't yet made up his mind to apply. He'd think about it over Christmas and decide by the New Year.

'Jake?' she said.

'Yes?'

'Have a good Christmas.' She took a sip of her tea and returned to work.

CHAPTER 18

Bridget waited until everyone else had left the office before heading off herself. In the end she'd had to tell Ffion to leave. Then, feeling like a captain last to leave a sinking ship, she switched off the lights as she left.

Leaving Kidlington behind, she battled her way back through the Oxford traffic towards the New Theatre. She was hoping to have a quick word with Guy Goodwin, and check that his account of his movements on the night of the murder tallied with what Julia had said.

The number of cars on the road was astonishing. Had so many people left it until now to do their Christmas shopping? Come to think of it, she still needed to find something to give her parents. Perhaps she'd drop in at the Christmas Market to see if she could pick up a last-minute present.

She left her car on St Giles and walked to the theatre, her head bowed against the weather. Snow was beginning to fall, swirling around her in the light breeze. It melted as soon as it hit the ground, but temperatures were forecast to drop overnight. There was a real possibility of a white

Christmas.

On arriving at the theatre, she was dismayed to find it closed. But of course, she should have guessed. It was Christmas Eve and there was no evening performance. She wondered what to do. She could call in at the Randolph Hotel in the hope of finding Guy there, but he was just as likely to be out. In any case, she doubted that the theatre director would say anything that would move the investigation on. Bridget was beginning to wonder whether David Smith's stabbing was simply a case of a random knife attack. Trying to find a reason why anyone might have wanted to murder him was proving fruitless.

She looked at her watch and realised that she was due to be back in Wolvercote in half an hour to meet Jonathan. She had let him down so many times in the past, but to leave him waiting outside for her in the cold on Christmas Eve would be unforgivable. She debated with herself for a moment, before deciding to head for home via the Christmas Market. Just for once, she would put family before work. Guy Goodwin could wait.

*

'I'm back!' Bridget called as she let herself into her house. She'd managed to dash over to the Christmas Market, scoop up an old-fashioned wicker picnic hamper packed with goodies for her mum and dad, and still get back to Wolvercote in time to meet Jonathan. With luck, she might even have time to get changed out of her work clothes before he arrived. They had planned to cook a Thai curry together – well, to be fair Jonathan was going to do the cooking, and she was going to watch and learn – and have a nice quiet evening with just her, Jonathan and Chloe, before facing the whole family tomorrow at Vanessa's. She'd already decided on the evening's music – Britten's *Ceremony of Carols* – and had even thought to buy a couple of cinnamon-scented candles at the market. Vanessa would be proud of her.

All the presents still needed wrapping, but she could find time for that in the morning.

'Chloe?' she called.

When there was still no reply, Bridget went upstairs to her daughter's bedroom. Chloe probably had her earphones plugged in as usual and hadn't heard Bridget coming home.

But Chloe's door was ajar and the room was deserted. *Damn,* thought Bridget. *Where is that girl?* Chloe knew she was supposed to be back for dinner this evening. It was supposed to be a special occasion – a rare chance for the three of them to sit down and enjoy some time together.

She called Chloe's phone but it rang and went through to voicemail.

'Hi, it's Mum here. Just wondering when you're going to be back. Don't forget that Jonathan's cooking tonight.'

She ended the call, then dialled again, this time the number for Olivia's house. If Chloe was out she would almost certainly be with her best friend.

When the two girls had been younger Bridget had often relied on Olivia's mum, Natalie, to pick them up from school and take Chloe home when Bridget was working late. Chloe had eaten at Olivia's house almost as frequently as her own home. Natalie had always said it was no problem, but Bridget felt guilty that she hadn't been able to return the favour as often as she'd have liked. Now that the girls were older they hopped onto the bus whenever they wanted to go anywhere and Bridget didn't see or speak to Natalie half as much as she used to. It was a friendship that she missed.

'Hello. Natalie here.'

'Hi, it's Bridget.'

'Oh, Bridget, how are you?'

'Fine, thanks. And you?'

'Busy!' She laughed. In the background a television was playing – some upbeat music and a round of applause. It sounded like a game show.

'Sorry to bother, you, but is Chloe with you again?'

'Again?'

Something about the way Natalie said the word set Bridget on edge. 'Don't get me wrong. I don't mind in the least. I know she loves coming over to your place.' Bridget tried to sound light-hearted, but the truth of what she was saying cut deep. Chloe did seem to prefer Olivia's house to her own.

The sound of more loud applause came across the line. 'Just a moment,' said Natalie. 'I'm going to move somewhere quieter.' A door closed and the background noise dropped in volume. 'Sorry about that. My parents are here, and it's wall-to-wall quiz shows with the volume turned up.'

Bridget had the feeling that Natalie was stalling for time. What was the problem? Was Chloe there or not? Why didn't Natalie just put her on?

'Actually,' said Natalie, 'we've hardly seen Chloe for a couple of weeks. I wondered if she and Olivia had fallen out.'

'Fallen out? She wasn't with Olivia last night then?'

'Last night? No. Olivia was here with her grandparents.'

Bridget didn't know what to say, so many thoughts were swirling around her head. If Chloe hadn't been with Olivia last night then where had she been? Why had Chloe lied to her? And, more to the point, where was she now?

'Bridget,' said Natalie sympathetically, 'would you like me to put Olivia on?'

'Would you?' said Bridget, dropping onto Chloe's bed. She suddenly felt very weary.

'Mrs Hart?' A timid voice on the other end of the line.

'Olivia, do you have any idea where Chloe is, only I don't seem to be able to get hold of her.'

'Well, um…'

'You're not in any trouble,' Bridget assured her. 'I just need to know where she is, that's all.'

'Well, I don't know for sure,' said Olivia, 'but she's probably out with her boyfriend.'

Boyfriend? What boyfriend? So this was Chloe's big secret, and the reason she was never at home these days. Bridget tried to remain calm. 'Do you have his number?'

'Sorry, no.'

'What about his name?'

'Alfie. He's called Alfie. He's in the upper sixth. He has his own car.'

If Olivia had intended to reassure Bridget with these last two pieces of information, she'd achieved quite the opposite. Chloe was only fifteen and she was dating a boy at least two years older. And one who drove his own car. Her daughter might be lying dead in a ditch, or worse. Bridget's mind was reeling.

'Thank you, Olivia,' she said numbly.

There was nothing more Olivia could tell her. She handed the phone back to Natalie who did her best to reassure Bridget that Chloe was fine.

But Natalie wasn't the one whose daughter had lied to her about her whereabouts these past two weeks. And Natalie didn't know the statistics for violent crime and teenage driving accidents by heart, like Bridget did.

Bridget was about to dial Chloe's number again, when the doorbell rang. She jumped to her feet and ran downstairs, yanking open the door.

But instead of Chloe, it was Jonathan.

'Hi!' He held up a canvas shopping bag. 'All the ingredients for a perfect Thai curry.'

'Jonathan, it's you!'

He gave her a bemused look. 'Who were you expecting? Father Christmas?' With his other hand he produced a sprig of mistletoe from his pocket and held it up, puckering his lips in anticipation of a kiss. Then, seeing the look on Bridget's face, he lowered the mistletoe and said, 'What's the matter?'

'Sorry.' Bridget's emotions were cartwheeling all over the place. 'It's Chloe. I don't know where she is.'

Jonathan stepped into the house and studied her face with concern. 'You've tried her phone.'

'Of course.'

'And she's not with Olivia?'

'No.'

'Then she's probably on her way home right now.'

'She's not,' said Bridget, tears beginning to roll down her cheeks. 'She's with her boyfriend.'

Jonathan raised an eyebrow. 'Boyfriend? Since when has she had a boyfriend?'

'I don't know. A couple of weeks, perhaps.' She told Jonathan what Olivia had said.

Jonathan clasped her shoulders. 'Bridget, you're letting your imagination run away with you. Chloe's a sensible girl. I'm sure she's fine.'

'I don't know,' said Bridget, pulling away from him. She didn't want sympathy and comforting words right now. She wanted someone on her side, taking her concerns seriously. 'This is how it all started with Abigail. She was Chloe's age when she started staying out late, not saying where she was going, lying about who she was with.' She ran a hand through her hair. 'I don't want Chloe making the same mistakes. I don't want the same thing to happen to her.'

'Of course you don't. I get that. As her mother it's only natural that you want her to be safe. But all teenagers do this sort of thing. Chloe needs to learn to make her own decisions. You can't keep her wrapped in cotton wool forever.'

He was so calm and reasonable that it was infuriating. Bridget knew she was being irrational, but she couldn't help herself.

'Are you going to report her missing?' he asked, when she said nothing.

'No.' She took a deep breath. She knew that Chloe wasn't really missing, she was just out. The police wouldn't treat a report of a teenager who'd gone off with her boyfriend seriously until at least twenty-four hours had passed. In the vast majority of cases, missing people returned safe and sound within a day. Bridget knew all that. But it didn't change the way she felt. This was her own daughter.

The sound of the key turning in the lock had her dashing to the front door again. She yanked it open just as Chloe pushed it from the other side.

Her daughter looked startled. 'Oh! Hi, Mum. Sorry if I'm a bit late.'

'Where the hell have you been?' demanded Bridget.

'Just out with friends,' said Chloe. 'What's the problem?'

'Which friends?'

'Olivia and –'

'Don't lie to me!' snapped Bridget. 'I phoned Olivia's house and you weren't there. But I did speak to Olivia, and she gave me the name of your boyfriend. Alfie! Were you out with him? Did he drive you home just now?'

A scowl swept across Chloe's face. 'It's none of your business.'

'Of course it is! I'm your mother! Why did you lie to me? Anything could have happened to you.'

'But nothing did.'

'That's not the point. I need to know where you are and who you're with. Why didn't you tell me you've got a boyfriend?'

'Because I knew you'd go off the deep end.'

'That's not true!' yelled Bridget.

'Well, I think you've just shown that it is. If you can't trust me to make my own decisions, I'm not going to discuss them with you.' She pushed past Bridget and marched up the stairs.

'Chloe...'

'I'm going to my room. Don't worry about dinner, I've already eaten with Alfie.' The bedroom door slammed shut.

Bridget stood at the foot of the stairs, shaking and almost in tears again. She was tempted to run up the stairs and bang on Chloe's door, but knew that was the worst thing she could possibly do.

Shit, she thought. *I'm handling this really badly.*

Jonathan took her hand and led her through to the lounge. 'Give her some space,' he counselled. 'She needs to cool off.'

Bridget knew what Jonathan really meant. She and Chloe both needed to cool off.

She sobbed into his chest, feeling useless. She didn't even know who was to blame anymore. Chloe for not telling the truth, or herself for not trusting her. She sank onto the sofa and buried her face in Jonathan's arms.

'Why am I such a terrible mother?' she wailed.

★

It was pitch dark around the back of the old house, but Dylan Collins wasn't afraid of the dark. There was nothing to be scared of, even when out on a midnight ghost-hunting expedition. Not if you understood that ghosts and hauntings were perfectly rational phenomena that could be explained by science. With the aid of the flashlight on his phone, he crept through the overgrown shrubbery to the boarded-up windows of the house. The building would have been elegant and fashionable once: a generously-proportioned family home with broad bay windows at the front, a balcony overlooking the rear of the property, and tall brick chimneys rising from its rooftop. A couple of other grand homes stood either side of the garden, but there were no lights in the windows that overlooked him. Snow fell lightly on his bare head, but he shook it off, concentrating on the task ahead of him. With the aid of a crowbar, he set about his work.

The house had stood abandoned for decades. Dylan had heard about it from one of the guys who sold him spliffs. It was used from time to time for illicit parties, or by homeless people in search of shelter, but he was pretty sure that he would have it to himself tonight.

The plywood boards that covered the kitchen window were old and damp, and already loose. Dylan prised them away, then climbed in through the empty window frame, long since glassless. Inside, the building smelled of mildew and decay. He shone his light around, noting the damp stains of mould that covered the walls and ceiling. Carefully, he hauled his equipment through the window after him.

The apparatus was fragile, painstakingly calibrated back in the Clarendon lab, and tested as extensively as he'd been able to under laboratory conditions. This was his first chance for a proper field trial, and he felt sure he'd chosen a good location for his experiment. A house this old had surely witnessed all manner of human drama over the years. Some faint trace of that would be imprinted on the very fabric of the building. According to stone tape theory, the bricks, stones, and perhaps even the timber that made the house might record the lives of its former inhabitants. Even if the recordings were too faint to be observed by human senses, his device should be able to detect their presence.

His equipment was heavy and cumbersome. He carried it carefully through the open doorway of the kitchen and into a downstairs hallway. His feet thumped loudly against bare floorboards as he manoeuvred the glass tube of the detector along the passage. A sudden movement up ahead made him stop. Scratching and scurrying sounds followed, as a startled rat fled from its hiding place and dashed away into the depths of the house. When it had gone, all he could hear was the pounding of his heart and the sound of his own ragged breathing, condensing into clouds before him. After a moment he resumed his careful exploration, further into the house, one foot in front of the other.

The first door he came to was closed. He gripped the brass handle and turned it carefully, waiting to see if any more creatures would come rushing out. But the only sound was the creaking of the floor beneath his feet. He carried his equipment into what looked like a dining room. A large table stood in the middle of the room, surrounded by high-backed chairs, and shrouded in a veil of thick cobwebs suspended from the ceiling rose. A shiver ran down his spine. It really was like a haunted house. He brushed the worst of the webs away from the end of the table and set his device down. Switching it on, he held his breath, hoping it had not been damaged. But all seemed well. The detector powered on, humming softly, and after a minute the digital readout lit up, glowing an eldritch green in the darkness. Picking it up, he began to move purposefully around the room.

Numbers flickered across the display, indicating faint traces of paranormal residue. He moved closer to the wall and watched as the reading increased. It was just as he'd hoped. The old house was a repository of psychic energy. He followed a slow path around the room, sweeping the end of the device up and down the wall. With mounting excitement he watched as the numbers on the display steadily increased. Creeping carefully around the edge of the room, he gradually homed in on one corner where the readings were particularly high. He lowered the detector and found to his surprise that the energy seemed highest next to the floor itself.

Dylan switched his device off and studied the area carefully. The floorboards at this end of the room were loose. They moved and squeaked as he pressed down with his foot. Kneeling down eagerly, he set to work once more with his crowbar. The wooden boards came away easily, and he lifted them one by one. The smell of earthy decay was stronger than ever. One board broke in half as he lifted it, the timber rotted through. He was lucky he hadn't put his foot through it. This place was a death-trap. No wonder the council had boarded it up.

Once he'd completed his task, he stared at the dark space that he'd uncovered. A gap of several feet separated the floor level from the bare soil on which the house stood. Stout timber joists ran perpendicular beneath the floorboards. Old pipes and electric cables snaked along them.

And there, in a shallow grave, lay bones. Human bones.

CHAPTER 19

The atmosphere at Bridget's house on Christmas morning was, by unspoken mutual agreement, civilised but barely cordial. Bridget had resolved to say nothing to her daughter that might imply criticism or that could be interpreted as a rebuke. Chloe, for her part, seemed to have no desire to discuss what had taken place the night before. As a result they had little or nothing to say to each other. Jonathan did his best to inject some good humour, but even his speciality scrambled eggs did little to ease relations. It was not an auspicious start to Christmas Day.

The prospect of spending the whole day at Vanessa's in the company of Chloe and her own parents did little to ease Bridget's stress levels. She knew that Vanessa would be in overdrive for the occasion, having spent months preparing for it.

The freezer would be stocked with so much baking there'd be enough to see them through to spring. Vanessa's two young children, Florence and Toby, would have applied their creative skills to making Christmas decorations out of coloured paper, glue and glitter. The turkey – a free-range black-feathered bird from an award-winning organic farm in Norfolk – had been ordered in August and delivered by courier in a presentation box the previous week. Vanessa herself would have been up since five o'clock in the morning, stuffing and basting the turkey and would now no doubt be making gravy from the giblets, or some such complicated culinary endeavour.

Bridget felt exhausted just thinking about it. She still hadn't wrapped any of the presents, but after a sleepless night worrying about both Chloe and the murder investigation, she couldn't face doing it now. Under the circumstances, it hardly seemed like a high priority, so after breakfast she carried them out to load into her car.

She stepped outside into a snow-filled sky. The air had turned markedly colder overnight, and snowflakes were falling thick and fast. Already the ground was covered by a thin layer of white, and the sycamore trees on the village green were dusted like icing on a cake. She stood on the doorstep for a moment, taking in the magical sight, and feeling her mood improve.

After all, she had no desire to spoil things for everyone else, no matter how overwhelming her own problems might feel. And as long as they didn't get snowed-in at Vanessa's, she resolved to be on her best, most appreciative behaviour. She loaded the presents into the boot of the car and went back inside to call the others.

They drove to Vanessa's house with Christmas classics blaring out of the speakers, and Jonathan and Chloe giving each other bemused looks.

'What's with the popular music?' asked Jonathan, as Mariah Carey proclaimed to the car's occupants that all she wanted for Christmas was them.

'It's Christmas Day,' said Bridget. 'I'm trying to be cheerful.'

If only it were that easy.

She parked her Mini on the drive behind Vanessa's Range Rover and, armed with the still unwrapped presents, rang the doorbell. The door opened, and Rufus, the family's Golden Labrador, bounded out to greet them, tail wagging enthusiastically.

A frazzled-looking Vanessa stood in the hallway. 'Bridget, at last. Thank God you're here!'

'Why, what's the matter?'

Had the oven broken down? Had Rufus devoured the chipolatas? Whatever had happened, Bridget couldn't believe that her sister's problems could begin to compare with her own.

Vanessa drew them into the hall and pulled her to one side. Bridget detected alcohol on her sister's breath and wondered how much she'd already had to drink. '*What's the matter*,' said Vanessa in a dramatic stage whisper, 'is that Mum and Dad have been here less than twenty-four hours but they've already caused more problems than you can possibly imagine.'

'Why? What have they done?'

'Well,' said Vanessa, taking a deep breath before launching into her tale of woe, 'first I got a phone call from Dad yesterday morning saying that they couldn't possibly travel on the train as planned because Mum had fallen and hurt her wrist and Dad couldn't manage the luggage on his own, so James had to drop everything and drive down to Lyme Regis and pick them up.'

'Why couldn't Dad drive instead?'

'Because he doesn't feel confident driving on motorways anymore. Anyway, as you can imagine, the traffic on Christmas Eve was horrendous and it took James hours to get there and back. And then it turns out that Mum can't manage the stairs anymore so we had to move the children's beds into the downstairs playroom for them and the children are sleeping on mattresses on the floor. *And*' – she dropped her voice even lower – 'Dad's bladder trouble means that he's up half the night using the toilet. Fortunately we've got the downstairs loo, but I barely slept a wink last night, there was so much toing and froing. I was terrified one of them would trip over in the dark and we'd have to rush off to the emergency department.' She paused for breath. 'I had no idea that Mum had become so frail. Dad does everything for her, but he's not half as strong as he used to be. They're really not coping on their own very well, and you and I are going to have to have a serious talk with them before they leave.'

'What about?' asked Bridget.

'About moving them back to Oxford where we can keep an eye on them.'

'Is that really necessary?' Their parents were only in their seventies. The way Vanessa was talking about them made them sound a decade older. She was no doubt exaggerating. Then again, it was ages since Bridget had seen her Mum and Dad. They had cut themselves off like hermits down in Dorset.

'I really could have used your help yesterday,' scolded Vanessa. 'Especially with James out all day.'

'You know I was working.'

'You're always working. Just some moral support would have been nice. Anyway, you could have popped in after work.'

Bridget refrained from explaining that she'd faced her own crisis last night with Chloe. Vanessa didn't look as if she could cope with any more bad news. It was disconcerting for Bridget to see her older sister falling to pieces. She was usually so much more in control.

An alarm beeped loudly from the kitchen and Vanessa jumped. 'I have to dash,' she said. 'I'm par-boiling the potatoes before roasting them, and they have to be just right. I even went to the trouble of buying goose fat from Fortnum & Mason.'

At least half of Vanessa's trouble was that she made everything so much harder for herself by setting such high standards. If only she could learn to lower her sights and to relax like Bridget she might be a lot happier. Then again, Vanessa's roasted potatoes were always a triumph. If anything could save the day, the potatoes would.

'All right, you go and deal with the food,' said Bridget. 'Leave Mum and Dad to me.'

Vanessa gave her a grateful look and disappeared into the sanctuary of her bespoke kitchen from Smallbone.

'Oh, God,' said Bridget, turning to Jonathan. 'This is a nightmare. Take me home already.'

'Chloe, come and see what we got for Christmas!' Florence and Toby appeared at the top of the stairs and beckoned for their older cousin to come and join them. Bridget wished she could go with them, but she couldn't put off seeing her parents any longer.

Whilst Chloe ran upstairs, no doubt glad of the lucky escape, Bridget took hold of Jonathan's arm. 'Come on. We'd better go into the lounge.'

'It'll be all right,' he said soothingly. 'I'm sure they can't be half as bad as Vanessa described.'

But it seemed that Vanessa hadn't been greatly exaggerating. Bridget's first thought on entering the lounge was that the thermostat must have broken. It was swelteringly hot in there. Still wearing her outdoor coat, she felt herself breaking out in a sweat. James, her brother-in-law, rose to greet them, dressed for summer in a short-sleeved shirt.

'Let me help you with those,' he said, taking the pile of presents from Bridget's arms. He kissed her on the cheek and shook Jonathan's hand. Bridget immediately divested herself of coat, scarf and cardigan. 'We've had to turn the heating up,' said James in a low voice. 'They say they feel the cold. Can I get you something to drink? Wine? Beer?'

'White wine, please,' said Bridget. Even she didn't normally drink before lunch, but she could do with a large glass right now. Jonathan accepted the offer of a beer.

Her parents were huddled together on the sofa. Bridget was alarmed to see for herself how frail her mother looked. 'Mum, Dad, how are you?' she said in her best jolly voice. 'How nice to see you both.'

Her father rose to his feet and gripped her hand in his. 'Bridget. How lovely to see you. It's been such a long time.' He had put on weight since she'd last seen him, but seemed in good health. He hugged her close.

Bridget kissed his cheeks and then turned her attention to her mum. She was struggling to extract herself from the sofa cushions with the aid of a walking stick, but was clearly having difficulty hauling herself up. Had she used a walking stick the last time she'd seen her? Bridget didn't think so.

'Don't get up, Mum,' said Bridget, leaning down to kiss her. Her mother seemed to have shrunk in size since Bridget had last seen her, her pale cheeks hollowed out. Was she eating properly? Bridget reached for her hand, but her mum cried out at her touch. 'Oh, I'm sorry,' said Bridget. 'I forgot you'd sprained your wrist. How is it?'

'Still very sore.' Her mother's face was unsmiling.

'I'm sorry I couldn't come round yesterday. I'm very busy at work at the moment.'

'So Vanessa told us.'

Bridget knew that her mum had never accepted Bridget's choice of career. When Bridget had first announced her intention to join the police force, her mum had given her a cold look. 'How could you?' she'd said. 'After what happened to Abigail.'

It was precisely because of what had happened to Abi that Bridget had decided to join the police. But her mother had never understood. Perhaps she had refused to understand. For her parents, the only way to deal with their daughter's murder had been to run away from it. They had turned their back on Bridget and Vanessa. They had sold their house in Woodstock. And they had spent their lives hiding away from reality in a bungalow in Lyme Regis.

Bridget knew also that her parents came from a generation where nice, middle-class mothers stayed at home to raise their children. Her mum couldn't have done more to provide a loving, caring home for her three daughters, but that still hadn't prevented Abigail, the youngest, from going off the rails and getting killed. Perhaps it was that truth that had shattered her parents' world. Abigail's murder hadn't only been calamitous. It had been shameful. And her mum and dad had been fleeing that shame ever since.

'Anyway,' said Bridget brightly, 'I want to introduce you to someone very special. Mum, Dad, this is Jonathan.'

'Pleased to meet you both,' said Jonathan, stepping forward. 'It's good you could come to Oxford for Christmas.'

Bridget's father struggled to his feet again to shake Jonathan's hand. 'It's been many years since we were here,' he said. 'The grandchildren have grown up without us seeing them,' he added wistfully.

Bridget's mum declined to shake hands with Jonathan. 'It's always so cold in Oxford in the winter,' she said.

'The climate's much better on the south coast,' agreed her dad. 'You should come and see us there more often.'

'Well it's certainly not cold in here,' said Bridget, fanning herself with a Christmas card from the windowsill. Her parents had complained for years about the weather in Oxford. But Bridget knew that it wasn't the weather that kept them away. It was fear of facing the trauma of the past. In any case, the bungalow in Lyme Regis was far too small to accommodate visitors. It was as if her parents had deliberately chosen such a small house in order to stop Bridget and Vanessa from staying. Suits me fine, thought Bridget. While her dad made an effort to be sociable, the coldness that her mother radiated was enough to keep even the most dutiful daughter at bay.

A thought suddenly struck her. Had her mother turned away from her and Vanessa after Abi's death because Abigail had been the favourite daughter? She wouldn't have been surprised. Abigail had always been the most warm, generous and loving of the three girls. It was impossible not to be charmed by Abi, even when she'd been at her most rebellious. Had her mother secretly wished that Bridget or Vanessa had been taken from her instead?

And yet her mother hadn't cried at Abigail's funeral, or any time afterwards. She always refrained from public displays of emotion. Instead, she had swallowed her bitter tears, slowly drowning in her own grief.

Suddenly Bridget felt an unexpected stab of pity for her mother's suffering. She held out her hands in a gesture of sympathy, but her mother drew back. 'Mind my wrist,' she complained.

The lounge door opened and James appeared with a glass of Sauvignon Blanc for Bridget and an opened bottle of beer for Jonathan. Bridget accepted it gratefully and knocked back a large mouthful. The hit of the alcohol immediately shored her up. She wondered how many glasses she'd need to make it through the rest of the day.

'Another sherry for you, Arthur?' asked James.

'I won't say no,' said Bridget's dad, handing his empty glass over for a refill.

Her mother, Bridget noted, wasn't drinking. She had always nursed a slightly puritanical attitude towards alcohol.

'So what do you do?' her father asked Jonathan.

'I run an art gallery.'

Bridget was grateful to her father for moving the conversation onward, but mention of the art gallery aroused little more than polite interest and the topic soon fizzled out after her mother expressed her incomprehension of modern art.

Is this what it's like being old? Bridget wondered. But her parents weren't *that* old. They had simply become frozen by their inability to come to terms with grief. She wondered if she could sneak off to the kitchen to help Vanessa with the food. But she knew that Vanessa would never risk Bridget's culinary ineptitude ruining the gravy or the bread sauce. She was immensely relieved when James appeared again and invited them to come through to the dining room.

Vanessa really had gone to town on the Christmas decorations this year. Tall white candles burned in two silver candelabras either side of the centrepiece, a magnificent display of white roses nestling in dark green foliage. Each place was set with silver cutlery, a crystal wine glass, a linen napkin in a silver ring and an expensive Christmas cracker. Clearly not willing to leave the seating arrangements to chance, Vanessa organised everyone into their places, positioning Bridget between James and her mother, whilst Bridget's father sat between Vanessa and Jonathan. Chloe and the children were at the far end. The vegetables, sauces and other trimmings were already on the table in matching earthenware tureens. Once everyone was seated, James made his entrance with the turkey on a large silver platter, its breast perfectly roasted a golden, honey brown. He brandished the carving knives as if about to perform a conjuring trick, then began to carve the meat.

'It all looks super, Aunt Vanessa,' said Chloe, and was rewarded with a beaming smile.

'Yes,' agreed Bridget. 'You've done an amazing job.' She downed the rest of her wine, and poured herself a glass of red to accompany the meal. If they could manage to keep the conversation away from controversial topics they might just make it through the day without killing each other. Surely even Vanessa would have the good sense to steer clear of politics and religion.

She was just about to help herself to some honey-glazed parsnips when she heard the unmistakable sound of her phone ringing from her bag.

Vanessa shot her a murderous look. 'Bridget, don't you dare answer that.'

The phone continued to ring. Bridget knew that after five rings it would go to voicemail. No matter how delicious the food, she simply wouldn't be able to sit through dinner not knowing who had called or whether they'd left a message. She stood up. 'I'll just be quick.'

But when she retrieved the phone from her bag and saw who was calling, she knew that this would not be a quick conversation after all. 'Ffion, what's happened?' She ducked into the hallway, closing the door behind her.

The voice of the Welsh detective across the line sounded unusually subdued. 'Sorry to disturb you on

Christmas Day, ma'am. But we've found a body.'

CHAPTER 20

The cold, damp room at the back of the Edwardian house on Lathbury Road was less than half a mile from her sister's house on Charlbury Road and yet it was a world away from the warm, comfortable home that Bridget had just left behind. Neglected and dilapidated, the building clearly hadn't been occupied for decades. Ancient wallpaper was peeling off the walls, the Persian rugs were covered in mildew, and the corners and light fittings of the room were festooned with cobwebs as thick as sheets. Bridget's nose wrinkled at the smell of decay.

The electricity was turned off and most of the windows boarded up, but bright lights had been erected on metal stands to illuminate the crime scene. Bridget pulled on a set of white plastic overalls and followed Ffion through the hallway to view the place where the skeleton had been discovered. Floorboards had been lifted to reveal a shallow space beneath the suspended timber floor. Vik, the head of the SOCO team, was at work, crawling around on his hands and knees in the dirt. He glanced up as Bridget entered.

'Merry Christmas, Bridget!'

'Merry Christmas to you too, Vik!'

Nothing, it seemed, could dent Vik's good humour, not even being dragged away from his dinner table to spend the day in a freezing cold house in the company of human remains. Bridget wondered if he too was perhaps secretly relieved to have an excuse to escape from difficult relatives.

'I hope this isn't ruining your Christmas dinner,' he said.

Bridget thought with some regret of the meal she'd been forced to abandon. She hadn't even managed a single mouthful before being called away. James had promised to keep her food covered for her, to be warmed in the microwave when she returned, a suggestion that had clearly appalled Vanessa, who never reheated food. Bridget, who was well used to microwaving days-old leftovers back to life, had no such qualms. In any case, going without lunch seemed a small enough price to pay for making what might prove to be a decisive breakthrough in the investigation.

Sarah Walker, the forensic medical examiner was also present at the scene. She turned from her examination of the corpse to give Bridget her preliminary findings. 'Definitely human remains,' she confirmed. 'Female, young adult.'

Bridget risked a quick glance into the dark void beneath the floor and shuddered. The flesh of the dead woman had long since rotted, leaving only skin and bones. 'You're sure of that?'

Sarah nodded curtly. 'You can tell from the overall size of the bones, the relatively rounded shape of the pelvis, and the narrow mandible.' She pointed to the jawbone.

'How long has she been here?'

'Judging from the condition, I'd say at least twenty years.'

The information confirmed Bridget's own hypothesis. Whilst it was always necessary to keep an open mind, it was likely that they were looking at the mortal remains of Camilla Townsend, the student who had gone missing that fateful night a quarter of a century ago and whose body had not been found. Until now.

'As you can see,' continued Sarah, 'decomposition is very nearly complete. The tissues have collapsed and all the body fat has broken down. Even the bones are starting to soften. These damp conditions accelerate the process of oxidation. And of course the underfloor is probably full of mice, rats and other creatures.' Mercifully, Sarah left the implications of that last observation unstated.

'I can't see any sign of clothing,' said Bridget. 'Had she been stripped?'

Sarah shook her head. 'I don't think so. There are still a few fragments of material left behind. But cotton clothes wouldn't have lasted longer than a few years under these conditions. Only synthetics endure.'

The scraps of material, Bridget knew, would enable the forensics team to discern what kind of clothes the woman had been wearing at the time of her death. That could be cross-checked with descriptions of what Camilla Townsend had worn the night she went missing.

Sarah stood up. 'We'll have to carry out more detailed analysis in the lab to be sure of all the facts. Especially dating the body. It'll certainly be an interesting challenge for Roy,' she added, as if she were describing an intriguing puzzle or board game she'd received as a Christmas gift.

Bridget wondered if Sarah, like her, had been dragged away from festive celebrations with family or friends, or whether she'd been spending her day on her own. If that were the case, then perhaps the call-out to examine the body had been a welcome distraction. Sarah certainly seemed to be enjoying herself. Bridget's thoughts drifted also to Dr Roy Andrews, alone with his books this Christmas. She wondered what his preferred reading material might be. Edgar Allen Poe? M R James? It was hard to imagine the dour pathologist sitting down to enjoy anything uplifting.

'I'm sure it will,' said Bridget. Perhaps this was the kind of puzzle that people like Sarah and Roy relished. The mortuary equivalent of completing the *Times* crossword.

'Oh yes,' said Sarah. 'He wanted to come with me to see what was what, but I told him he'd just get in the way.'

Bridget stared at Sarah, needing to be sure she'd understood correctly before putting her foot in it. 'You were with Roy this morning?'

'Yes,' said Sarah. 'He invited me around to his place for lunch. As I had nothing else planned, I accepted.' She gave Bridget an unreadable look. 'He's a surprisingly accomplished chef, for a bachelor.'

Bridget had no idea what to make of this new revelation. She was delighted to learn that Roy and Sarah hadn't spent Christmas alone, but was mystified by the nature of their relationship. She hadn't even known that Roy and Sarah were acquainted with each other, although it was perhaps inevitable that they encountered each other professionally from time to time. What did the doleful Scotsman and the reserved doctor have in common, other than an interest in cadavers and their causes of death? And were they more than just friends? A gap of at least twenty years separated them, but that wasn't necessarily an obstacle to true love.

Bridget shook her head, unwilling to venture too far down that particular avenue right now. 'Who discovered the body?'

'It was Dylan Collins,' answered Ffion. 'The physics student. He was here last night carrying out some kind of experiment into the paranormal. He'd brought some weird-looking contraption along with him.'

Bridget recalled the equipment she'd seen Dylan working on at the Clarendon Laboratory and his attempt to explain it to her. She hadn't realised that he actually intended to go ghost-hunting with it. But she really ought to have guessed. Why else would he have gone to the trouble of constructing a ghost detector?

'When he found that some of the floorboards in this room were loose,' continued Ffion, 'he lifted them up and discovered the skeleton underneath.'

'But what led him here in the first place?' asked Bridget. 'Did his detector actually work?' The idea that a ghost had left its imprint in the walls and floor of this old house was intriguing. Yet Bridget didn't believe in the supernatural.

'I don't think he detected a ghost,' said Ffion sceptically. She pointed to the hole in the floor. 'Look. There are copper pipes and electrical cables running along the joist. I think his gadget just homed in on those.'

'Like a metal detector,' suggested Vik. 'That sounds about right.'

Bridget nodded. 'So where is Dylan now?'

'Uniform have taken him to the station to take a full statement. He's pretty shaken up by all accounts.'

'I'm not surprised,' said Bridget. Dylan might have been searching for psychic waves or whatever, but hadn't bargained on discovering anything as visceral as a human body. 'So what's the story with the house?' she asked Ffion. 'Who owns it? And why is it abandoned?' She had no doubt that her efficient constable would already have the answers at her fingertips.

'I had a word with the neighbours. The couple next door told me that the house belongs to an elderly woman who went into a nursing home thirty years ago suffering from early onset dementia. She's completely senile now, but with no relatives to take legal possession of the house, there's nothing anyone can do about it until she dies. The council boarded up the windows and doors, but it's not difficult to break in. The neighbours told me that it attracts squatters and vagrants.'

'Thirty years,' mused Bridget. 'We'll need to check the date carefully. But if that's true, then the house would have been empty when Camilla went missing. Assuming it's her, she might have been killed here, or her body brought to the house afterwards.'

Vik poked his head up from where he'd been crawling under the floor with his torch. 'I just found this.' He levered himself up out of the hole and handed Bridget a piece of chewed plastic. 'Rats must have carried it away from the body but they weren't able to get their teeth into it properly.'

Bridget turned the card over in her gloved hands. 'It's a Bodleian Library card. It's twenty-five years out of date.' But the name on the card was clearly legible. Camilla Townsend. A formal identification of the remains would need to be made from Camilla's dental records, but there was already little doubt in Bridget's mind. A historic missing person case had finally been brought to a close. And Bridget's murder enquiry had become an investigation into a double murder, the two cases inextricably linked. David Smith had been arrested on suspicion of Camilla's death, and had spent a lifetime searching for her abductor, only to be murdered himself just days before her skeleton was unearthed. The irony made the whole affair feel even more tragic.

The most obvious link between the two victims was the theatre director, Guy Goodwin. And yet he had an alibi for both murders. Bridget wished now that she'd spoken to Goodwin on Christmas Eve. She would be sure to rectify that oversight at the very first opportunity.

'We also found this,' said Vik. He handed her an evidence bag containing a knife. 'It was lying between her ribs. I'd stake money on this being the murder weapon.'

Bridget examined the knife. It was a kitchen knife, its blade stained brownish-black. Dried blood, no doubt. She watched from a safe distance as the SOCO team completed their photographing of the skeleton and Sarah and Vik began supervising the bagging up of the remains ready to be taken to the lab for analysis. There was little more that Bridget could do here today, and she was aware that she was now simply getting in the way of the experts.

'Will you be wanting to speak to Dylan Collins, ma'am?' asked Ffion as they left the room and returned to the hallway.

'Later.' Bridget checked the time. It was already mid-afternoon on Christmas Day, and she had no wish to keep Ffion away from whatever she'd been doing when she'd been called to the crime scene. 'Why don't you head back and enjoy what's left of the day? We'll meet again first thing tomorrow morning.'

'Will do.'

Bridget watched her constable leave the house, peeling off her white protective coveralls once outside. Then she turned back inside. An old rickety staircase led upstairs. Out of curiosity, Bridget started to climb, the wooden treads creaking loudly with each step. The upstairs of the house was lighter, as not all of the windows were boarded up. The smell of decay and damp was less on the upper storey, although here too water had entered the house and left its mark on walls and ceilings. Bridget used her flashlight to peer into the darker corners of the rooms, revealing bedrooms, a bathroom and even a nursery, still with a cot and an antique rocking horse. The building was a shrine to a lost age.

Yet even upstairs there was evidence of modern intruders – empty beer cans and wine bottles, cigarette stubs and burns on the carpets, and graffiti on the walls. Bridget had a soft spot for old houses, and it saddened her to see such a beautiful old building falling into rack and ruin. She wandered from room to room, finding nothing but vandalism and decay. She wondered if the building could ever be saved, or if it would have to be eventually demolished.

From the window of the nursery, she peered out over the overgrown garden. Beneath the light covering of snow, it was practically a jungle, making Bridget's own unkempt garden in Wolvercote look well-tended by comparison. Huge rhododendron bushes flanked the perimeter, and tangled brambles of blackberry and rose snaked across the lawn, which now consisted mainly of nettles dotted with tall stems of milk parsley. No doubt it was a haven for wildlife, but the neighbours must hate living next to such an eyesore.

The south-facing plot backed onto the gardens of the large houses opposite. Dusk was steadily closing in and the curtains of their downstairs windows were already closed against the night. Warm light leaked through the gaps around their edges. But the upstairs windows were mostly dark. A sudden movement at a window in the house immediately opposite caught her attention, and with a jolt she realised she was looking at the house on Staverton Road that she'd visited two days previously when she had gone to interview Trevor and Cheryl Mansfield, the lecturers from Harvard.

The figure at the window ducked back, as if conscious of Bridget's attention. It was too far away in the dim light for her to make out any features of the person who'd been standing by the window, but Bridget could have sworn that whoever it was, they were watching the house on Lathbury Road. She lingered a while longer, but there was no further movement in the house opposite. The watcher had gone.

CHAPTER 21

'I'm not in trouble, am I? I didn't mean any harm.' Dylan Collins sat huddled in the chair of the interview room at Kidlington, his thin arms wrapped protectively around his knees. He was wearing a black T-shirt featuring an image of a skull. *How appropriate*, thought Bridget.

'You're not in any trouble, Dylan,' she assured him.

'You promise?'

'I promise. In fact, you've greatly assisted our investigation through your actions.'

He nodded, drawing his knees up to his chin. One hand went to his nose and touched it lightly, but he seemed a lot calmer now than when he'd called the police to report his find. By all accounts, he'd been almost incoherent at first, and it had taken some considerable patience by the call handler to make sense of what he was saying. The first officers to arrive at the scene in the middle of the night had been sceptical and irritated by what they assumed was some kind of prank call. But they had changed their minds immediately once Dylan had shown them the bones beneath the floor.

'So,' said Bridget, 'can you explain to me what you were doing at the house?'

'Hunting ghosts. I already said so. Why does no one listen to me?'

'But why at that house in particular?'

'It seemed like a good place to look. It's an old house. And it's empty. I knew there'd be no one to interrupt me on Christmas morning.'

'I see.'

'I wasn't expecting to find a skeleton,' he added.

No, thought Bridget. *I bet you weren't.* But perhaps that was one of the hazards of being a ghost hunter.

'But at least I know now that my detector works. When can I have it back?'

'I'll ask for it to be returned to you immediately,' said Bridget. 'It's not relevant to our investigation.'

'I could build you one, if you like. You could use it to find bodies.'

'Thanks. I'll bear that in mind.' Bridget studied the rather fragile youth more closely. He was so thin that she wondered if he was eating properly. 'Are you going to be all right on your own over Christmas? Isn't there anywhere you can go?'

'I'll be fine,' he said quickly. 'I don't want to go anywhere. Please don't say I have to.'

'You don't have to do anything that you don't want to. I was just concerned for your welfare.'

'There's no need to be. I'm used to being alone.'

'Luke Henderson told me that your mother's dead. Is that true?'

'Yes,' said Dylan, studying his knees, which were still tightly bound within his arms.

'What about your father?'

'Don't have one. Or at least, I never knew him. Mum was the only family I've ever had, and she's gone.'

'I see.' Bridget turned these facts over in her mind. It was perhaps no wonder that the young man was so disturbed, given his upbringing. She wondered whether it might also explain his obsession with ghosts. 'What got you started in the paranormal, Dylan?'

'I don't know. It was after Mum died. I didn't want her to be dead. I couldn't get my head around it. One second she was there, the next she wasn't.'

Bridget frowned. 'You saw her die?'

A tiny nod.

'And that's when your interest in ghosts began?'

'Yes. I thought, she can't have just gone. She must have gone somewhere. And so I started reading up on paranormal phenomena. Spirits. Seances. The occult. I've been studying it ever since. That's why I came to Oxford to study Physics. I wanted to make my own ghost detector.'

'Well, you've succeeded at that, Dylan. And I'm grateful for your help.'

He looked up. 'Is that it? Can I go?'

'Yes. I'll get an officer to drive you back to your house.'

'And I can have my detector back?'

'Certainly. It's the least we can do for you.'

She led him from the room and into the safe hands of a female officer. 'Take good care of this young man,' she said. She drew a twenty-pound note from her purse and gave it to him. 'Buy yourself something to eat with this, Dylan. Don't spend it on drugs.'

In return, he gave her a shy smile. 'Thanks. I will. I mean, I won't.'

★

It was fully dark when Bridget returned to Vanessa's house, tired but buoyed up by the discovery of the body. It was a grim piece of news for Christmas Day, but if the forensic work confirmed the identity of the body as Camilla Townsend, as Bridget felt certain it would, then a long-standing missing person case could finally be resolved, and Camilla's parents informed. Bridget was equally convinced that it was also a key step forward in untangling the mystery of who had murdered David Smith. The chances of that being a random knife attack had diminished to almost zero in her mind.

She was about to ring the doorbell when Vanessa pulled the door open. She stood in the doorway, noticeably unsteady on her feet. Bridget wondered just how many glasses of wine her sister had consumed in the hours Bridget had spent away.

Vanessa eyed her reproachfully. 'How could you do that to me? On today of all days. You know how much time I've spent preparing. I know you think that I obsess about trivia, and that your job is *so* much more important than what I do, but have you ever stopped to think where you'd be without me?'

'Please, Vanessa, not now,' begged Bridget, pushing past her into the hallway. The house felt even hotter than before, and she wondered if the heating had been turned up further to keep her parents happy, or if it was simply the contrast with the penetrating chill of the house on Lathbury Road. She pulled her coat off and hung it on the stand.

'Yes, now,' said Vanessa. 'It's high time we talked. Do you know how many times I've had to look after Chloe when you've dashed off to work, or failed to come home on time? She's even had to stay here overnight when you've been held up at work, and it was me she confided in when she got drunk at a party.'

Bridget flinched at the reminder of all her failings. Vanessa had always had a talent for finding the chinks in Bridget's armour, especially at times like now when she was at her most vulnerable.

Vanessa seemed to sense her weakness. 'You often don't even seem to remember that you have a daughter,' she declared.

'That's not fair,' said Bridget. 'I've always done my best for Chloe.' She wanted to tell Vanessa about all the sacrifices she'd made for Chloe's sake, compromising her career and yet also missing out on time with her daughter, just to keep things going. She wanted to explain to Vanessa that with her comfortable life and supportive husband, she couldn't even begin to understand the choices Bridget had been forced to make as a single mother. She wanted to protest that none of this was her fault anyway, but that Ben must take the blame for being such a lousy husband. But she was too tired to start an argument now.

Vanessa, however, had only just begun. 'So. While you were off doing whatever it was that was so terribly important, I've had a simply awful time here. After all the effort I put into preparing the meal, do you know what Mum said?' She didn't wait for Bridget to respond. 'That the vegetables were undercooked. Undercooked! I explained that they were *al dente* but she wasn't having any of it. Then Dad went off on a rant about politics. James and Jonathan did their very best to humour him, but I can safely say that the whole meal was a disaster. Chloe's been on her phone practically the whole time, and then to cap it all, James and Jonathan insisted on doing the washing up.'

Bridget regarded Vanessa wearily. 'And for some reason that wasn't a good thing?'

'It was good for *them*. They got to escape to the kitchen and do a little light domestic work over a couple of beers, while I had to put up with Mum and Dad moaning about their ailments, complaining about the weather and the traffic in Oxford, and generally pushing me to my limit.'

'I'm sorry,' said Bridget.

Vanessa seemed almost disappointed by the apology. Perhaps she'd been hoping for a real bust-up. She really was quite drunk. 'It's like you're taking this case personally,' she complained. 'Why does it matter to you so much?'

Because Abigail is dead and I couldn't do anything to help her, but maybe I can do something this time, she wanted to shout. But she held her tongue. It was useless to try to explain what drove her. Vanessa would never understand.

The kitchen door opened and James appeared. He took in the strained atmosphere between the two sisters at a glance. 'Ah Bridget, you're back. We saved your lunch for you, and some Christmas pudding. Why don't you go and sit down in the lounge and I'll heat it up and bring it through.'

'Thank you,' said Bridget, realising just how famished she was.

'Well, now it's your turn,' said Vanessa. 'You can entertain Mum and Dad for what little remains of the day.' She pushed open the door to the lounge and ushered Bridget through. 'She's back,' she announced to the room at large.

From Vanessa's account of the day, Bridget was expecting to see a family at war. Instead, everything appeared normal. Her parents were back in their places on the sofa. Chloe was playing a board game with her cousins on the floor. Rufus the dog was fast asleep in front of the hearth.

'You're back, love,' said her father. 'Come and take the weight off your feet.'

Bridget took a seat in the armchair facing the sofa. 'I'm sorry I had to leave like that,' she said.

Her mother looked unconvinced. 'On Christmas Day of all days. I never understood why you decided to join the police in the first place. Couldn't you have found yourself a nicer job? One with normal working hours?'

Bridget resisted rising to the bait. She'd had this discussion so many times before, she'd long since lost count. 'I really wouldn't have gone unless I had to.'

'Oh, of course not,' said Vanessa, her tone dripping with sarcasm. 'Just like all the other times you've abandoned me, Chloe or Jonathan. It must have been something absolutely pivotal. A matter of life and death.'

Bridget gritted her teeth. She knew she ought not to say anything about where she'd been, but Vanessa seemed unwilling to let the matter drop. The pressure that had been building up these past few days, with the ongoing murder enquiry, the argument with Chloe, her mother's continuous moaning, and now the grisly discovery at the house on Lathbury Road, suddenly reached critical point. 'If you must know, I've just been to view the exhumation of the body of a woman who went missing twenty-five years ago. Her remains were found beneath the floor in a house less than half a mile from here.'

Stunned silence greeted her pronouncement. The overheated room suddenly felt chilly. Chloe looked up. Vanessa's eyes widened and she reached out an arm to steady herself.

'So that's why I had no choice,' said Bridget. 'Someone has to do that job, so that everyone else can spend their Christmas with their family in the safety of their home.'

The door opened and the two men entered, James bringing a tray with Bridget's hastily reheated lunch, and Jonathan carrying a very welcome glass of red wine. They stopped in the doorway, taking in the scene.

The silence lengthened. Vanessa lowered herself onto a chair, her legs almost collapsing beneath her. Chloe rose to her feet, taking Toby and Florence by the hand. 'Come on, let's go and play upstairs,' she said to them. 'You can show me the rest of your presents.' She gave Bridget a reassuring smile as she led the two small children from the room, and Bridget's heart fluttered in gratitude and admiration at her daughter's sensitivity and sense of responsibility.

Once the children had gone, Bridget's mother was the first to react. To Bridget's surprise, her voice was free of the griping and complaining that she had exhibited so far. Instead, a much younger version of her mother seemed to be speaking – one more like the mum Bridget remembered from her childhood. 'Missing for a quarter of a century. The poor girl's parents. To go for so long not knowing what happened to their daughter, not even knowing if she's alive or dead. I can scarcely imagine their pain.'

Bridget nodded. 'We'll be contacting them as soon as we've confirmed that it's definitely their daughter.'

'They'll be relieved, I'm sure,' continued her mum. 'Even though this is perhaps the last thing you might think they want to hear. I remember when Abigail went missing. Every hour of waiting felt like a week. Every day felt like a year. All I wanted was some news, any news, however bad. Just to know *something*. And then when the police came to tell us that they'd found a body...'

'Not now, Maureen love,' said Bridget's father, laying a hand on his wife's arm. 'Not on Christmas Day.'

But her mum pulled her arm away with surprising vigour. 'Why not now? If you can't talk about your loved ones at Christmas, when can you talk about them?'

'Go on, Mum,' encouraged Bridget. 'Tell us how it was. Tell us what it was like for you when Abigail died.'

Vanessa murmured her agreement. James passed the tray of food to Bridget and she balanced it on her knees. But she didn't touch the meal just yet. This was the first time her mother had ever spoken properly about these events, and the conversation was long overdue. Twenty years overdue.

It was like a dam had burst, and emotions repressed and internalised for so long were finally allowed to break free. Her mum spoke with eloquence and passion about Abigail, the rebellious daughter who had always pursued her own path.

'When she was alive, I used to think she'd be the death of me. But when she died, a part of me died too. I know that I wasn't able to be a good mother to the pair of you after that. I should have done more, but I just couldn't. I'm sorry.'

'You have nothing to be sorry about,' said Vanessa, in floods of tears now. 'I couldn't bear it if anything happened to one of my children.'

'Me neither,' said Bridget. 'If anything happened to Chloe... it would be my worst nightmare.'

'Losing a child is the harshest blow anyone can suffer,' said their dad. 'It rocks your world to its foundations. After she died, we ran away. There's no other way to describe it. We just couldn't face staying in the house in Woodstock. Everything reminded us of her. The pain was too much to bear.'

Now Bridget felt hot tears coursing down her cheeks. Her own world had been shaken to pieces by Abigail's death. To lose a sister… it had been the defining point of her life, perhaps just as devastating as losing a child. After all, how could you measure grief? It was boundless, all-consuming. It was still with her today. She began to understand now why her parents had behaved the way they did. Perhaps she couldn't completely forgive them, but she could at least move forward again.

'But I want you to know I'm very proud of both of you,' said her mum at last. 'I know that I haven't been able to show it always, and it's one of my biggest regrets. I'd have liked to see more of the grandchildren, too, but at the back of my mind I was afraid. Afraid of getting too close, in case something happened… I couldn't bear to go through that a second time. Does that make any sense?'

Bridget nodded. 'It does, Mum. It finally does. If only you'd been able to say something before.'

Vanessa looked to be drowning in tears. 'It's the news that we've been waiting for. All these years, we just needed you to say something, so we could hear how you felt.'

'I know, love. I understand that now. And I'm sorry it took so long.'

At that point, Jonathan and James were also wiping their eyes.

That evening, when Bridget and Jonathan curled up in bed together, she felt that something long broken had finally started to heal. She held him close, the tension that had held her body rigid the previous night now completely dissipated.

It had been the saddest, but in some ways the happiest Christmas she had ever known.

CHAPTER 22

It was shortly after eight-thirty on the morning of Boxing Day when Bridget joined Ffion in the deserted incident room at Kidlington. It was supposed to be a holiday, but the events of Christmas Day had put paid to that idea. Bridget had promised Vanessa that she and Jonathan would call round later that evening, and she intended to keep that promise come what may. Chloe, too, had promised to be there, boyfriend or no boyfriend. The outpouring of emotion the previous evening had worked magic, bringing everyone together in the way that no amount of admonishing or cajoling had ever achieved. Perhaps the secret to life wasn't really so hard after all. All you needed when things got tough was to dig up a body...

Ffion was already in the office when Bridget arrived, and gave the impression that she'd been there for some while. There was nothing unusual about that. The Welsh detective was always one of the first in. But Bridget had hoped that Ffion might have made the most of a lie-in. After all, young people were supposed to stay up late and enjoy themselves.

Bridget couldn't help feeling a little concerned by the

fact that Ffion hadn't gone back to visit her family in Wales for Christmas and seemed more than happy to be at work. She hoped it wasn't a sign of another unhappy family situation. Once this case was closed, she'd insist that Ffion take a few days off to make up for all the hours she was putting in over the holiday season. Not even Ffion was a machine that could keep going for ever without a break, and with her own family now firmly on a path of "truth and reconciliation" Bridget was rather keen on the idea that everyone should try to overcome their grievances at Christmas and let bygones be bygones.

Ffion looked up as Bridget entered. 'Morning, boss. I've got the files ready for you.' A collection of dusty box files was arranged over several desks. 'I've sorted everything into order.' She indicated the first desk. 'These are witness statements taken from everyone who knew Camilla at Pembroke College, or who was involved in the production of *Twelfth Night*, or who was at the after-show party at Freud's.' She pointed to the second desk. 'These are the files relating to the arrest and questioning of David Smith. And this' – she motioned to the third desk, piled high with at least as much paperwork as the entire police investigation – 'is the fruit of David Smith's own enquiries.'

Bridget stared at the mounds of paperwork in dismay. Where to begin? But she already knew in her heart what she had to do first. The most difficult job of all couldn't be postponed. She needed to contact Camilla's parents and inform them what had been found. Even though the skeleton hadn't yet been formally identified, the Bodleian Library card that had been found in the grave made it almost certain that the remains were Camilla's. Bridget didn't want information about the discovery of the body to leak out and for Camilla's parents to read about it first in a newspaper.

'Do we have contact details for Camilla's parents?' she asked Ffion. 'Are they still alive?' Bridget did a quick mental calculation. Camilla, if she had still been living would be around forty-five years old now, making her parents likely to be in their seventies.

Ffion picked up a sheet of paper and slid it across the desk. 'Here's the last known address and telephone number. If they've moved on, we'll have to make enquiries and find out what's happened to them.'

Bridget read the relevant information. An address in the town of Godalming in Surrey. She wondered if Camilla's parents, like her own, had fled from their family home after their daughter's disappearance. Yet something told her they would have stayed. A missing girl wasn't the same as a dead one. There was always the chance, however faint, that a missing person would one day return home. Bridget felt certain that Camilla's parents were still at the same address, hoping, perhaps without even admitting it to each other, that one day they would see their daughter walk back to her home. Well, Bridget was about to quash that faint hope.

She hesitated before picking up the phone. How would they react to the news? Then she remembered what her own mother had said the day before, that not knowing what had happened was the worst part of all. She dialled the number and waited to be connected.

A ringing tone indicated that the line was still in use. After several rings, a woman's voice answered. 'Hello?'

'Could I speak to Mrs Judith Townsend, please?'

'Yes. Speaking.' Her voice sounded weary and flat. Bridget wondered what kind of Christmas the Townsends had gone through. It was just over twenty-five years since their daughter had gone missing, at the end of Michaelmas term immediately before Christmas. Every Christmas must be a time of agonising pain for them.

'I'm sorry to have to call you on Boxing Day. My name is Detective Inspector Bridget Hart of Thames Valley Police.'

An audible inhalation of breath at the other end of the line greeted her pronouncement.

'There isn't an easy way to say this, but we think we

may have found the body of your daughter, Camilla. I'm very sorry to have to break this news to you at Christmas.'

Mrs Townsend's voice was quavering. 'Is it definitely her?'

Bridget chose her words with care. 'We'll need to check her dental records to make a formal identification. But at the moment we're fairly certain that it's her.'

There was silence on the line.

'Mrs Townsend, are you with someone? Is your husband there with you?'

'Yes, yes, he's here. And don't worry, I'm fine.' The voice was still faint but Bridget detected a note of relief. 'Thank you for letting us know. We'll be able to give her a proper funeral now.'

'Of course,' said Bridget. She knew how important it was for relatives to have somewhere they could visit to pay their respects and remember their loved ones. 'I can't give you much more information until we've carried out further investigations, but do you have any questions at this stage?'

'No. It's enough to know that she's been found at last.'

Bridget tried to say a few more words of comfort and explain what would happen next. The poor woman would need some time to process what she'd just heard. Bridget, too, found that she was trembling when she put the phone down, and had to take a few deep breaths to steady herself. She couldn't get the image of her own parents out of her head, and how they must have suffered on first learning of the discovery of Abigail's body in Wytham Woods.

'It's for the best, ma'am,' said Ffion, as if the young constable could possibly know how it felt to lose a child. 'All the studies show that when someone is missing for many years, the distress is even greater than when they're confirmed dead. Until that happens, there's no way for the relatives to put the fact behind them and begin the grieving process. People remain trapped in a never-ending state of despair.'

Bridget nodded. Whatever Ffion may lack in personal experience, her grip of the facts was impeccable, as usual.

'I just hope that they can begin to make sense of what happened now. And if we can find out who was responsible for Camilla's death, then we'll be playing our part in that.'

She made herself a coffee and sat down with Ffion to go over what they already knew. It seemed more likely than ever that Camilla's death was connected to the more recent death of David Smith, the man who had devoted his life to finding out what had happened to her. If the same person was responsible for both killings, then it had to be someone who was in Oxford twenty-five years ago and who had now returned, or had never gone away.

Bridget lifted her gaze to the list of candidates she had written on the whiteboard. Guy Goodwin and Julia Carstairs were the only two she knew of. Guy Goodwin was the man that David Smith had long suspected, and now Bridget came to think of it, Guy's alibi for both the recent murder and the historic one had both been supplied by Julia Carstairs. Guy's movements on both occasions would need to be probed far more rigorously.

'What did the original police investigation conclude about Guy Goodwin and Julia Carstairs?' she asked Ffion.

Ffion reached for the file and produced the relevant witness statements. 'Both Guy and Julia were interviewed along with the entire cast of *Twelfth Night*. Guy and Julia both reported seeing Camilla at the after-show party, and that was the last time they saw her.'

'And this party took place at Freud's on Walton Street?' Walton Street was less than a mile from the house on Lathbury Road where Camilla's remains were found. Too far to drag a body, but well within walking distance if the intended victim had still been alive prior to reaching the house.

Ffion clearly understood the significance of the question. 'That's right.'

'What did Guy and Julia claim they did after the party?'

Ffion thumbed through the sheaf of paper. 'Apparently they stayed to the end of the party and then went back to Guy's room in Worcester College together. They were a couple at the time.'

'I wonder if anyone else can vouch for their movements?' wondered Bridget aloud.

'I don't know,' said Ffion. 'We'll need to read through all the statements and see if anyone reported seeing them. But the police probably weren't particularly interested in what Guy and Julia were doing at the party. Their focus would have been on sightings of Camilla.'

'We could track down the people who were at the party and ask them what they remember about what Guy and Julia did that night, but I doubt anyone will be able to recall much after so many years.'

'No.'

'What about David Smith? Did the police have any evidence to implicate him in Camilla's disappearance?'

'Only circumstantial. He was supposedly seen by someone lurking about outside the party, although he denied that when interviewed. More significantly, both he and Camilla had been a couple at the beginning of term, but they had a row and broke up some weeks before the end of term.'

'What was the row about?'

Ffion consulted the notes. 'It seems that David accused Camilla of sleeping with Guy in order to secure her part in the play.'

'Interesting.' Bridget recalled Julia's vehement denial that there had been anything going on between Camilla and Guy. Her response indicated that there may well have been truth in the accusation, and Julia's jealousy of Camilla seemed hardly to have diminished even after the passing of a quarter of a century. 'So if Camilla and Guy were sleeping together, then both Guy and Julia remain firm suspects.' She looked again at the two names on the whiteboard. 'If Guy murdered Camilla for some reason, it's conceivable that Julia would lie to the police in order to protect him.' Thinking back to her own interview with Julia Carstairs, Bridget wouldn't have been surprised if half of what the actress told her was untrue.

'But there's someone else I think we should add to the list of suspects,' said Ffion. 'Someone who was in Oxford twenty-five years ago, and who's returned now.'

Bridget cocked her head to one side. 'Who can that be?'

'Camilla's tutor at Pembroke College. Dr Trevor Mansfield.'

Bridget stared at her DC in growing astonishment. 'The same Trevor Mansfield who's now a lecturer at Harvard but has returned to Oxford for Christmas to visit his mother?'

'The very same.'

'And whose house backs directly onto the abandoned property on Lathbury Road.' Bridget felt goosebumps rising on her arms as she recalled the shadowy figure she'd seen watching from the house the day before. 'Well, in that case,' she said, 'I think we should pay Dr Mansfield a visit, don't you?'

*

The house in Staverton Road resonated with the sound of children's voices and laughter when Mrs Mansfield opened the door to Bridget and Ffion later that morning.

The old lady didn't appear remotely surprised to see them standing at the door. She peered at Bridget through her glasses, her eyes as bright as buttons. 'Inspector, I had a feeling we might be seeing you again. We couldn't help noticing your colleagues at the house opposite. And on Christmas Day too! You've clearly found something there of great significance.'

Bridget wondered whether Mrs Mansfield knew exactly what had been found at the house. Was there even a possibility that she had known for many years?

'Do you know much about the history of the house in Lathbury Road?' asked Bridget.

'Why, yes. It belongs to a lady called Mrs McBride. But it's been empty for many years now, perhaps thirty. Yes, I would say that it's been thirty-one years since Mrs

McBride had to move into a nursing home. Dementia,' she explained in a hushed voice. 'It happens to a lot of older people, you know.'

Bridget refrained from comment. Cheryl Mansfield had said that her mother-in-law was ninety-one. But the old lady's brain was clearly functioning perfectly.

'The house has been empty ever since,' she continued. 'Mrs McBride has no surviving relatives, and had never made a will, so it was unclear what the legal position was with regard to the upkeep or sale of the house, as she was unfit to make any decision. The council applied for a possession order, but the court denied their request. So now they're essentially waiting for her to pass away so that the estate can go to the Crown, and it can be sold off.'

'I understand that it's been used by squatters over the years.'

'Yes. Squatters, drug addicts and vandals. The council boarded it up to try to keep people out, but it hasn't been entirely effective. They still get in from time to time. I expect it's in a terrible state of repair by now. These old houses need such a lot of care and attention to stop them falling to pieces. But listen to me, rattling on. Where are my manners? I'm sorry, do come inside.'

She let them into the hallway, and then showed them into the front room that Bridget had visited the previous occasion. 'I assume that it's Trevor and Cheryl that you'd like to speak to again?'

'Just Trevor, if that's all right,' said Bridget.

The guarded look Bridget had observed on her previous visit flashed across the old woman's face once more. 'Yes, of course. He's upstairs helping his great-nephew construct a railway track. I'll fetch him down for you. May I take your coats?'

Although the old woman's voice remained civil, it had taken on a certain coldness. Bridget noticed that no tea and biscuits were offered this time. Perhaps that was too much to expect when Mrs Mansfield had clearly guessed the reason for their visit. Camilla's story had been all over the news after she went missing, and if Trevor had been interviewed at that time by the police in regard to her disappearance, then no doubt his mother was fully up to speed on the case. If she'd observed the police activity at the house overlooking her rear garden and deduced that a body had been found, then she must know exactly what Bridget and Ffion were doing here now. A fresh visit from the police after so many years could hardly be welcome.

Bridget and Ffion took seats in the front room. The newspaper crossword that Mrs Mansfield had been working on the other day now lay on a coffee table next to Bridget's chair. It had been fully completed.

'She knows, doesn't she?' whispered Ffion.

'I think she probably does.'

Trevor Mansfield appeared in the doorway, wearing the same sweater, slacks and slippers he had been wearing when Bridget had last spoken to him. With his wireframe glasses, trimmed silver beard and receding hairline, he appeared the picture of a harmless academic. Nothing had changed on the outside, yet now when Bridget observed his keen penetrating stare, his measured and unflustered composure and relaxed smile, she saw a man fully in command of his emotions. Could this man be capable of killing and covering up the murder of a student, and then ruthlessly murdering a man decades later in order to prevent his crime from being revealed?

He took a seat opposite Bridget. 'So, I presume this visit is about the murder of David Smith? Or is it about some other matter? Perhaps it's related to what's going on at the house opposite?'

'I'm sorry to have to inform you that we've unearthed human remains at the property.'

Dr Mansfield leaned forward. 'A body?'

'The remains have been there for some time, at least a couple of decades.' She watched his face as he absorbed the information.

'A man or a woman?' he asked.

'A woman.'

He leaned back, a look of resignation on his face. 'And you think I might know something about it.'

'Dr Mansfield, can you confirm that you were interviewed by the police twenty-five years ago regarding the disappearance of one of your students, Camilla Townsend?'

He flinched visibly at the mention of Camilla's name. 'Have you found her? Is it Camilla's body in that house?'

'Please just answer the question.'

He sighed. 'Yes, I was questioned about Camilla's disappearance. She was my student, after all. But there was nothing useful that I could tell the police.'

'Perhaps you could give us your version of events once more. Tell us what you remember about Camilla's disappearance.'

He stared at the wall opposite, as if picturing in his mind's eye the events of a quarter of a century earlier. 'It was nearly the end of Michaelmas term. The students were getting ready to leave Oxford for the Christmas vacation. Camilla was involved in a play, and she asked me if I'd like to go along and see her perform. Sometimes student theatre can be of a very high standard, and I had nothing particular to do that evening, so I agreed to go along. It was a performance of *Twelfth Night* at the Burton Taylor Studio. Camilla was playing the part of Viola.' He gave Bridget a sharp look. 'You mustn't imagine for a moment that it was in any way unprofessional of me to go and watch her perform, or that perhaps I was infatuated with Camilla. She was a good student, and admittedly very pretty, but my relationship with all my students was always strictly professional. Perhaps with hindsight it was unwise of me to go and see her that evening, but *Twelfth Night* has always been one of my favourite Shakespeare plays, and as I said, I had nothing better to do. Anyway, I went to the theatre, and that's the last time I saw her.'

'Was this the final night of the play?'

'Yes, it was.'

'You didn't join her at the after-play party?' enquired

Ffion.

'No, certainly not. I wasn't asked. I understood that was just for the cast and the other students involved in the production. It was only after she was reported missing that I learned about the party.'

'Can I ask where you were the rest of that night?'

'I was here.'

'And can anyone vouch for that?'

'My mother can.'

'I see.' Bridget doubted very much that a jury would accept Mrs Mansfield's assurances of her son's innocence. But she couldn't rule out the possibility that Trevor was telling the truth. Not everyone she interviewed turned out to be a liar. 'You're no doubt aware that Camilla's boyfriend was arrested in connection with her disappearance?'

'Of course, yes. But he was released without charge as I understand.'

'That's correct. Did you know him?'

'Not really. He wasn't one of my students. What was his name... David something?'

'David Smith. The name doesn't mean anything to you?'

'Should it?'

She waited to see if he would make the connection himself. He stared at her, comprehension slowly dawning. 'Not the same David Smith who was murdered at the Turf Tavern?'

'Yes. Quite a coincidence, don't you think? After his arrest, David Smith dropped out of university. But he stayed in Oxford, giving ghost tours to tourists in the guise of Gordon Goole, and writing and publishing his own books about ghosts to supplement his income. Just like the one your wife bought on Sunday night.'

The book that Cheryl had bought from Gordon Goole lay on the coffee table, next to the completed crossword. Trevor Mansfield stared at it in horror. 'I had no idea,' he murmured. 'David Smith...' He seemed at a loss for words.

Bridget waited for him to recover from his shock, whether real or feigned.

'I'm sorry, Inspector, but I never knew Camilla's boyfriend, and even if I had, I wouldn't necessarily have recognised him after all this time. People change.'

'Some do, some don't,' said Bridget, recalling her own experience at a recent college gaudy earlier in the year. 'Anyway, like I said, David Smith was Camilla Townsend's boyfriend. First she was murdered and now he's been killed. Obviously we're looking for a connection.'

'I'm sorry, but I can't help you there.'

'Can I ask why you really went to Harvard? You had a good position at Oxford, you have family here. There must have been a compelling reason.'

'The truth is, it wasn't easy for me after Camilla disappeared. Even if you haven't done anything wrong, there are always rumours. You find yourself something of a social outcast in the Senior Common Room. I simply wanted a fresh start.'

It sounded like an honest answer. 'One more thing. On Sunday evening at the Turf, you took a phone call from Harvard, is that right?'

His face clouded over and Bridget sensed she'd touched a raw nerve. 'I'd rather not go into details about that, if it's all the same with you, Inspector.'

'It's not necessary for you to divulge any details about your call, Dr Mansfield. However, the problem I have is that at the moment we only have your word regarding this phone call. Given that this is your alibi for the time David Smith was killed, we need to confirm that the call took place. Can you at least tell me who it was with?'

'I see,' he said stiffly. He seemed to be debating with himself what to tell her. 'All right, then, if you must. The call was with one of the faculty deans at Harvard. I can give you his name and contact details if you want to check with him.'

'Thank you. I'd be grateful.'

Reluctantly, he wrote a name and a telephone number on a sheet of notepaper. 'And now I assume that will be all?'

'For the moment,' said Bridget.

CHAPTER 23

'So what did you make of him?' Bridget asked Ffion after they'd finished interviewing Trevor Mansfield at his home in North Oxford. It was the first time for Ffion to meet the Harvard lecturer, and Bridget was keen to hear her opinion. The young detective constable was an astute observer who never missed a thing.

'Shifty,' said Ffion. 'He was definitely hiding the truth about that phone call to Harvard. His mother knows more than she's letting on, too. I don't trust either of them.'

Bridget knew that Ffion had a policy of not trusting any of the witnesses involved in an investigation, but she was minded to agree with her assessment of Trevor Mansfield and his mother. And yet Trevor's wife, Cheryl, had seemed so nice. It was difficult for Bridget to reconcile her first impressions of the couple with the idea that Trevor was a scheming murderer and that his mother had helped cover up his crimes.

'So, where to now?' asked Ffion.

'The Randolph Hotel. I'm pretty sure that's where we'll find Guy Goodwin.'

The Randolph had long enjoyed a reputation as

Oxford's finest hotel. The building, which was located on the corner of Beaumont Street and Magdalen Street, was very imposing. Built over five storeys in the Victorian Gothic style, it was a mass of arched windows, pointed rooftops and tall chimneys. Its pale golden brickwork was clearly intended to match the Cotswold stones of the colleges it nestled amongst.

Inside, its interior was as opulent as you might expect from a traditional five-star hotel at the heart of the university town. A deep carpet patterned in crimson and gold led up to a mahogany desk manned by a receptionist in grey uniform. To the left of the desk, a broad staircase swept up to the guest bedrooms. Thick, patterned wallpaper lined the walls, as if the decorators had taken every possible measure not to leave any surface unadorned. Even the doorways were flanked by ornate pillars and crested with Gothic arches in dark wood.

Bridget approached the desk, waiting patiently while a guest made arrangements to summon a taxi. When it was her turn, she flashed her warrant card at the receptionist. 'I believe that you have a Mr Guy Goodwin staying with you. I'd like to see him.'

'Mr Goodwin? Yes, he certainly is staying with us. I'll try his room for you right now.' He dialled a number on the keypad of his phone. 'Mr Goodwin? I have a Detective Inspector Bridget Hart from Thames Valley Police waiting in reception for you. Yes?' He lowered the receiver and covered it discreetly with one hand. 'Mr Goodwin would like to know if you'd like to speak to Miss Carstairs too.'

'No,' said Bridget. 'I would not.'

The receptionist took her brusque reply in his stride. He was clearly well-trained at handling awkward guests. 'Mr Goodwin will be down shortly. Perhaps you'd like to wait in the bar?'

'We'll wait here, thank you,' said Bridget. The temptation to grab a quick coffee whilst waiting was strong, but the last thing she needed was Guy doing a runner.

She didn't have long to wait. Guy Goodwin descended

the staircase after a few minutes, looking cross. With his thick head of black hair that reached to his collar, bushy eyebrows, and deep-set charcoal eyes, he presented an intimidating front. He stood almost a full head taller than Bridget, frowning at her, his hands thrust deep into the pockets of his faded jeans. To complete the studied look of theatre director, he wore a turtleneck sweater in black cashmere.

'Inspector Hart? You asked to see me?'

'Perhaps we could talk in the bar?' suggested Bridget. The lure of that coffee was proving too much to resist after all. If she could pair it with one of the delicious cream cakes that were on display, she could kill three birds with one stone. Sugar, caffeine, and an interview with her prime suspect. It was too good an opportunity to miss.

'All right,' said Guy. 'But I don't have long. I need to be back at the theatre for rehearsals this afternoon.'

'We'll try not to take up too much of your time, Mr Goodwin,' said Bridget with a pleasant smile.

Once their order had been brought to their table, Bridget got straight to the point. 'We'd like to talk to you about Camilla Townsend.'

Guy's stern features immediately darkened further. 'Julia mentioned something about that. But I thought you were investigating a murder.'

'We are,' said Bridget. 'In fact, we're now investigating two murders.'

'Two? You don't mean –'

'We believe that we have unearthed the remains of Camilla Townsend. We've reopened the investigation into her disappearance and are now treating the case as murder.' She took a welcome sip of her cappuccino, and sat back to watch his reaction.

Guy's heavy brow was now so furrowed that his eyebrows bunched together in a continuous dark line. 'But how did you find her? And where?'

'That's confidential information for now,' said Bridget. 'Maybe we can start with how well you knew her. She was in a student production of *Twelfth Night* that you directed.'

'Yes, of course. Everyone knows that. But that was ages ago.'

'But the party that followed the end of that production was the last time Camilla Townsend was seen alive.'

'Yes, yes. I understand.' His face cleared as he began to recover from the shock of hearing about Camilla's body. Now that he was sitting calmly, he seemed much less scary than when he was agitated or shouting directions at a group of actors on-stage. Bridget could easily appreciate what Julia Carstairs saw in him. He was a very attractive man, if you liked the dark, mercurial type. Bridget had fallen for that look herself when she married Ben, but look how that had worked out. Some men were dangerous to know, and Guy Goodwin struck her as one of those.

Her thoughts circled inevitably back to Chloe, and the mysterious Alfie. Was he too a rugged, handsome tempter? Bridget had so many pearls of hard-earned wisdom to dispense to her daughter, but she knew that Chloe would never listen to what she said. Life's most important lessons always had to be learned the hard way, it seemed.

Guy was watching her through flinty, expressionless eyes.

'So how did you first get to know Camilla?' she prompted.

'Dear Camilla,' said Goodwin, his expression intensifying once more. 'She had a natural talent for the stage. She would have made a great actress. If she'd lived,' he added. He sipped his espresso thoughtfully. 'I knew her through acting, of course. We inhabited the same circle. Actors form a small, cliquey group. They just can't help it.' He laughed. 'It's because they're all so damn insecure. None of them wants to be first to leave a room in case the others immediately start gossiping about them. The world of theatre is a bitchy place, full of backstabbing.' He frowned, as if realising that his choice of word might be inappropriate. 'I don't mean literally. No one's ever killed another actor to get a part, at least as far as I know.' His brow furrowed again, but this time his eyes revealed a flash of humour. 'Or maybe they have, now you mention it.'

'I didn't mention it,' said Bridget. 'I asked you how you got to know Camilla.'

His voice was impatient again. 'Yes, yes. Like I say, we met through the stage. We were at different colleges, but we were both involved in theatrical productions. She was an actress, I was interested in directing.'

'Would you say that you were close?'

'No.' His denial was flat and final.

Ffion took up the thread. 'David Smith believed that you were sleeping with Camilla.'

Now Guy smiled grimly. 'You see what I mean? Jealousy. It infects everyone in this world. Why would I have wanted to sleep with Camilla? I was with Julia at the time.'

'Perhaps Julia wasn't enough,' suggested Ffion. 'Camilla offered herself to you in exchange for a part in your play, and you said yes.'

Guy scowled at the accusation. 'Despite what you might hear, not everyone in my industry is a sleazeball. I'm not in the habit of abusing my position to get what I want, and Camilla was a nice girl – she wouldn't have slept around just to get a part in a play.'

'You admit that you wanted to sleep with her, though?' said Ffion.

Guy ran a hand through his thick hair. 'Now you're twisting my words.'

'Camilla got the best part, though, didn't she?' said Bridget. 'Viola. It was the part that Julia wanted for herself.'

'Camilla was better for the role than Julia,' snapped Guy. 'She was perfect for the part, whereas Julia... she has many fine assets, but there's talent and then there's narcissism. Don't get me wrong, Julia's not a bad actress. She does well enough with the roles she's given, but she's not star material. Never has been. She lacks the depth of character needed to pull off a complex role.'

Bridget could only imagine how Julia would react if she could hear her lover talking about her in this way. 'Your relationship with Julia Carstairs came to an end while you were at university. When was that, and why?'

'It fizzled out shortly after Camilla went missing. It was a difficult time for all of us. Accusations were tossed about. Arguments became heated. You've seen what Julia is like. She's a passionate woman. Too emotional.'

'And jealous,' added Ffion.

'Jealous, yes.' Guy nodded his agreement. 'Irrationally so. Like I've already explained to you, there was no reason for her jealousy, but Julia didn't see things clearly. She rarely does.' Guy took another sip of his espresso and Bridget took a bite of her cake. She wondered how much longer Guy and Julia's newly rekindled relationship had to run. She wouldn't put money on it lasting into the New Year.

'What about David Smith?' she asked. 'What was his involvement with the play?'

'None whatsoever. He auditioned for the part of Malvolio, but I had a better actor for that role. David was surplus to requirements.'

'You couldn't have found another part for him?'

'I didn't need to. Oxford's full of budding thespians. I had my pick of the crop. I know that you'll twist this and say that I turned him down so that I could have Camilla all to myself, but that's not how it was. David simply didn't have what it took. Hardly surprising that he ended up giving ghost tours for a living.'

'Actually,' said Bridget, feeling an urge to speak up for the murdered man, 'he made a very good ghost tour guide.'

'I'm very glad to hear it.'

'So tell me about the last performance of *Twelfth Night*,' said Bridget. 'What do you remember about that night?'

'It was a terribly long time ago, Inspector. If you want a reliable account, you'd be better off reading the statement I gave to the police at the time.'

'I've read the statement. I'd like to hear it again from

you.'

Goodwin rested his chin in one hand and gazed up at the ceiling as if struggling with his memory. He was a half-decent actor himself. Bridget suspected that he had perfect recall of what had happened that momentous night. When he spoke, it was clear that the details were still etched vividly in his mind. 'It was a fabulous production. We all knew it. After the last curtain call, everyone was on a real high. It's always like that when you've had a good run. The reviews were glowing and everyone was up for a big celebration. We went to Freud's on Walton Street for a party. Do you know it?'

Bridget knew of the trendy café-bar, but it wasn't a place she frequented. The crowd was too young, the setting too noisy.

'I know it,' said Ffion.

Guy nodded his appreciation. 'It's a great place. On that night, it was packed and there was a really good atmosphere. Everyone was there. Actors, stage crew, critics, as well as friends and partners. All the people who are drawn to the world of the stage, like moths to a flame.'

Bridget wondered if Guy always spoke in such flowery terms. Perhaps it was a hazard of his occupation, or maybe it was just another act. 'You saw Camilla at the party?' she asked.

'Of course. She was the star of the show. Everyone wanted to congratulate her on a stunning performance.'

'And Julia was there?'

'Sure. Like I said, everyone was.'

'How long did you stay?'

'Oh, pretty much until the end. I was the director, it was expected. There were only a few stragglers left behind by then.'

'Was Camilla still there when you left?'

'No. She'd gone. But I didn't see her go. She might have left alone, or with one of the other people at the party. I told the police this at the time.'

'What about Julia?'

'I left with her. And if you've read my statement, you'll know that we went back to my room in college and spent the rest of the night there together. The first we heard of Camilla's disappearance was at breakfast the next morning. Her housemates reported that Camilla hadn't returned after the party. We all assumed she'd gone back to someone's room. But she was never seen again.' He tailed off, a look of melancholy casting a dark shadow across his face. 'And now you say you've found her body? So she's been dead this whole time.'

'So it would appear,' said Bridget. 'Fast forward twenty-five years. Where were you on the night of December the twenty-second, between the hours of ten and ten-thirty?'

Guy seemed wrongfooted by the abrupt shift. 'Uh... that was the night after I first bumped into Julia at the theatre. She was there with her friends to see the show, and she came backstage to see me afterwards. We got talking and went for a drink together. We certainly had a lot to catch up on after so many years. Marriage, divorce –'

'That was Saturday night,' interrupted Bridget. 'I asked you about Sunday.'

'Right, yes... I was coming to that. We arranged to meet up again. I agreed to send Julia a message as soon as I'd finished at the theatre, and she was to come and find me.'

'And where did she find you?'

'It was here, at the Randolph.'

'So explain again exactly what your movements were between ten and ten-thirty on Sunday night.'

Guy seemed flustered. 'I left the theatre just after ten and sent Julia a text. Then I came back to my room here and she joined me shortly afterwards. She's been staying with me ever since.' He rolled up a sleeve to reveal a chunky watch. 'And now I really must be pressing on. The show opens again this afternoon, and as you may have heard, I've lost my leading lady. We have a lot of work to do if we're going to avoid a catastrophe.' He offered

Bridget a broad grin. 'But you know what they say about theatre?'

'The show must go on,' concluded Bridget. It was clearly her cue to leave.

★

With most of her team still on leave, there was little Bridget could do now until everyone returned to work. It was frustrating but couldn't be helped. At least she had managed to interview her two most promising suspects on a day when she had expected to be putting her feet up at home. That was progress, she supposed. But where exactly had it got her?

'I want to find out more about this phone call that Trevor Mansfield took from Harvard,' she told Ffion when they were back in the office. 'He was very evasive about the whole matter. As a minimum, we need to check that the call took place as he described.'

'Dr Mansfield's given us the contact details of the faculty dean at Harvard,' said Ffion. 'Although it might prove tricky to get hold of him during the holiday period.'

'We certainly can't call him up on Boxing Day,' agreed Bridget. Once again, it seemed that the Christmas holiday was getting in the way of the investigation. But there was nothing she could do about that.

'Anything else you want me to do?' asked Ffion.

'Not for now,' said Bridget. 'Today's supposed to be a holiday. I'm sure you have something exciting you'd like to go to. A party, perhaps?'

'Mm,' said Ffion noncommittally. 'What about you, ma'am? Any plans for the rest of the day?'

'Family.' Bridget had no desire to explain the myriad complications of her personal life. 'So I'll see you back here tomorrow. The rest of the team should be back then, too. I'll give Jake a call in Leeds and ask him to get down here as soon as he can.'

Her mention of Jake was met with silence. Bridget

decided it was time that she tackled this issue head on. She adopted her best "nice but firm" tone. 'Listen, I know that you two have had a falling out. I'm sorry that you're no longer together, but I need all the members of my team to cooperate with each other.'

She left unspoken the implied threat. If two of her team members were unable to work together for personal reasons, then she would have to consider getting one of them transferred. But which one? Ffion with her sharp mind, keen analytical skills and computer wizardry? Or Jake with his emotional empathy, steady temperament and reassuringly tall physique? She didn't want to lose either of them.

Ffion shook her head. 'You don't need to have any worries on that score, ma'am. I can work alongside Jake. No problem.'

'Good. Then we'll say no more about it. Until tomorrow, then.'

'Until tomorrow.'

She made a note for herself to call Jake, and also to check what was happening about getting hold of Camilla's dental records. Nothing, she suspected, since everyone would be on holiday. It was frustrating when she was chomping at the bit to get on with the case that the world in general was caught up in a Christmas-induced haze of food, alcohol and officially-sanctioned relaxation.

Bah, humbug! She needed to watch herself, or at this rate she'd end up treading on everyone's toes and becoming a disruptive team member herself.

Before leaving the office she called Chief Superintendent Grayson on his home number to update him on the latest developments. The Chief sounded even more miserable than her, forcibly stuck at home with his wife and the rest of his family and compelled against his will to be jolly, but even he agreed that nothing more could be done until the following day.

'I hate this time of year,' he moaned, sounding slightly tipsy. 'Everyone's expected to be so bloody cheerful all the time, but I can't stand being stuck indoors with all my relatives.'

Bridget tried to picture her boss being cheerful, but couldn't imagine it. She didn't envy Grayson's relatives one little bit.

'I'm not even allowed to escape onto the golf course for the afternoon,' he went on. 'Do you need me to come into the office?'

'No, sir, I can deal with everything.'

'Hmm.' Grayson sounded disappointed. He was obviously hoping for an excuse to get out of the house. 'Let's just get this damn holiday over with,' he growled, 'and then everything can get back to normal.'

'Yes, sir.'

The phone call had provided an unusually candid window into Grayson's personal life, and made Bridget feel slightly better. However strained her own family relationships might be, at least she didn't have Grayson to put up with.

Then again, she reflected, perhaps she and Grayson weren't as dissimilar as she'd always imagined. It was clear that they would both prefer to be working on an investigation than stuck at home making small talk with relatives. It was a novel and somewhat disconcerting notion.

She drove home keen to put the tribulations of work behind her and enjoy some time with her newly reconciled family. Since her mother had opened up, and a truce had been declared with Chloe over the boyfriend issue, she found that she was actually looking forward to getting home.

Perhaps she could spend the afternoon with Jonathan, snuggled up on the sofa, watching a film together whilst eating some of the leftovers from Christmas Day. The only food she'd seen since breakfast was what she'd eaten at the Randolph, and a coffee-and-cream-cake diet would never count as a sensible choice even in her wildest fantasies.

She'd left Vanessa's house the previous night loaded up

with containers filled with cold turkey, sausage meat stuffing and thick slices of ham, not to mention homemade mince pies, Christmas cake and pudding. Vanessa had given her more food than there'd been in the picnic hamper Bridget had given her parents. She wouldn't have to cook for a week, and that could only be to everyone's benefit.

'I'm back,' she called, as she entered the house.

'Oh, I wasn't expecting you until later,' said Chloe. She was on her way down the stairs and the first thing Bridget noticed was that she was wearing her padded jacket, woolly hat and scarf.

'Going out?'

'I'm just going round to see Alfie.'

'You haven't forgotten that we've arranged to go round to Vanessa's later, have you?'

'Of course not, Mum.'

'You're not planning to be late?'

'No. I told Alfie that I won't be able to stay with him for long.'

'Well, then,' said Bridget, not sure what to say for the best. Her daughter had recently developed a habit of staying out far later than she promised. But Bridget knew better than to push the issue. She would just have to settle for Chloe's reassurance.

Chloe seemed to be reading her mind. 'It's not like your own track record's very good, Mum.'

'What do you mean?'

'Well, you've been working on Boxing Day. You even went to work on Christmas Day. Aunt Vanessa nearly blew her top after you left.'

'I can imagine.' Bridget could tell from her daughter's voice that she had secretly enjoyed the commotion Bridget caused by abandoning her meal and heading off in search of a dead body. It wasn't the kind of thing most mothers did. At Christmas or any other time of year.

'So you won't be late back?' she repeated.

'No, I promise. I just want to see Alfie for a bit.'

Bridget nodded. It was apparent that Chloe was completely bewitched by her boyfriend. Bridget recalled how she herself had been with Ben, in the days before the cracks in their marriage had begun to appear. Blissfully head over heels.

But thoughts of her ex-husband set off warning bells in her head.

'I'll tell you what,' she said, an idea coming to her suddenly. 'Why don't you bring Alfie round to dinner this evening? I'm sure Aunt Vanessa won't mind. You know how she loves to make a fuss of her guests. It would be nice to meet him.'

Chloe gave her a suspicious look. 'You mean to check him out?'

'No, I mean to get to know him a little,' said Bridget, dismayed that her true motive had been so transparent.

'I'm not sure. I don't know if he'd want to. Aunt Vanessa can be quite intimidating.'

It was a fair point. And perhaps it was unreasonable to drag a teenage boy in front of his girlfriend's family unawares. It might be better to give the young couple more time to come to terms with the idea, and for Bridget to arrange a more low-key occasion to make Alfie's acquaintance.

'Will you at least invite him? I don't want to appear rude.'

'Maybe.'

'All right,' said Bridget. 'Just remember –'

'– don't be late.' Chloe slipped out of the front door with a trace of a smile on her lips before Bridget could say another word.

Entering the kitchen, she found Jonathan making coffee.

'I suppose you heard all that,' she said to him.

'I caught the gist. But I thought it would be diplomatic for me to keep out of the way.'

'You mean you didn't want to get caught in the rift between me and my daughter.'

He handed her a cup of filter coffee with a wry smile. 'That too. But in fact, the rift appears to have healed.'

'I hope so,' said Bridget. She had certainly done her best to heal the wounds in the fractured relationship. And she was willing to accept that at least half the blame for the original argument lay with her. She couldn't control her own daughter, she knew that. All she could do was try to give good advice and be there to pick up the pieces when Chloe needed her.

But there was one part of her life that she did have some control over. Work.

'I'm sorry,' she said to Jonathan, 'but before I can properly relax this evening, there's one more job I have to do.

Picking up her phone, she dialled Jake's number.

★

Jake stared at the screen of his laptop, his brow furrowed in frustration. He'd been trying all afternoon to fill in the online application form for the job in Halifax. The first part of the form was easy enough – providing details of his education and work experience – but he'd been stuck on the next part for hours.

Please state why you are applying for this particular role.

It was a simple enough question, and he'd thought he knew the answer. Because he fancied a change. Because he wanted to get away from Oxford and return to the North of England where he fitted in better. Because he felt embarrassed and awkward working in the same office as Ffion.

But none of those reasons was the kind of thing he could write on the form.

He tried again. *To make the most of my varied skillset in a new and challenging environment,* he typed. No, no, no. *To pursue a new direction in my career based on…* No. Delete.

It was hopeless. Why couldn't he write a simple reason that didn't sound like he'd lifted it straight out of a handbook of management jargon?

Perhaps the answer was that he didn't really know himself why he wanted the job.

'Another slice of cake, love?' His mum bustled into the dining room where he was hunched over the table, his fingers resting uselessly on the keyboard. She bore a plate with yet another slice of her homemade Christmas cake. He hadn't been home for two days yet but already he must have put away at least a pound of the rich fruitcake with its marzipan and icing covering. Not to mention half a chocolate log and a couple of dozen mince pies.

Christmas dinner the day before had consisted of roast turkey with all the trimmings followed by a huge portion of Christmas pudding smothered in rich, creamy custard, exactly the way his mum had made it when he was a boy. Jake wasn't complaining. He loved it, and couldn't understand why some folk didn't like a turkey dinner at Christmas. Ryan had told him that goose was better, and Andy's wife was planning to cook a duck. Jake couldn't get his head round that. Why did people insist on complicating things?

He patted his stomach, which was straining at his waistband. 'Sorry, Mum, but I really don't think I can eat another thing.' That wasn't something he'd ever heard himself say before, but this Christmas at home in Leeds he'd finally been beaten where food was concerned. Or at least, he was very close to admitting defeat. 'Perhaps you could leave it on the table for me,' he suggested. 'I might feel like it later.'

His mother beamed and came over, putting the plate next to his laptop. 'What are you up to all on your own in here, love? Something secret?'

'No, no, nothing secret.' He quickly folded the screen of the laptop so that she couldn't see what he was up to. 'Just something I need to do for work.'

'This is supposed to be your holiday.'

'I know.'

He wasn't completely certain why he didn't want his

mum to know what he was doing. She would have been delighted to hear that he was thinking of moving back north. All she'd ever wanted was for him to live nearby, get married to a nice local lass and produce a couple of grandchildren that she could spoil rotten.

And yet after graduating from university in Bradford he'd moved south, and then split up with his longstanding northern girlfriend. His mother was still reeling from the shock of that breakup. He hadn't dared tell her that he'd briefly hooked up once again with Brittany, only to split up with her for a second time. The disappointment would have been too much for his mother to bear.

So why was he unwilling to tell her that he was applying for the job in Halifax? Was it because, if he was entirely honest with himself, he was beginning to have second thoughts?

He'd been desperately looking forward to spending Christmas at home, and the first day of being pampered and fed by his mum had been fantastic. But a restlessness had soon set in. By Boxing Day morning and his fifth slice of cake, his mother's undivided attention was starting to feel a little smothering. Part of him wanted to be back in Oxford. He thought of his flat on the Cowley Road, and imagined the heavenly aromas coming from the curry house and the Chinese takeaway next door. Even the memory of washing powder and soap suds drifting up from the launderette below had the power to induce a fond nostalgia.

Was it possible that he was even starting to feel a little homesick?

He was wrestling with the question when his phone vibrated in his pocket. Checking the screen he was astonished to see that it was his boss calling. Bridget wouldn't phone on Boxing Day unless it was urgent. 'Do you mind, Mum?' he said. 'I need to take this call. It's from work.'

His mother sighed and left the room.

'Hello, ma'am. Did you have a nice Christmas?'

'Well, it would have gone a lot more smoothly if we hadn't found the skeleton of a young woman beneath the floor of a house in North Oxford on Christmas morning,' Bridget answered, deadpan.

He almost laughed, thinking she must be joking, before realising she was deadly serious. 'Camilla Townsend?' he asked.

'We think so. Jake, how long are you planning to stay in Leeds? I could really use you back here.'

Suddenly he knew without a shadow of a doubt that his place wasn't in Leeds or Halifax, but in Oxford, with Bridget and the rest of the team, Ffion included. He'd never imagined that news of a dead body could be so welcome.

'I can be back at work tomorrow morning,' he said. 'Will that be soon enough?'

'Perfect,' said Bridget. 'I'll see you then.'

CHAPTER 24

It felt good to have everyone back at work. Jake was looking more cheerful than Bridget had seen him in a long while, despite having got up well before light to drive back down from Leeds. His time off with his family had obviously done him a power of good. He'd made the return journey to Oxford in remarkably quick time and Bridget suspected that he might not have stuck strictly to the speed limit. She'd ridden in his souped-up car to London once, in hot pursuit of a suspect, and still occasionally woke up sweating in the middle of the night with the memory of it.

She'd expected some resistance from Ryan Hooper when she'd asked him to cut short his leave, but apparently there was a limit to how many Netflix boxsets and mince pies even Ryan could consume before growing restless, and he'd agreed readily enough to change his plans. Even Andy Cartwright had reluctantly consented to leave his young family and return to work when she'd explained about the skeleton beneath the floorboards. Bridget wondered if he too was secretly relieved by the chance to get away. Perhaps the excitement of a double murder investigation held more appeal than yet another game of Snakes and Ladders with the kids.

Grayson was back in his glass office, pretending to be busy with some paperwork. But Bridget was pretty sure that he was just waiting for her to brief him on the latest developments. 'Keep me informed,' was always the Chief Super's motto. He gave her a surreptitious glance, before returning to his work.

Ffion, of course, had continued to work right through the holiday period without a single day off, but she still didn't show any signs of flagging. She seemed to be thriving. Bridget hoped she wasn't overdoing it.

By contrast, Ryan's two days off appeared to have done him no good whatsoever, judging from the strong black coffee and handful of aspirins he required to get him back up to speed.

'Welcome back, everyone,' said Bridget, taking her place in front of the whiteboard. 'I hope you all had an enjoyable Christmas and didn't eat and drink too much.'

'Don't say that,' groaned Ryan, looking green. 'I barely managed to squeeze into my trousers this morning. I thought I was going to have to borrow an old pair of my Dad's!'

Bridget joined in the light laughter that accompanied his remark. She, too, was feeling a little stuffed after the enormous Boxing Day meal that Vanessa had produced the previous evening. But she was pleased with herself for keeping her promise to be there with the rest of the family. She, Jonathan and Chloe – but not Alfie, who had been unable to come, or more likely hadn't been asked by Chloe – had turned up at Vanessa's, and the whole family had enjoyed the meal together, and then watched a classic *Miss Marple* on television. Her parents had agreed to stay until the New Year and were causing Vanessa much less trouble, despite her mother's various ailments.

'Right,' said Bridget. 'To business. While Santa was attempting to squeeze his generously-proportioned frame down the chimney, physics undergraduate and amateur paranormal investigator, Dylan Collins, was busy snooping around an abandoned property in North Oxford in search of spooky activity. He found more than he bargained for beneath the floorboards of the old house.' She pointed to a display of photographs showing the dilapidated house on Lathbury Road and the grisly remains that had been found there.

The mood in the room turned immediately more serious as Bridget explained exactly what Dylan had unearthed. 'Evidence found on the scene strongly suggests that these are the mortal remains of Camilla Townsend, an undergraduate who was reported missing some twenty-five years ago following the final performance of a student production of Shakespeare's *Twelfth Night*, in which she was playing the part of Viola. Dental records will confirm her identity, but we've already recovered Camilla's library card from the scene, and our working assumption is that this is indeed Camilla's body.

'Camilla was the girlfriend of David Smith, the ghost tour guide known as Gordon Goole, who was stabbed and killed at the Turf Tavern two days before Christmas. During the original police investigation, he was arrested on suspicion of her murder but no charges were brought and the case against him was dropped. But David, as you already know, spent the last twenty-five years conducting his own private investigation into Camilla's disappearance. Ffion?' Bridget nodded in her constable's direction.

Ffion stood up to address the room. 'David Smith's prime suspect was Guy Goodwin, the director of *Twelfth Night*. He's now a professional theatre director and is back in Oxford directing *West Side Story* at the New Theatre.'

'That's a massive coincidence,' said Ryan.

'Wait until you hear the rest of it,' remarked Bridget.

Ffion continued. 'Guy's girlfriend, both at the time of Camilla's disappearance, and also again now, is Julia Carstairs, the actress. They appear, at least on the face of it, to have just bumped into each other by chance a few days ago. Julia has provided an alibi for Guy both for the recent murder and the historic one.'

Bridget wrote the names of Guy Goodwin and Julia Carstairs on the whiteboard beneath the heading "suspects".

'Another coincidence,' she said, 'is that the property where Camilla's remains were found backs onto a house owned by the mother of Dr Trevor Mansfield. Mansfield was on the ghost tour with me the evening when the stabbing took place, and he was also Camilla Townsend's tutor.' She added Trevor Mansfield's name to the list of suspects.

'You've got to be kidding,' said Ryan.

'We have to seriously consider the possibility that the two deaths are linked,' said Bridget. 'My working hypothesis is that David Smith saw something on the evening of the ghost tour that gave him a clue to the killer's identity, and that he was killed to stop him revealing what he'd found out.'

'What do you think he saw?' asked Jake.

'If we knew that, I think we'd already have solved the case,' said Bridget. 'But it must be linked to one of the people who was on the ghost tour.'

'Or who was in the Turf afterwards,' said Ryan. 'What about Bill Tomlins?'

'The carousel owner? I think we can probably rule him out,' said Bridget. 'We know that he was at the scene of David Smith's murder, but we have nothing to link him to Camilla Townsend.'

'Except,' said Ryan, 'that I asked around at the market and discovered that he's been coming to Oxford at this time of year for the past thirty-odd years.'

'So he was here when Camilla went missing?' Bridget was unable to keep the dismay from her voice. She had hoped to narrow down her list of suspects, but it seemed that instead the field of candidates was growing. She added Bill Tomlins' name to the board.

'What about this student, Dylan Collins?' asked Andy. 'What exactly was he doing in that house on the night of

Christmas Eve?'

'Looking for ghosts,' said Bridget. 'And in a manner of speaking he found one. But Dylan's far too young to have had anything to do with Camilla's death. He wasn't even born when she went missing. The same goes for his friend Luke.'

'So we've narrowed it down to four?' said Jake.

'I think so.'

'What about Julia Carstairs' friends, Liz and Deborah? They were at the Turf on Sunday night, and they were also students at Oxford at the same time as Julia.'

'We can't rule them out, then.' Bridget added the two names to the list of suspects on the whiteboard. 'So, let's see what we can find out. Ffion, can you go through the witness statements from Camilla's missing person file, and find out if Liz or Deborah were at the party at Freud's the night she went missing? Jake, I'd like you to get in contact with the faculty dean at Harvard and see if Trevor Mansfield's story checks out. We need to know whether he was telling the truth about being on the phone at the time of the murder, so we'll need to find out exactly when the call took place and how long it lasted. Put in a request for his mobile phone records too. We need to nail it down.'

'It'll still be night-time over in the States,' said Jake. 'But leave it with me. I'll see what I can do.'

'Ryan, I'd like you to go to the Randolph Hotel and find out if any of the staff can confirm that Guy Goodwin returned to the hotel on Sunday night at the time he said he did.'

'Righto,' said Ryan. 'What about you, ma'am?'

Bridget's face darkened. 'I'll go and let Grayson know what we're doing, and hope that he's happy with the state of progress.'

★

It didn't take Ffion long to establish that Liz and Deborah had indeed been at the party at Freud's the night that

Camilla Townsend went missing. They had been guests of Julia and had also gone to see her perform in *Twelfth Night*. She read their statements carefully, but there was nothing to indicate that they had been particularly close to Camilla.

She put the file to one side, reflecting on where the case was going. She was pleased to be at the very heart of the investigation, having been the first to hear about the discovery of the skeleton at Lathbury Road, and to make the connection with the murder of David Smith. Her Christmas hadn't gone entirely as planned, and she hadn't got round to going to the race meeting on Boxing Day, but she couldn't say she was sorry. It had felt good to be the one to call Bridget on Christmas Day and inform her that a body had been found. And she'd enjoyed spending the following day together with the boss going through all the old case files and then paying a visit to Dr Mansfield and Guy Goodwin. It had helped to take her mind off the fact that Jake was gone, and that they were never going to get back together.

She was missing him more than she cared to admit.

The soap and candles he'd given her were obviously a goodwill gesture, and she appreciated the thought. But if he imagined that she could forgive him that easily he had badly misjudged her. Ffion didn't give her affection easily, and when she did, she expected loyalty in return. Jake had let her down badly, and hurt her more than he could know.

She couldn't be sure whether he even wanted her back. In the immediate aftermath of the breakup, he'd begged enough times to be forgiven, but when she'd repeatedly refused, he'd withdrawn into himself, no longer speaking to her or looking her in the eye. He'd avoided her, just as she'd shunned him.

He hadn't even asked her why she wasn't going home for Christmas. It seemed he didn't care. Well, that was fine with her. She'd been hurt by him once, just like her own mother had hurt her. She wouldn't allow either of them to hurt her again.

Ffion didn't believe in second chances.

*

It seemed that the faculty dean at Harvard was an early riser, and was quick to reply to Jake's email requesting a telephone interview. Jake hadn't even been sure that the dean would reply. He was under no obligation to help British police with their enquiries, but in fact the dean seemed keen to talk.

A phone call was arranged and Jake answered it a minute later. 'Hello, Dr Charlton, thank you very much for agreeing to speak to me.'

'No problem at all. Only too pleased to help the authorities.' The dean's voice was deep but friendly.

'So,' said Jake, 'as I explained in my email, we're investigating a crime here in Oxford' – he was careful not to mention the word "murder" – 'and we'd like to eliminate Dr Trevor Mansfield from our enquiries. We're hoping that you can corroborate what he's told us about his movements last Sunday night.'

'That would be Sunday night by British time?' queried Dr Charlton.

'Sorry, yes.' It was the first time Jake had worked on any investigation with an international angle, and he was feeling a little out of his comfort zone. Authority figures made him anxious at the best of times, but speaking to the dean's disembodied voice from the safety of the opposite side of the Atlantic Ocean seemed to help. 'That would be around five pm your time,' he said, consulting the chart of time zones he had ready on his computer screen.

'Sure,' said the dean. 'What exactly is it that you want to know?'

'Simply whether you spoke to Dr Mansfield, and if so at what time did the call begin and end.'

'I can easily answer that question for you. In fact, I remember the conversation very well.'

Jake waited, his pencil hovering over his notebook.

'I called Trevor at around five fifteen my time, so that

would be ten fifteen your time. He was in quite a noisy pub at the time, and it was difficult for him to hear me, so he took the call somewhere quieter. We spoke for around ten minutes in total.'

Jake jotted it down. 'So, just to confirm, the call began at five fifteen your time, and ended at five twenty-five.'

'Give or take,' confirmed the dean. 'A few minutes either way.'

'Thank you very much, sir. That's extremely helpful.'

'Pleased to be of assistance.'

Jake was ready to end the call, having obtained the information he needed, but something about the dean's voice made him stay on the line.

After a pause, Dr Charlton spoke again. 'Is it possible for you to tell me the nature of the crime you're investigating?'

'I'm sorry,' said Jake. 'I'm afraid that's confidential.' He had no desire to get Dr Mansfield into trouble with the dean, especially since Dr Charlton's account seemed to have removed any doubt about whether he'd been telling the truth.

'Of course. Naturally,' said the dean. 'It's just that, there's something I'd like to share with you. This information is also confidential. I wouldn't normally be in a position to say anything, but as you are a law enforcement agency, and you're telling me that a crime has been committed, I feel it would be negligent of me to hold this back.'

Jake waited, half-afraid to breathe, and wondering what the dean might have to tell him.

'The reason I called Trevor on Sunday was because he's currently suspended from his duties as lecturer here at Harvard.' The dean paused, as if struggling to select the right words. 'A female student has made an accusation about Dr Mansfield of inappropriate behaviour.'

'What kind of inappropriate behaviour?'

'I don't want to go into any details over the phone, especially as we're still conducting our own internal investigation, but suffice to say that the allegation is of inappropriate sexual conduct.'

'I see.'

'That's all I wanted to say,' said the dean. 'I'll leave it with you to decide whether this sheds any light on your present investigation, whatever the nature of that may be.'

'Thank you,' said Jake. 'You've been most helpful.'

CHAPTER 25

Bridget stared at the names and photographs on the whiteboard in frustration. They were six days – and two bodies – into the investigation and the list of suspects was stubbornly refusing to be whittled down. Ffion's latest news that both Liz and Deborah had been present at the party on the night Camilla Townsend was last seen didn't help the situation at all. She racked her brains trying to remember exactly what the two women had been doing on the night of the ghost tour at the Turf Tavern.

As far as she could recall, Liz, Deborah and Julia had all been talking with Cheryl Mansfield while Bridget was speaking to Lynda Henderson and her daughter. When the men returned from the bar with drinks, Bridget had extricated herself and gone to join Cheryl and the other women, while Jonathan spoke to Gordon Goole. Then Julia had gone to the bar to buy more drinks and Bridget had headed off towards the ladies' toilets. But she had no clear information about what Liz and Deborah had done next. Although they had remained in the vicinity of the pub courtyard, nobody had reported seeing them until some time after the murder. The place had been far too crowded for anyone to see much at all.

And although Julia Carstairs and Guy Goodwin had given each other an alibi for the night of the historic murder, neither Liz nor Deborah had been asked to account for their movements after leaving the party at Freud's. Both Liz and Deborah had the means and opportunity to commit both murders. But what might their motive have been?

Trevor Mansfield seemed a more likely suspect. Not only had he been present at the Turf on the night of the stabbing, but he'd also been Camilla's tutor. And the fact that the skeleton had been found in the house backing onto his was stretching coincidence too far.

Jake came over to her, looking excited. 'I've just come off the phone to Dr Charlton, the faculty dean at Harvard.'

'And?'

'He confirmed that he spoke on the phone to Dr Mansfield on Sunday night, and the time of the call matches what Dr Mansfield told us. But the call was only ten minutes long, not twenty like Mansfield claimed, so it doesn't let him off the hook completely. He might still have had time to carry out the murder. But there's more.'

Bridget raised her eyebrows in expectation.

'The reason for the phone call was that Dr Mansfield is currently under investigation at Harvard. He's been accused of sexual misconduct towards one of his female students.'

Bridget felt herself staring open-mouthed at Jake. 'A sexual abuser?' The image that Trevor Mansfield liked to project with his tartan slippers and chunky sweaters may be that of a harmless and homely old don, but beneath the façade a less savoury individual was beginning to emerge. Bridget recalled the glimpse of a harder, more determined man she'd seen beneath the surface. Was his mask finally slipping?

'I wonder if there have been any similar allegations in the past?' she asked.

'I don't know.'

Bridget knew that back in the days when Mansfield was a tutor at Oxford, only a brave undergraduate would have dared to make a complaint against her tutor. She would have been more likely to brush off an inappropriate advance as banter or harmless flirting. But it was worth checking with the university to see if any allegations had been made against him. If a complaint had been filed, it might explain why he left Oxford to go to the United States.

'Check with the university,' she told Jake. 'I want to know if there's anything else Trevor Mansfield hasn't disclosed to us.'

'Will do,' said Jake.

Her phone rang as he was leaving and she picked up.

'Ma'am? It's Ryan. I'm at the Randolph Hotel right now, and I've spoken to the receptionist who was on duty on Sunday night.'

'Yes?'

'Guy lied when he told us that he went straight from the theatre to his hotel room. According to the receptionist, he didn't return to the hotel until well after half past ten, and when he did, he was arm in arm with Julia Carstairs.'

Bridget felt her anger rising. 'So they both lied to us. Julia told me that Guy sent her a text and she went to the hotel to meet him. When I spoke to Guy, he confirmed her version of events.'

'I thought you ought to know about it as soon as possible,' said Ryan.

'Yes, thank you, you've done well. You'd better get back here now.'

She ended the call, her mind whirring. So both Julia's and Guy's alibis were blown, and since they had only each other to confirm their whereabouts on the night of the party twenty-five years ago, that too was looking decidedly flimsy.

'Ma'am, I think you should see this.'

She looked up to see Andy hovering in front of her desk. 'What is it?'

'It'll be better if I show you.'

She followed him across to his desk, where his computer monitor was displaying a CCTV still from Sunday night. 'What am I looking at?'

'This is from the camera located closest to the entrance to the Turf Tavern. It's the one where I spotted Bill Tomlins the carousel owner going to the pub.'

'Yes?'

'After you showed the photograph of Guy Goodwin this morning, it jogged a memory. I thought I'd seen that face before. So I've been trawling back through the CCTV footage from Sunday night and guess what?' He indicated the screen and pressed play.

Bridget watched as a lone male figure in a black padded jacket strode confidently up Broad Street in the direction of the Turf. He walked briskly, his hands thrust into his pockets against the cold. The man crossed over the road by the Weston Library, just as Bill Tomlins had done, but some five minutes earlier, at a time just before the murder took place.

Andy froze the screen and they both stared at the features of the man moments before he would pass out of the camera's view beneath the Bridge of Sighs. There was absolutely no doubt. The dark and handsome features of Guy Goodwin were unmistakable, his long, untamed hair curling over the collar of his jacket.

'That's him all right,' said Bridget. 'So instead of waiting for Julia at his hotel he went to meet her at the Turf. Is there any footage of the pair of them leaving?'

'No, that's the odd thing,' said Andy. 'I can't find him again. He appears to have done a vanishing act.'

'Not necessarily,' said Bridget. 'There are two entrances to the Turf – this one on New College Lane and another on Holywell Street. Or they could have met in New College Lane and then headed off in the opposite direction towards Queen's Lane and the High Street. The bottom line is, he lied to me and that's a good enough reason for bringing him in. Jake, wait for Ryan to get back, then the pair of you can go and fetch him. And I don't care what state his rehearsal is in.'

★

Jake and Ryan set off for central Oxford in Jake's Subaru, a marked police car on their tail. Jake wondered if Bridget was expecting Guy Goodwin to get heavy with them when they made their arrest. Jake wouldn't mind if he did. The theatre director could do with being taken down a notch. Jake had taken a dislike to him at first sight. He was the kind of bloke who took women for granted, and seemed to believe they could get away with anything. It would be good to bring him back to the nick in handcuffs.

'So how was your Christmas then, mate?' he asked Ryan

'Oh, you know, too much food, too much booze, too much telly.'

'Just the way you like it, then?'

'Can't complain. How about you?'

'Yeah, good.' The traffic lights on the Banbury Road turned red and Jake slowed the car to a stop.

'So,' continued Ryan, 'me and Andy were wondering whether you'd be coming back to Oxford at all after the Christmas break.'

'What?' said Jake, startled. 'Why would you think that?' He was sure he'd kept his job searches a secret. He certainly hadn't mentioned anything to the guys in the office, especially not to Ryan, who could never be trusted to keep his mouth shut.

'Logical deduction,' said Ryan, looking smug. 'I thought you might be looking for a fresh start, now that relations between you and Ffion have turned into a total car crash.'

'Well, cheers, mate. Thanks for putting it like that. It's good to know I can always depend on your sensitivity and delicacy.'

'I tell it like it is.'

The lights changed and Jake moved off, saying nothing. What Ryan had just said rankled. He hadn't realised that the rest of the team had picked up on the tension between himself and Ffion. He didn't want to be the cause of any awkwardness in the office. If he was going to stay in Oxford, and he certainly intended to, then he was going to have to find a way to get along better with Ffion.

'So you've no plans to leave?' persisted Ryan.

'Where would I go?' asked Jake, playing the innocent.

'Ee bah gum, 'appen Yorkshire,' said Ryan in a ridiculous accent. 'There's nowt like a proper cuppa Yorkshire tea.'

Jake shook his head and kept his eyes firmly on the road ahead. There really was no response to that.

He parked directly outside the theatre on George Street, leaving the uniformed officers in the marked car to wait for them. He was pretty sure that he and Ryan had enough muscle to handle the theatre director without backup.

'*West Side Story*,' said Ryan, glancing up at the large billboard above the theatre's entrance. 'Music by Leonard Bernstein, lyrics by Stephen Sondheim, based on the plot of *Romeo and Juliet*.'

Jake shot him a curious look. 'You seem to know quite a lot about it.'

Ryan feigned a look of offence. 'I'm not entirely ignorant. I used to do a spot of acting when I was at school. Drama was my favourite subject.'

'Well, you're full of surprises.'

'Hidden depths, mate. That's me all over.'

The matinée performance of *West Side Story* was due to begin shortly, and the entrance foyer was packed with a throng of people presenting their tickets. Jake and Ryan approached the usher manning the door to the auditorium and directing people to their seats.

'Tickets, please?'

Jake flashed his warrant card at her instead. 'We're here for Guy Goodwin.'

The usher looked indignant. 'Now? But the show's due to start in twenty minutes. Can't it wait?'

'No,' said Jake. 'It can't. So if you could direct us to Mr Goodwin?'

But before she could answer, a woman came storming out of the auditorium in a cloud of heady perfume, causing Jake and Ryan to take a step back or risk being bowled over.

'Julia?' said Jake. 'I mean, Miss Carstairs?'

She stopped directly in front of him and looked up. 'Oh, yes, you're the sergeant, aren't you?'

'DS Jake Derwent,' he mumbled, aware that everyone in the foyer had turned to stare at them. Some faces registered disapproval; others awe. Julia's talents were obviously known and appreciated by at least a few of the audience members.

'You know Julia Carstairs?' hissed Ryan under his breath. 'She's, like, famous!'

Jake registered a moment's astonishment that Ryan was apparently a fan of the actress. He wouldn't have put Ryan down as an afficionado of TV crime drama, but the blokey sergeant seemed full of surprises today. 'I met her the other day,' he said casually.

Julia was oblivious to the commotion she was generating. 'I was just leaving.'

It was obvious from her appearance that she'd been crying. Her eyes were raw red, and mascara had run down her cheeks, giving her a vulnerable look. Jake felt a touch of sympathy for her. It had been obvious to him from the start that Guy Goodwin was a self-absorbed bastard, and it required no great leap of deduction to guess that Julia's relationship with him had come to a messy end. 'Are you all right?' he asked.

'No, I bloody well am not!' she declared, surveying the packed foyer. Now that she was aware she had an audience, she seemed happy to play her scene for all it was worth. Fresh tears sprang from her eyes, and she began to wail. People stood and stared.

'Maybe we should go somewhere a little quieter to talk,' suggested Ryan.

Julia regarded him with disdain, then turned back to Jake. 'No,' she declared. 'Anything I have to say can be said in public. I've nothing to hide.'

'I really do think it would be better if we went somewhere private,' said Jake, gently taking her arm. He escorted her to a quiet corner of the bar where he persuaded the barman to serve her a double brandy. Guy Goodwin could wait for ten minutes.

'You boys not having one?' she asked, clutching her glass in both hands.

'We're working.'

'Of course, silly me.' She knocked back half her drink in one go.

'We're actually here for Guy Goodwin,' said Jake.

'That bastard!' said Julia. The sobbing stopped, to be replaced by a hard-edged anger. 'I'm finished with him!'

'What happened?' asked Jake.

'All I did was make a suggestion about how the show might be improved and he flew off the handle. He told me that I'm a mediocre actress who doesn't deserve anything better than bit parts in soaps and low-brow melodrama. He said my best role was when I had to play a corpse.' She dissolved into tears again.

'He's wrong,' said Ryan, leaning forward earnestly. 'I think you're a great actress. I saw you when you played that murderer's wife. You were brilliant!'

Julia's face cleared and she gazed at Ryan in gratitude. 'That's the kindest thing anyone's ever said to me.'

'So, … about Guy,' said Jake.

'You're welcome to him!'

'We have reason to believe that the alibi you provided for him was false.'

Julia studied Jake's face uncertainly. '*False* isn't a very kind word to use, is it?' She turned hopefully to Ryan, who smiled. 'But, yes, I suppose that you could put it that way.'

'So when you told us that you met Guy back at his hotel room after the ghost tour, that was a lie,' persisted Jake.

Julia glared at him in defiance. 'It wasn't a lie, exactly. I just made it up, that's all. It's called improvisation.'

'So were you trying to keep Guy out of the investigation?'

'I just wanted to protect him from getting embroiled in a murder enquiry. The bad publicity could have ruined his show.'

'And what about the other alibi that you gave him? The night that Camilla Townsend went missing? Was that improvisation too?'

Julia knocked back the rest of the brandy and banged the empty glass back on the table. 'That wasn't improvisation. Guy asked me to lie for him.'

'He asked you to lie?'

'Yes.'

'So what really happened that night?' pressed Ryan.

'We had a blazing row, that's what happened. Guy was flirting outrageously with Camilla, even though he was supposed to be with me. I already suspected that they were sleeping together, which was why he'd given her the part of Viola, even though I was obviously better suited to the role. Anyway, Guy denied sleeping with her, but told me that he'd like to. I stormed out after that. I don't know what Guy did.'

'So you broke up with him that night? Then why did you agree to lie for him?'

She regarded her empty glass shamefaced. 'Guy can be very persuasive. There's an animal magnetism to him. He's always been able to get me to do whatever he wants. The next morning, he was full of remorse, apologising to me and telling me that he'd been drunk and didn't know what he was saying the night before. He told me that he'd only ever loved me, and begged me to forgive him. So, naturally, I did.'

'Naturally.'

'Well, it's over now,' she said. 'I've finally seen him for what he is. A monster! As far as I'm concerned, you can lock him up and throw away the key.'

Jake nodded and stood up. 'Thanks. I think we might be about to do just that.'

CHAPTER 26

By the time Jake and Ryan returned to the foyer of the theatre, the show was just starting. A clash of cymbals and blast of brass heralded the opening bars of the overture.

Julia showed them to the pass door leading backstage and gave them directions to the theatre manager's room where she said they would find Goodwin. But she refused to accompany them any further.

'I don't want to see that man again for as long as I live,' she declared.

'Okay, thanks,' said Jake. 'So what are you going to do now?'

'I'm going back to the Malmaison to make up with Liz and Debs. If they're willing to take me back, that is. I'm sorry to say that I've treated them rather badly these past few days.' She sounded uncharacteristically contrite.

'And what then? Will you be staying on in Oxford?'

Julia brightened up at the thought. 'We're staying until the end of the week. Christmas may be over, but when the girls are together, the party never stops.' With that she spun on her heel and vanished into the street outside.

'Quite a woman,' said Ryan, staring after her.

'Yeah. Now quit drooling. We've got work to do.' Jake pushed open the pass door, and found himself suddenly in the underbelly of the theatre.

He hadn't been to a theatre performance in years, generally preferring the cinema or a comedy club. But he still held fond memories of going to the Alhambra in Bradford for the Christmas pantomime with his mum and dad as a kid. *Jack and the Beanstalk*; *Snow White*; and his all-time favourite – *Aladdin*. He'd loved the music, the familiar stock characters of the wise-cracking dame, the goodies and the baddies and of course the hero and heroine, but most vivid in his mind was the impression of the theatre itself. It had blown him away, with its huge domed and decorated ceiling, row upon row of red velvet seats, gilded boxes and glittering chandeliers. Every seat in the auditorium was always taken, and the applause at the end of each show was thunderous. In his mind a theatre was a magical place. Even catching a glimpse of the director and actors at the rehearsal the other day had brought back that familiar feeling in the pit of his stomach that here was a place where dreams were made.

So it was a terrible shock to find himself backstage.

The narrow corridor ahead was dimly lit and dusty. Electrical cables snaked along the low ceiling, and scenery was propped up precariously against one wall. At six foot five, Jake had to keep his head down to avoid banging it on a beam or an air-conditioning pipe.

A stage hand appeared, calling for the Jet girls and the Shark girls to be ready. Jake stepped back abruptly as a door flew open and half a dozen young women in brightly coloured swinging skirts flooded out on their way up to the stage.

'Blimey, it's like a rabbit warren,' said Ryan.

They found the theatre manager's office eventually, more by chance than from Julia's directions, which turned out to have been somewhat inaccurate. Jake knocked on the door and entered.

He wondered if Guy would be upstairs by now, watching his new leading lady, but perhaps he was leaving it until the last possible moment, or else couldn't bear to watch the impending disaster unfold. But for whatever reason, he was here, seated in front of a desk littered with programmes and unwashed mugs. The walls of the small room were plastered with old posters for shows going back to the nineteen-sixties. A second man sat across the desk. He was in his late fifties, with a receding hairline and thick, black-rimmed glasses. Judging from Julia's rather vague description, this was presumably Jim Banks, the theatre manager. Banks held a programme from an old production of *My Fair Lady*. Perhaps they were reminiscing about the good old days.

Both men looked up at the intrusion and Banks shot angrily to his feet. 'Who on earth are you? And what do you think you're doing, barging into my office?'

'DS Jake Derwent and my colleague DS Ryan Hooper. We're here for Mr Goodwin.'

Guy shot a contemptuous look in their direction. 'Well, I can't speak with you now. The show's already starting. I was just about to take my seat, ready to watch.'

'I'm afraid that won't be possible, sir,' said Ryan, stepping forward.

'Not possible?' Guy rose up, filling the small office with his physical presence. His dark brows knitted together furiously. 'What do you mean?'

'What we mean,' said Ryan, 'is that you are under arrest on suspicion of murder.'

'No!' protested Guy. 'You're making a stupid mistake.'

'I don't think so, sir,' said Jake. 'But you made a stupid mistake when you lied about meeting Miss Carstairs on Sunday night. You told us that she'd come to your hotel room, but that wasn't true was it?'

'That vindictive bitch,' said Goodwin, spittle flying, his large hands balling into fists. 'Did she tell you that? You can't trust a word she says.'

'She didn't need to tell us. You were caught on CCTV

walking towards the Bridge of Sighs at the time you claimed to be in your hotel room. Julia merely confirmed what we already knew.'

'Hellfire and damnation,' said Goodwin, 'I told her we should never have lied about that.' His broad shoulders sagged as the fight drained out of him.

'But you can't arrest him now!' exclaimed the indignant theatre manager. 'He's the director!'

Guy raised a palm to calm Banks down. 'By your patience, no,' he proclaimed. 'My stars shine darkly over me.' He hung his head, letting long, black hair fall over his face.

'I beg your pardon?' said Jake.

'Sebastian, from *Twelfth Night*,' explained Banks. 'It's a quote from the play.'

'I think what Mr Goodwin means,' commented Ryan as he snapped a pair of handcuffs over Guy's wrists, 'is that his luck's finally run out.'

CHAPTER 27

Somehow Bridget had known she hadn't seen the last of Guy Goodwin at the Randolph Hotel. He'd put on a good performance for her benefit that day, but there had been one or two moments when the mask had slipped and he'd been unsure of his response. Perhaps he should have asked Julia to give him some acting lessons. Or perhaps he should have learned his lines better. Bridget was certain that at least some of what he'd told her had been a fiction. It was her task now to sieve the truth from the lies.

There were no cream cakes or espressos on offer in interview room two at Kidlington. Guy sat across a bare table from her and Jake, his solicitor at his side, referring to his notes. The solicitor, a rather confident young man with an air of arrogance about him, had already been briefed by Bridget in advance of the interview, and was fully aware that his client had lied about his whereabouts at the time of the two murders, and that both David Smith and Julia Carstairs believed he'd been having an affair with Camilla Townsend in the days and weeks immediately prior to her disappearance. An affair that, Bridget contended, had led Guy to murder her and conceal her body in an abandoned house very close to the party that the cast and crew of *Twelfth Night* had attended following its final performance.

Now that Bridget had the theatre director on her own turf, she felt much more confident about extracting the truth from him. Sitting opposite, his head bowed, he looked dejected and dishevelled. The long unruly hair that had formerly lent him an edge of dangerous allure now looked merely scruffy and unkempt. He'd said nothing since arriving at the station, other than to confirm his name and address. Perhaps he was still smarting from Julia's betrayal. Guy had obviously been counting on her continued support to get him off the hook. Well, perhaps he ought to have thought harder about that before telling her what a lousy actress she was. Jake and Ryan had filled Bridget in on the juicy details of the breakup. It had happened even more quickly than she'd thought it would, and in spectacular fashion. And Julia had already taken her revenge, blowing his alibi not only for the time of David Smith's murder, but also the historic murder twenty-five years previously. *A woman scorned,* thought Bridget with a wry smile.

'So,' she said, once the recorder was switched on and the caution had been given, 'do you now admit that you went to the Turf Tavern on Sunday night shortly after ten o'clock, and that you met Julia Carstairs there?'

Guy's solicitor cleared his throat. 'I have advised my client to answer *no comment* to all your questions during this interview.'

'No comment,' said Guy, in response.

'I can keep you here all afternoon if you're not going to cooperate,' said Bridget.

Guy put his head in his hands. 'Oh, what's the point? Why deny what everyone already knows is true?' He looked up. 'Yes, I went to meet Julia that night, but I didn't actually go into the Turf. I texted Julia to say I was coming and we met beneath the Bridge of Sighs. I certainly didn't murder David Smith. I didn't even see him. In fact I had no idea that he was there. The last time I saw David was more than twenty years ago.'

'So why did you lie when questioned, claiming that you waited for Julia at the Randolph?'

'It was all Julia's idea. She was the one who lied to you.'

'But why would she lie?'

'She's an actress, damn her! She's a professional liar. I would have thought you'd have brought her in for questioning rather than me.' Guy glared across the table, breathing heavily, then calmed himself back down. 'Look, Julia knew that if my name came to your attention, you might jump to the wrong conclusion. She wanted to avoid any suspicion falling on me.'

'That plan rather backfired,' remarked Bridget.

'Yes, it did. I should never have gone along with it.'

'Are you going to try and put all the blame on Julia?'

'What do you mean?'

'Julia told us that it was your idea to lie about you and her being together in your room in college on the night that Camilla vanished.'

Guy shifted uneasily in his seat. Next to him, his solicitor, who suddenly appeared less than confident in the strength of his client's case, fiddled with his cufflinks.

Bridget pressed home her advantage. 'According to Julia, the pair of you didn't leave the party together. She says that you rowed about Camilla, split up, and went your separate ways. So which was it? A happy-ever-after ending or a tragedy? It was certainly a tragic ending for Camilla.'

'All right, I admit it. Julia and I had a stupid row at the party.' Guy ran a hand through his dark hair in an exasperated gesture. 'What you need to understand about Julia is that although she appears to be confident, like a lot of people in show business she's basically insecure. She needs people to tell her how wonderful she is all the time. She was hurt that she didn't get the part of Viola and insanely jealous of Camilla. She became fixated on this ridiculous notion that Camilla and I were sleeping together, and the argument came to a head at the party. She stormed off and I went back to college alone. Then the next day when Camilla had vanished and the police were asking awkward questions... well, I guess I just panicked. I persuaded Julia that she should say I was with her.'

'Why would you do that?' persisted Bridget. 'Unless you had something to hide.'

'Well I hadn't.' He sounded as petulant as a spoilt child. 'But Julia wasn't the only one who imagined there was something going on between me and Camilla. Theatre companies gossip horribly. When a rumour gets going, it's almost impossible to put a stop to it.'

'No smoke without fire,' offered Jake.

Guy rounded on him crossly. 'Is that all you have, then? Gossip and tittle-tattle? Am I to be convicted on the basis of hearsay?'

'You just have to say *no comment*,' said his solicitor.

'I'll say what I bloody well like!' roared Guy.

Bridget regarded him sternly. 'What I suggest is that you start telling the truth. Did you or did you not sleep with Camilla Townsend?'

'I didn't. It's the truth.'

'According to Julia,' said Jake, 'that night at the party you told her that you wanted to sleep with Camilla.'

Guy nodded miserably. 'Yes, I was so fed up with Julia's jealousy and accusations that I lost my temper. Julia just kept asking me over and over about Camilla. It was as if she wanted me to tell her the worst. So in the end I snapped.'

'And was it true? Did you want to sleep with Camilla?'

Guy let out a long breath. 'Well, I don't suppose there's any point denying it. She was a very attractive girl, and we worked together closely on the play. It would have been weird if I didn't fancy her.' He glared at Bridget. 'Satisfied?'

'No. Your story changes every time you open your mouth. Let's get to the bottom of this. Did you or did you not sleep with Camilla Townsend?'

'No!'

★

The interview with Guy Goodwin had come to an end without any clear conclusion, and Bridget took Jake aside to discuss what they'd learned, if anything.

'He admitted that he met Julia at the Turf,' said Jake. 'And he told us that he lied about his alibi the night Camilla disappeared. He even went as far as admitting that he was attracted to Camilla.'

'That's all completely circumstantial,' said Bridget, 'Besides, he only tells us what we already know, and not until he's forced to. There's no reason to believe he's told us everything.'

'What about this story that he met Julia under the Bridge of Sighs and didn't go into the Turf?'

'We need to speak to Julia again and find out precisely where they met.'

'I agree ma'am,' said Jake. 'To tell you the truth, I wish I'd brought Julia Carstairs in for further questioning when I saw her at the theatre.'

'What are you thinking?'

'I'm thinking that now we know that Julia and Guy split up after the party, then she had just as much opportunity to attack Camilla as Goodwin did. And she arguably had a stronger reason. Jealousy.'

Bridget nodded. 'What did she say her plans were?'

'She was going back to the Malmaison to make up with her friends. It sounded like they were planning to hit the town.'

Bridget checked her watch. It was already late afternoon. She'd kick herself if she let Julia Carstairs get away. 'Then let's take your car. We're going back to the prison.'

CHAPTER 28

Julia Carstairs was quite possibly the most glamorous person Bridget had ever brought into the station for questioning. Quite a few heads turned as the moderately famous actress was escorted into the interview room that Guy Goodwin had occupied just an hour earlier.

Julia glanced around the barely-furnished room with disdain. 'Have I been arrested?' she demanded.

'No,' said Bridget patiently. 'Like I explained, you're being interviewed under caution.'

She hoped that the actress wouldn't put on too much of a performance during questioning. Julia had made enough of a fuss when Bridget and Jake arrived at the Malmaison to pick her up. It hadn't been difficult to locate her. She, Liz and Deborah were at the bar, about to down their cocktails. The three friends had clearly made up and were busy gossiping together. No doubt Liz and Deborah were only too keen to hear the sordid details of Julia's short-lived fling with Guy Goodwin, however much they might have resented being abandoned by her. They'd looked on open-mouthed as Bridget and Jake escorted her outside to a waiting police car. 'Is there no end to this drama?' she'd wailed, throwing up her arms in dismay.

Now she was conferring with her solicitor while Bridget and Jake prepared themselves for the interview. She had refused the offer of a cup of tea from the vending machine, but to Bridget's astonishment, Ryan had volunteered to run across the road to Starbucks and fetch her a skinny latte. 'He'll probably be asking for her autograph when he gives it to her,' said Jake.

When the formalities were done, Bridget began her questioning. 'I'd like to begin this interview back at the beginning, when you were an undergraduate at Oxford. You were involved in a production of *Twelfth Night*, directed by Guy Goodwin.'

'Yes. I played Olivia.'

'And Camilla had the part of Viola. The part that you wanted. Why do you think you were passed over for the role?'

Julia fidgeted with her hands. 'Like I told you before, I believed that I should have been given the part. I can only assume that Camilla exerted some kind of influence over Guy.'

'Some kind of sexual influence?'

Julia pursed her lips before speaking. 'I'm only repeating what everyone thought at the time. The gossip was rife.'

'Do you have anything more concrete than gossip?'

'No.'

'All right, then,' said Bridget. 'Let's move on to the party at Freud's after the final performance. You were there with Guy, and Camilla was present too. Is that correct?'

'Yes.'

'Originally you told me that you and Guy left together and spent the night in his room, but you have now changed your account. Would you care to repeat what you told my sergeant?'

'I said that Guy forced me to lie and say that I was with him.'

'Forced you?'

'All right, then. Asked me.'

'So you didn't leave the party with Guy, after all?'

'No. We had a blazing row. I stormed out and went back to my own room. I didn't see Guy again until the following day.'

'I see,' said Bridget. 'And did anyone see you?'

'What do you mean?'

'I mean, can anyone vouch for your movements after you left the party?'

Julia stared across the table at Bridget in astonishment. 'You're suggesting that I had something to do with Camilla's disappearance?'

'I'm asking you whether anyone can confirm that your version of events is true.'

Julia took a sip of her latte before responding. 'At the party, everyone was congratulating Camilla on her performance. I thought I'd made a rather good Olivia, but no one seemed to think I deserved any praise. And then when Guy finally admitted that he preferred her to me, I freaked out. I was mad. But I didn't do anything to harm her. You have to believe me.'

If sincerity could be ranked on a scale from one to ten, Bridget would have awarded Julia at least a nine for her current performance. But she still hadn't supplied an alibi for herself. 'Let's return to the present. On Sunday night, after a gap of twenty-five years, you found yourself in Oxford on a ghost tour hosted by none other than Camilla's old boyfriend, David Smith, who was subsequently stabbed to death shortly after the tour ended. It seems extraordinary that you should be present at the times and places of both murders. How do you explain it?'

The solicitor leaned forward. 'My client is not obliged to respond to such conjecture.'

But Julia didn't seem to care about obligations and legal proceedings. 'I can't explain it,' she said, ignoring her solicitor and looking Bridget directly in the eye. 'I wish I could, but I can't.'

'You invented a lie about Sunday night, saying that you'd met Mr Goodwin at the Randolph Hotel when in actual fact he came to the Turf to meet you. Why make up something like that if you had nothing to hide?'

'I was acting on instinct,' said Julia. 'When I heard that David Smith had been murdered, I wanted to protect myself and Guy from any involvement. In my line of business you become paranoid about protecting your privacy. If the newspapers got hold of the story they would have made our lives a misery.'

'Julia,' said Jake, 'can you tell us precisely where you met Guy that night? Please tell us exactly what happened. Don't leave out any details.'

'I'd arranged to meet Guy that night when he finished at the theatre. I was checking my phone all evening for messages. I received a text from him when I was at the pub with you' – Julia looked at Bridget – 'but I knew that if I said where I was going, Liz and Debs would stop me. So I told them I was going to the bar. In fact, I went straight to the exit and walked down that narrow passage that leads to the Bridge of Sighs.'

'St Helen's Passage,' said Jake.

'Yes. Guy was waiting for me beneath the bridge. It was rather romantic, really.' She smiled, then seemed to remember what Guy had said about her acting abilities. 'That bastard. He always had the power to make me do whatever he wanted.'

'So you met him there,' said Jake. 'Not inside the grounds of the Turf.'

'He was definitely waiting outside,' said Julia. 'Believe me, if I'd found him holding a bloody dagger, I wouldn't hesitate to tell you.' She frowned as if lost in thought. 'But there was something else, now I think about it.'

'What?'

'As I was leaving the Turf, I almost bumped into David. Of course I didn't realise then that he was the David Smith I knew back in the day. He'd changed so much, and he was all dressed up in his tour guide outfit. Besides, I hadn't given him the slightest thought for years.'

'You saw him?' asked Bridget, incredulous. How could Julia have only just remembered such a significant detail?

'Yes. He was standing in the alleyway. He looked kind of lost. I said goodbye to him and thanked him for a lovely evening, but I don't think he even heard me. He had this frozen expression on his face.' She mimed a horror-struck look to demonstrate. 'I thought at the time, he looked as if he'd seen a ghost.'

'A ghost?' repeated Bridget sceptically.

'Was there anyone else with him?' asked Jake.

'Not that I remember. I'm pretty certain he was on his own. But I was in rather a hurry. I left him there and went to meet Guy.'

★

'What did she mean by, "He looked as if he'd seen a ghost?"' asked Bridget. Leaving Julia Carstairs in the care of the duty sergeant who seemed only too happy to oblige, she and Jake were returning to the incident room. 'Was she inventing that whole story to cover what she really did?'

'I don't know, ma'am. I'm not sure whether she has a vivid imagination or a terrible memory, or both.'

'Or is just a bare-faced liar,' concluded Bridget. 'Guy Goodwin and Julia Carstairs – they make a fine pair. They're as bad as each other.'

'So what do we do now?'

'We take Julia back to her hotel and we release Guy Goodwin. We don't have enough evidence to hold him, and certainly not enough to charge him for murder. Meanwhile, I want to find out if there's been any news on Trevor Mansfield. He's another dark horse.'

Back in the incident room, Ffion had done her job, checking with the university's HR department whether any kind of complaint had been filed against Dr Mansfield during the period he'd been a tutor at Oxford. 'Nothing,' she said. 'Although that doesn't necessarily prove he didn't harass his students.'

'No,' said Bridget. 'But we have to assume he's innocent unless we have some evidence to the contrary.'

'I suppose so,' said Ffion grudgingly.

Bridget mulled over her options. Based on what they now knew, it would be worth paying Mansfield another visit. The fact that he too had been around at the time of both Camilla's and David's deaths and was unable to provide a cast-iron alibi for either of them hadn't gone away. And then there was that nagging coincidence that the house where Camilla's body had been hidden backed onto the house where he had been living at the time she went missing. It would be interesting to see how the Harvard lecturer reacted when Bridget revealed that she knew the reason the faculty dean had phoned him on Sunday night.

But that would have to wait until the morning. It was too late to do any more tonight.

*

Ffion was shutting down her computer and pulling on her green leather jacket when Jake sidled nervously up to her desk.

'Do you have a moment?' he asked. 'Before you go home?'

She wondered what he had in mind. It was clear from his body language that he was gearing himself up for a big announcement. Jake always wore his emotions openly, the way a dog revealed its feelings by the way it wagged its tail if it was happy or twitched its ears forward when alert. She'd found it one of his most endearing features when they'd been together. That same transparency had revealed his guilt when he'd cheated on her. If Jake had been a dog, his tail would now be tucked between his legs, and his eyes downcast. She hoped he wasn't going to beg her to take him back yet again. That gate was already shut, bolted and securely padlocked. She was tired of repeatedly saying no.

'What is it?' she asked. The office was emptying fast. Bridget had already left, and so had Grayson. So if there had to be a scene, at least there wouldn't be too many witnesses.

'Can we go somewhere quieter?'

'It's quiet enough here.' She didn't want to encourage him. Whatever he had to say, it would be better if he just got it over with.

He breathed a sigh of resignation. 'All right, then. Listen. I've been thinking things over a lot recently. The bottom line is, after everything that happened between you and me, I decided it would be better if I left. So I found a job in Halifax.'

'Halifax?' The news was a shock. Ffion hadn't realised quite how seriously the break-up must have affected him if he felt the need to put a hundred and fifty miles between them. Perhaps her attitude towards him had been a little too cold. Now it was her turn to feel guilty. 'You're planning to move back up north?'

'I gave it some serious consideration. But on balance, I'd prefer to stay here.'

Good, she wanted to say. *I'm glad*. She would have hated for him to leave, and would have missed him terribly, despite all their difficulties. But she didn't want to offer him false hopes of reconciliation. 'I don't have any problem with that,' she said, keeping her voice free of inflection.

He scratched his nose, a sure sign that some further declaration was imminent. Ffion braced herself.

'Look,' he said. 'I know we can't be a couple again. You've made that perfectly clear. I had my chance, and I blew it, and I'm sorry for the mess I made. And I'm not asking that we can be friends. Not exactly.' He paused, clearly trying to assemble the right words in his head. If this was a prepared speech, stage fright had made him stumble over his carefully-rehearsed lines. After a moment he seemed to recover his flow. 'But you're a bloody good detective, Ffion, and as long as I'm still in Oxford, I want us to be able to work well together. As professionals. What do you say?'

At last it seemed safe for her to show her true feelings. Her lips slowly broadened into a grin. 'It's a deal. And for the record, you're a bloody good detective too, Jake.'

CHAPTER 29

This time it was Cheryl Mansfield who answered the door to Bridget and Jake. The reception she gave them was as frosty as the weather outside. 'I suppose you want to speak to Trevor again?' she asked, all traces of the friendliness she had shown to Bridget on the evening of the ghost tour now gone. 'If you'd like to wait in the lounge, I'll tell him that you're here.'

'Thank you.' Bridget wondered exactly how much Cheryl knew about her husband's predicament. Had he told her that he'd been suspended from his teaching post at Harvard? And if so, had he revealed the true nature of the allegations against him?

She and Jake went through to the now familiar front room. All was as before, and yet in Bridget's mind, the glittering gold and silver decorations that adorned the tree now seemed tarnished, as if the sordid truth of Trevor's misdemeanours had stained them. Certainly the feeling of contentment that had pervaded the house on her first visit had long since dissipated.

Trevor Mansfield, when he entered the room, was clearly very agitated. He stood by the door, not making any attempt to conceal his hostility. 'Inspector Hart again. I wonder if I should insist on a lawyer being present for this interview?'

Bridget did her best to play down his concerns. 'You're perfectly entitled to arrange for a solicitor to be present if you like, Dr Mansfield, but it's quite unnecessary and would just prolong the whole procedure. We just have a few questions for you, and then we'll be on our way.'

'I see. Well, I'll certainly do my best to answer any questions that you have. I'd like to be of assistance if I can. Why don't you take a seat?'

'Thanks,' said Bridget, taking her usual chair beside the coffee table. She waited until Trevor too was comfortably seated, although comfortable probably wasn't the right word. He sat bolt upright, perched on the edge of the sofa, every sense alert as he awaited her questions. Jake withdrew his notebook, and waited too. They were like the cast of a play, all eager and ready for the performance to begin.

It was time for the curtains to rise.

'Last time I visited, I asked you about the night that Camilla Townsend went missing. You told me that you went to watch her perform in *Twelfth Night* at the Burton Taylor Studio that evening, and that you returned home straight afterwards.'

Trevor Mansfield's lower lip twitched. 'Yes, that's right. I did.'

'Did you speak to Camilla at all during that evening? Before or after the play, for instance?'

Mansfield's eyes were as wary as a cat's. 'I did see her briefly that afternoon. I said I was looking forward to the performance and told her to break a leg because that's what people say to actors, isn't it? That was the very last time I spoke to her.'

'You didn't see her again after the play ended?'

'No.'

'And you didn't go to the party at Freud's?'

'No. I told you that before. The party was for students.

I wasn't invited. I didn't even know that it was taking place.'

'I see. Can you describe the exact route that you took after leaving the theatre?'

He paused, as if afraid to speak. Eventually, he said, 'I walked home that evening. It was dry that night and not particularly cold for the time of year, and it's not so far to walk back from town.'

Jake scribbled a note. 'So, you walked?'

'I walked,' agreed Mansfield. 'In fact, I believe that I may have stopped off for a pint at The Royal Oak. It's a pub on the Woodstock Road.'

'I know it,' said Jake. 'So, let's be clear. Did you or did you not call in for a pint?'

He hesitated. 'I did.'

Bridget leaned forward. 'In your statement to police at the time of the original enquiry, there was no mention of stopping at a pub.'

'It must have slipped my mind, or else it didn't seem important at the time.' He frowned. 'I probably wasn't even asked about how I walked home. I was never a suspect.'

Jake smiled warmly. 'No one's saying that you're a suspect now, sir. We just want to be clear about the facts.'

The sergeant's relaxed manner went a fair way to mollify the lecturer. 'Good, as long as we're clear about that.'

'So what time did you leave the pub?'

'Well, I guess that it would have been at closing time. In those days, pubs usually closed at eleven. So that would have been when I left.'

'And would anyone be able to verify that?'

'I doubt it. Not after such a long time.'

'So,' said Jake pleasantly, 'you stopped at the pub for a drink, left at eleven, and then what?'

'I came straight back home.'

'So you would have arrived back here at, say, a quarter past eleven.'

'That sounds about right.'

'You didn't go anywhere else?' asked Bridget.

'I walked straight back here. I didn't see Camilla, and before you ask, I was alone.'

'And once you'd returned you didn't leave the house until the following day?'

'Correct.'

'Can anyone verify that?'

'My mother. You can ask her.'

'Thank you,' said Bridget. 'We will.'

'So, is that it?' asked Mansfield, rising from his seat.

'Not quite,' said Bridget. 'Regarding the telephone conversation you had with the faculty dean at Harvard on Sunday night –'

'What of it?' he interrupted.

'The dean has indicated to us – in confidence, of course – the nature of that phone call.'

Trevor Mansfield sank back into the sofa, a look of defeat spreading across his face. 'He had no right to do that.'

'I expect that he felt an obligation to us, as a law enforcement agency. Be that as it may, the nature of the accusation that has been made against you by one of your students may have a bearing on the Camilla Townsend enquiry.'

Mansfield swapped his defeated expression for one of anger. 'I knew that if you found out about that, you would leap to the wrong conclusion. That's why I didn't say anything. You must understand that this accusation that has been made is quite false. There's no point me going into details about what I'm supposed to have done, because the allegations are quite honestly ridiculous and fanciful. And completely unsubstantiated, I might add. I will defend my innocence until my last breath, and any reasonable person would dismiss these accusations as the delusions of a fantasist. Unfortunately in this day and age, the word of a mentally unstable young woman is given credence over the word of a lecturer with an unblemished record.'

Unblemished, except for the inconvenient fact that one of your Oxford students was murdered, thought Bridget, but she didn't see the point in going over all that again. Trevor's speech had been an impressive and impassioned protestation of innocence, and she wasn't here to judge a man without knowing the facts.

'Thank you,' she said. 'We have no more questions for you now, but I would like to speak to your mother before we leave.'

'I'll ask her to come and speak to you.' He left the room, his shoulders slumped. He looked to have aged several years since Bridget had first seen him a week earlier. She hoped that if all the various allegations that were piling up against him proved ultimately to be untrue, that he would recover from the strain.

A minute later, Mrs Margaret Mansfield entered the room, closing the door behind her. 'Inspector Hart, DS Derwent, how may I help you?'

Bridget rose to greet her. 'Please do take a seat.'

'There's no need,' said the old woman in clipped tones. 'I am perfectly capable of standing.'

'Very well. I won't keep you any longer than I have to, Mrs Mansfield. You'll no doubt be aware that we are now investigating two murders – that of David Smith at the Turf Tavern last Sunday evening, and also that of Camilla Townsend, which we believe took place twenty-five years ago, most probably the same night that she went missing.'

She gave a nod.

'Do you remember that night, Mrs Mansfield? The night that Miss Townsend disappeared?'

'I do. I remember it perfectly well, Inspector. One doesn't easily forget when such a terrible tragedy occurs. The newspapers were full of stories about that poor girl for weeks afterwards.'

'What can you tell me about your son's whereabouts that night? Especially after around eleven o'clock.'

'I can tell you precisely where Trevor was that night.

He was here, with me.'

'Was anyone else present?'

'No, it was just the two of us. My other children are older and had already moved away from the family home. My husband sadly died a few years prior to that.'

'I'm very sorry to hear that. Can you be absolutely certain that Trevor was at home all evening?'

'Not all evening. He went to the theatre to see *Twelfth Night*. But he was definitely home by eleven o'clock.'

'By eleven?' Jake's pencil was moving rapidly over his notebook.

'That's right. At least, I think so.' Mrs Mansfield seemed suddenly less sure of herself. 'What time did Trevor tell you?'

'We'd like to hear what you recall about that night, Mrs Mansfield,' said Bridget hurriedly.

'Well, it was definitely some time around eleven. Perhaps eleven thirty.'

Bridget saw her chance and went for it. 'What time did you go to bed that night, Mrs Mansfield?'

'I'm not sure. I tend to go to bed quite early. I'm an early riser, you see. Always have been. So I don't like late nights.'

'Perhaps about ten o'clock,' suggested Bridget. 'Or ten-thirty?'

'I don't know.'

'I see. So, when your son returned that night, would it be a fair assumption that you were already in bed?'

Margaret Mansfield stared at Bridget dumbstruck. Her mouth opened, but no words emerged.

'So perhaps,' concluded Bridget, 'your recollection of that evening isn't quite as perfect as it might be.'

★

'It's my firm belief,' said Bridget to her assembled team, 'that the deaths of David Smith and Camilla Townsend are linked. My theory is that whoever murdered Camilla also murdered David, and my best guess is that they killed him because they realised that he had recognised them and deduced that they were the killer.'

No one in the room contradicted her, so she carried on. 'Let's list all the potential suspects.' She turned to the whiteboard, which now held six names. 'Top of the list is Dr Trevor Mansfield, Camilla's tutor at the time of her death and now a lecturer at Harvard University. Only his mother can provide him with an alibi for the night of Camilla's disappearance, and by her own admission she can't be certain what time he returned home that night. He was also at the Turf Tavern the night that David was killed. We now know that he's currently suspended from his position at Harvard while an investigation is carried out into allegations of sexual harassment against a female student.'

'And Camilla's body was found in the house right behind his,' pointed out Ryan.

'Exactly.'

She pointed to the next name on the board. 'Equally likely is Guy Goodwin, the man who directed the student production of *Twelfth Night*, and is now back in Oxford with *West Side Story* at the New Theatre. By his own admission he came to the Turf Tavern at the time of David's murder, and he has no alibi for the time of Camilla's death. Again, by his own admission, he was sexually attracted to Camilla, and may have had a fling with her.'

Bridget moved on to her third suspect. 'Julia Carstairs, actress. We've now established that Julia also has no alibi for the time of either murder. We know that she was jealous of Camilla, both professionally because Camilla had been given the part of Viola instead of her, and more pertinently, because she believed that Guy was having an affair with Camilla behind her back.'

Bridget paused. The other people on her list seemed less likely, but couldn't be ruled out. 'Then there are Julia's two friends, Liz and Deborah. While we have no obvious motive for either of them, they were both present at both murders. They remain as suspects for the moment. Then finally there's Bill Tomlins. We know that he's been coming to Oxford at Christmastime for many years. We know that he was at the Turf Tavern at the time of David's murder. He even admits to seeing David lying stabbed. And we know that he and David knew each other, because of the altercation they had at his carousel ride.'

Bridget cast her gaze over the six names on the whiteboard. Frustratingly they still had no way of eliminating any of them.

'What are you thinking, ma'am?' asked Jake.

'I've been mulling over something Julia Carstairs said, and I think it might be the key. Julia claimed that she saw David Smith when she was leaving the Turf, and that he looked, in her words, like he'd seen a ghost. What if David had just at that moment seen someone he knew from the past? A person he wasn't expecting to see back in Oxford. Someone he'd just encountered, or who he had just recognised?'

'That could be any one of the people you've listed,' said Ryan. 'No doubt they've all changed a lot since their student days. Smith might suddenly have twigged where he'd seen them before. If they realised that he'd recognised them, they might have decided to kill him to keep him quiet.'

'Yes,' said Bridget. 'But all these people seem too obvious. Remember that David Smith had been obsessing about Camilla's murder for more than twenty years. Even if he had recognised Julia, or Trevor, or Guy, or one of the others, what could he possibly have realised that night that suddenly made it necessary to murder him?'

'Well,' said Jake, 'I don't know if this is a daft idea, but what about Geoff Henderson?'

'What about him?' Bridget had almost forgotten the unassuming accountant from Beaconsfield while she'd been busy chasing celebrities. After Ffion had visited Beaconsfield to speak to Luke, they'd had no reason to consider the quarrelsome family any further.

'It's just something that Luke Henderson told us when we were interviewing him. He said that one of the reasons his parents were so keen for him to study at Oxford was that they wanted him to follow in their footsteps.'

'That might have meant any number of things.'

'Yes, but with Luke studying Law, he's not going to be qualified to become an accountant like his father. So, I think that what he meant was that his parents were students at Oxford too, perhaps even at New College. Then by coming to study at Oxford, he'd be following them.'

'It's possible, I suppose.'

'Would they have been around at the time of Camilla's murder?' asked Ryan.

'They're the right age to have been Camilla's contemporaries,' said Ffion.

'But even if they were,' said Bridget, 'how could Geoff Henderson have been involved with Camilla? He isn't an actor.' It was very hard to imagine the stiff accountant ever being caught up in the bohemian world of the theatre.

'Hang on,' said Ffion. 'I think I might have something.' She rummaged in the collection of files that they'd recovered from David Smith's house, sifting through a selection of grainy coloured photographs. In them, the cast members were all in costume, the men often with fake moustaches or beards, the women in wigs. It wasn't easy to recognise them. Eventually Ffion pulled out a slightly faded photo and pinned it to the whiteboard.

Everyone gathered around to take a closer look.

'This was taken just before the final performance of *Twelfth Night*,' she explained. 'It shows all the cast and crew.'

Bridget peered closely at the young faces. There was Guy Goodwin in the centre, his dark features not quite as wild as they were now, but impossibly handsome in his youth. To one side of him stood Julia Carstairs, more brunette than blonde in those days, clinging to Guy's arm proprietorially, and to his other side, Camilla Townsend, her fresh face captured for one of the very last times before her untimely death.

Bridget didn't recognise any of the other people in the photo. 'What am I looking for?'

'There.' Ffion's green-painted fingernail reached out to a man standing at the end of the back row, his face half-turned away.

The young man was moderately handsome, but couldn't match the striking good looks of Guy Goodwin in the front row. He clearly lacked the self-confidence of the director and starring actors, and seemed more comfortable at the back, a step removed from the limelight. He was slimmer in the photograph than he was these days, and had more hair, but now that Ffion had pointed him out, there could be no doubt in Bridget's mind. In fact the resemblance to his son, Luke, was striking. 'It's Geoff Henderson. What on earth is he doing there?'

Ffion passed her the programme for the play. Geoff Henderson's name was listed at the back with the stage crew. 'He was props manager.'

'So not an actor, but backstage. No wonder that no one remembered him.'

CHAPTER 30

Geoff Henderson had lived an inconspicuous and unexceptional life. Never on stage, always in the background. Successful in his chosen career, but not outstanding. Affluent, but not conspicuously so. His well-proportioned four-bedroom home was just like all the other houses in Beaconsfield, his dark grey BMW no different from the executive saloons parked on every driveway in the quiet suburban street where he lived with his wife and two children.

Geoff Henderson might never have dressed up in elaborate costume, yet he wore the perfect disguise for a killer.

Bridget rang the doorbell of the Henderson family home, Jake towering behind her. Two uniformed officers waited in the marked police car parked behind Bridget's Mini, drawing the curious glances of an elderly lady who was out walking her tartan-clad Highland terrier.

The front door swung open and Bridget was met by the surprised and displeased face of Lynda Henderson. Lynda's eyes flicked from Bridget to Jake and finally to the police car, at the sight of which she visibly flinched. On a

258

street like this, the arrival of the police would set curtains twitching and tongues wagging for days. Well, that was just too bad.

'Mrs Henderson. Is your husband at home?'

'Geoff? Why? What do you want this time? That Welsh woman said you'd finished asking all your questions.'

'Could we come in, please?' said Bridget.

Lynda had no choice but to invite Bridget and Jake into her immaculate home. A tempting aroma of baking wafted from the kitchen, something chocolatey, and drew a rumble from Bridget's empty stomach. She'd eaten just a single slice of toast and marmalade that morning and now regretted her uncharacteristic forbearance. She'd have been better off with a plate of fried bacon and scrambled eggs to keep her going.

She caught a glimpse of Lucy through the open lounge door to her left. The girl was sitting cross-legged in a comfy chair reading a book. She gave Bridget a shy smile over the top of her paperback, before Lynda pulled the lounge door closed with a bang. There was no sign of Luke. Presumably he was still in bed, like indolent teenagers the world over.

Geoff appeared at the top of the stairs, dressed casually for the weekend in chinos and a shirt. 'What's going on, Lynda?'

'Geoff!' cried his wife. 'The police are here. They're asking to see you.'

'Me?' He descended the stairs. 'Perhaps we can go through to the kitchen.'

He led the way into the large modern kitchen, which was as immaculately presented as the hallway. Stainless steel appliances stood next to a wooden island unit, and recessed ceiling lights cast a white glow over the surfaces. Through the spotless glass door of the oven, a chocolate sponge cake was rising. The washing-up from Lynda's baking session appeared to have already been done, and the granite worktops were clean and sparkling with nothing out of place. Lynda positioned herself at her husband's side, her arm looped about his.

'Mr Henderson,' said Bridget, 'we would like you to come with us to the station to answer questions relating to the historic murder of Camilla Townsend and the more recent murder of David Smith, otherwise known as Gordon Goole.'

'Now?' asked Geoff, looking bemused.

'Yes, now.'

'All right.'

It was Lynda who reacted with vehemence. 'This is outrageous. Geoff has nothing to do with either of those murders. How dare you come into this house and accuse him of something like that!'

'I haven't actually accused him of anything,' said Bridget. 'I'd just like him to come to the station and answer some questions.'

'But can't he answer your questions here? And why did you have to bring a police car and make such a scene? Are you arresting him?'

'Hush, Lynda.' Geoff laid a hand on his wife's shoulder. 'Everything will be fine. You stay here with the children and I'll go to Oxford and speak to the police.'

'Do you need me to call a lawyer?'

'I don't think that will be necessary.'

Lynda looked deep into her husband's eyes for reassurance. He bowed his head and planted a kiss on her forehead. She leaned into him and wrapped her arms around him. Bridget looked away, caught off-guard by this intimate moment between husband and wife that seemed to exclude anyone else. Jake, too, averted his gaze, standing awkwardly while the couple embraced.

'If we could make a move,' said Bridget after a moment, 'the car's waiting outside.'

'Yes,' said Geoff, pulling away from his wife at last. 'I'm ready now.'

★

Rarely had a suspect agreed to come back to the station

with Bridget with so little fuss. Geoff Henderson sat opposite her now in interview room two, just as calm as he'd been at home. It was disconcerting to see him behave that way.

Dressed in his smart casual clothes, his hair neatly combed, his face clean-shaven, he had clearly put his brief youthful flirtation with the bohemian world of theatre far behind him, and embraced the sober adult world of business. His son, Luke, might claim to despise the corporate world that his father inhabited, but it nevertheless paid for his own university education, as well as enabling the family to enjoy a comfortable lifestyle in a nice house. It also meant that Lynda didn't need to go out to work. Instead she could stay at home looking after her children and baking cakes to her heart's content in her spotless kitchen.

Bridget stopped herself. Why was she being so uncharitable towards this family?

There was something about that too-perfect home that had unnerved her. She didn't think it was simply the contrast with her own cramped and untidy cottage in Wolvercote. After all, she didn't feel the same about Vanessa's house in North Oxford, which was like something out of the glossy pages of *Good Housekeeping* magazine. Perhaps the difference was that Vanessa's house was a real home, and her family was a happy and contented one. Geoff Henderson's family, by contrast, was so tightly wound that it was close to breaking point.

And yet Geoff Henderson was the eye in the centre of the storm. He had remained still and calm throughout the journey from Beaconsfield, gazing serenely out of the window at the passing scenery as if he had never before seen fields, trees and clouds, or expected never to see them again. He had declined Bridget's offer to arrange for a solicitor to be present.

Not a wise move, in her opinion. Although she had nothing more than circumstantial evidence against Geoff Henderson, by the end of this interview she hoped to have something stronger.

With the preliminary introductions done and the recording machine switched on, Bridget started the interview by sliding the photograph of the whole cast and crew of *Twelfth Night* across the table towards him. 'Mr Henderson, do you recognise this photograph?'

The photograph elicited a smile. 'I haven't seen this for years.' He studied it carefully, a fondness at the memories it evoked apparent in his eyes. 'It was taken just before our last performance. Guy wanted something to remember it by.'

'And can you identify this person for me?' Bridget pointed to the young man on the back row of the photograph.

Henderson didn't need to look again at the photograph before answering. 'That's me.' There was an unmistakable note of pride in his voice. 'I was props manager.'

'Perhaps you could explain to us what that involved?' Images of skulls and bloody daggers sprang to mind but Bridget knew she was mixing up her Shakespeare plays. There were no daggers in *Twelfth Night*. Not during the performance, at least. She tried to think what props might be needed but came up blank.

'*Twelfth Night* uses a lot of props, or *property*, to give the correct word,' said Henderson. 'The term can refer to anything that's used onstage, apart from scenery and costumes.' He seemed more animated than she'd seen him before, younger somehow, as if talking about his student days had ignited a dream long since snuffed out. 'Candlesticks, wine bottles and glasses, a suitcase, the fraudulent letter to Malvolio, the letter that Malvolio writes to Olivia, the swords used in the duel between Sir Andrew Aguecheek and Viola when she's dressed as Cesario.' He smiled. 'Not real swords, of course.'

'You mentioned the character of Viola just now. She was played by Camilla Townsend.' Bridget tapped the picture of Camilla in the group photograph. 'Do you know what happened to her?'

'Yes,' said Henderson quietly. 'She went missing.'

'And are you aware that she was the girlfriend of David Smith, known latterly as Gordon Goole?'

'Yes. Although I didn't know what had happened to David after he dropped out of university. It was a complete surprise to discover that he was giving ghost tours in Oxford. If I'd known that, we would never have gone on the tour that evening. I thought it would be a bit of fun to round off the day. But it wasn't.'

'Can you tell me exactly what happened that day?'

'We'd come up to Oxford to collect Luke. As you know now, he was obliged to stay on for two weeks after term ended, to do some work. It was supposed to be a punishment for his misdemeanours with drugs, but from what he's told me, he rather enjoyed it. It's the first time he's actually done any kind of manual work. With hindsight, I think that Lynda and I have rather spoiled him. Lynda's very protective towards her children – perhaps over-protective.'

'So you were in Oxford to collect Luke.'

'Yes, and we decided to make a day of it. Last-minute Christmas shopping at the market, lunch out at Brown's, a matinée performance of the pantomime, then the ghost tour to round the evening off. I think Lynda wanted to make it up to Luke, and we both thought that it would be nice to spend some time together as a family. It didn't work out exactly as planned. Luke was resentful the whole time, and Lucy, our daughter, is at a difficult age. She would rather have been out with her friends. As it was, she spent the whole time with her nose glued to the screen of her phone. Even the visit to the theatre was a disaster. We'd have been better off going to see *West Side Story* at the New Theatre. But Lynda loves tradition, and she still thinks of the children when they were small and adored going to the panto, but they were both bored. So perhaps it shouldn't have been such a surprise that the ghost tour turned out to be a catastrophe too.'

'How did your son's friend, Dylan, end up being there?'

'We certainly didn't invite him along. But Luke told him, and he joined us next to the carousel at the start of the tour. I could hardly turn him away. I think that's perhaps where it all started to go wrong.'

'What do you mean?'

He smiled ruefully. 'David would probably never have known who I was if Dylan hadn't kicked up that fuss about ghosts being recorded in the stones, or whatever it was. But I drew attention to myself by getting involved in the argument. I wish I hadn't done that now.'

'So he recognised you?'

'Not at first. He had little reason to know who I was. Who remembers the props manager from a play? I wasn't like Julia. I could tell that David knew exactly who she was the instant that she and her two friends joined the tour. I recognised her immediately too, even though I hadn't set eyes on her for a quarter of a century. You can hardly miss Julia. She's a star, shining brightly in the firmament. Not like me, standing unnoticed in the shadows. That's how I've always been. A bystander. A nobody.'

'So David didn't recognise you at first. I assume that at some point he did.'

'It was in the pub. I noticed him giving me a curious look. He came up to me and said, "Don't I know you from somewhere?" But I denied it. I said I didn't think so. But it didn't completely satisfy him. Later he came looking for me.'

'When was this exactly?'

'Some time after Luke had gone off to meet Dylan. Lynda asked me to go and find him, so I went looking. But I didn't find Luke. Instead, David found me. He must have followed me when he saw me walking away, and he eventually cornered me near St Helen's Passage.'

Henderson had Bridget's full attention now, and she sensed him waiting for her next question as if he required a cue from her to proceed. She was happy to oblige him. 'What happened then?'

'He had finally realised who I was. He asked me if I was

the props guy for the performance of *Twelfth Night*. I admitted that I was. There was no point trying to deny it. He told me that Camilla sometimes used to talk about me. That was a shock. It was the first time in twenty-five years that anyone had spoken to me about her. I was scared about what might happen next. My reaction must have given away my feelings. Then I saw the look of realisation on his face and I knew that he'd guessed the truth.'

Jake stopped taking notes and looked up. The ticking of the clock on the wall seemed unnaturally loud. Bridget was aware of the blood pumping in her ears. 'What was the truth, Geoff?'

'I killed her. I killed Camilla Townsend.'

Bridget held her breath, hardly able to believe that it had been this easy to elicit a confession. But Geoff Henderson was clearly a man tormented by his past. His overwhelming emotion seemed to be relief that he could finally tell his story after holding it a secret for so long.

'David looked at me, and I knew that the game was up. He had no evidence, of course. But I could tell by the look in his eyes that he had guessed everything. If he went to the police, the investigation would be re-opened. I had sailed under the radar the first time, but I couldn't be certain that if the police interviewed me again they wouldn't find something. I couldn't take that risk. I had a wife and family depending on me. And so I killed him.'

'How?'

'There was a steak knife on a plate nearby. I grabbed it, and I stabbed him in the heart. It was far easier than I'd hoped. He went down without a struggle. He hardly even made a sound. I looked around, expecting someone to have seen, but no one had noticed. We were in the darkness of St Helen's Passage, and fortunately for me, there was no one else nearby at the time, otherwise I would have been caught immediately. And so I walked away and returned to my family. Luke was back too by then. I could scarcely believe that I'd got away with it.' He paused, lowering his gaze to the table.

This really was a first. Bridget had never had a suspect confess so easily to one murder, let alone two. 'So why are you telling us this now?'

'Because once Camilla's body was found, I knew that it was only a matter of time before you came to arrest me. You can't imagine what it's like living like that. I've spent most of my adult life in fear of being caught. With two deaths on my conscience, the burden's become too heavy. I just wanted to confess.'

Bridget didn't normally feel much sympathy for the perpetrators of crimes, but in this case she could imagine the strain that Henderson must have been under for all these years. She could understand that it was a relief for him to finally come clean.

'Let's talk about Camilla, now,' she said. 'What happened the night she vanished?'

Henderson took a deep breath before beginning his story. A faint smile played on his lips as he began to remember those far-off days.

'Camilla was beautiful. I fell completely in love with her. She wasn't like the other girls in the play. Julia, for example, was so wrapped up in herself that she never even gave me a second glance. For people like Julia Carstairs, the stage crew were nothing. As far as she was concerned, we existed solely to enable her to give a seamless performance. But Camilla was different. She appreciated my role in making the play possible. She knew that without the stage crew to support her and the rest of the cast, there wouldn't even be a play. She always thanked me when I gave her the right prop to go onstage. Camilla was kind.

'I think those weeks I spent behind the scenes preparing for *Twelfth Night* was the happiest time of my entire life. I'd always loved everything about the theatre – the actors, the costumes, the drama, the greasepaint, the camaraderie, the sense of a heightened reality, and now I was part of it. And for the two and a half hours of the performance nothing mattered except the play. Even when part of the scenery collapsed, or someone forgot their lines, there was always this sense that *the show must go on.*'

'You were telling us about Camilla,' prompted Bridget, steering him back on track before he lost himself entirely down memory lane.

'I didn't know at the time if she felt the same way about me as I felt about her. I knew that she'd been David's girlfriend, but they'd broken up before rehearsals for the play began. Some people whispered that she and Guy were sleeping together, but I never believed that. They were just malicious rumours. But I was too shy to say anything to her. I bided my time.'

'At this time in your life, you hadn't yet met Lynda?' queried Bridget.

Geoff frowned at the interruption. 'Actually, Lynda and I had been dating for a while, and we were happy together. But Camilla was very different to Lynda. She wasn't only beautiful, she was kind and gentle and considerate and had a way of making you feel special. She cast a kind of spell over me. Looking back, I think that I may have allowed myself to become rather deluded. Perhaps I mis-read her natural kindness as a come-on. But if she hadn't been so considerate, nothing more would ever have happened. You see, it was Camilla who insisted that I went to the party after the last performance. I wasn't planning to go. I was too shy and awkward to enjoy parties, but she said, "You are coming, aren't you Geoffrey? We couldn't have done the show without you." So I joined them all at Freud's.'

'Did Lynda go with you?'

'No. She didn't approve of my theatrical friends. She thought they were vain, and that I was wasting my time getting involved with them. And so I went to the party alone. Privately I was glad. I didn't want her to come with me. I wanted to be free, so I could see Camilla again.

'But almost as soon as I arrived, I realised I'd made a mistake. I didn't fit into that world, not really. I'd gained access to the circle by helping out with props, but apart from the other members of the stage crew, no one paid me any attention. The actors just wanted to hear how fantastic they'd been. I realised then that actors can be very insecure. They need their egos bolstering all the time. But Camilla was tired of people telling her how amazing she was. She left the party early and I followed her, thinking that was what she wanted. I offered to walk her home and she agreed.'

He paused to take a sip of water.

'Camilla lived in a shared student house in North Oxford,' he said. 'Lathbury Road. Next door was an abandoned house. Back then it wasn't as derelict as I believe it is now. Students used to go there for parties sometimes. I persuaded her to come into the garden with me, even though it was late and she said she was tired. But when I tried to kiss her she resisted. At first I thought she was just playing hard to get. After all, she'd let me walk her home, hadn't she? She'd gone into the garden with me. She must have known how I felt, and I thought she felt the same about me. So I kissed her harder and she screamed. Then I don't know what happened. I must have lost my mind. I stabbed her with a penknife I carried in my pocket. When I realised what I'd done I was horrified. She started to lose blood, and I tried to stop the wound, but it was useless. I was too scared to call for help. Instead I stayed by her side and watched her die. I can't explain my actions. Looking back, they weren't rational. But love isn't rational, is it? It's a kind of madness.'

A heavy silence hung in the room. For a while no one spoke. Geoff Henderson stared at the table. Beside Bridget, Jake was also motionless.

Bridget was enthralled and saddened by this confession. Geoffrey Henderson had clearly been a young man in the grip of a delusion that had caused him to commit a terrible crime. She wondered how many people were walking that fine line between reality and fantasy at any one time and how many of them could so easily slip onto the wrong side of the law. She waited for him to continue.

'I waited a while until I was certain that she was dead. Then a kind of cold certainty took over. It was self-preservation, I suppose. I broke into the house and dragged her body inside. I knew I had to hide the body. In one room I found a loose floorboard. I pulled it up and was able to lift some more boards using my knife. There was just enough space to slide her body into the hole. I tossed the knife in after her and replaced the loose boards. Then I ran away. I've been running every day since that night.'

CHAPTER 31

The interview with Geoff Henderson had come to a close. Bridget knew that Grayson would be delighted to hear of the positive outcome, but she wasn't yet ready to deliver the news to him. She drew Jake into an empty meeting room and closed the door.

Jake eyed her nervously. 'What's up, ma'am?'

'His story. Do you believe it?'

'Don't you, ma'am? He confessed easily enough, and it was a full and detailed confession.'

'Except that one of the details wasn't quite right.'

'The penknife.'

'Camilla wasn't stabbed with a penknife, and there was no penknife with her body. The murder weapon was a long-bladed kitchen knife.'

'It's a small detail. Perhaps when he said a penknife, he was confused.'

Bridget shook her head. 'He didn't sound confused, and he had a keen memory for props. He would never have made a mistake like that. Besides, a knife like the one that was found would be useless for prising up floorboards. You'd need a short-bladed knife.'

'Like a penknife.'

'Exactly. But no penknife was found at the scene.'

Jake frowned, his thick ginger eyebrows drawing together. He stroked his nose carefully. 'You think he's covering for someone?'

'Yes, I do.'

'Who?'

'The person he mentioned over and over again during the interview. The person he's sworn to protect. And the person he most fears to lose.'

'His wife. Lynda.'

'Exactly.'

'You think that she killed Camilla?'

'I think that's the part of the story he left out, or changed. Perhaps Lynda picked up on his infatuation with Camilla and became jealous. What if she waited outside the party and saw him leaving with Camilla. What might she have done?'

'Follow them?'

'Back to Camilla's house. And then, when she saw Geoff kissing Camilla in the grounds of the old house...' It wasn't necessary for Bridget to say any more.

Jake nodded. 'It's just speculation, of course, but it fits.'

'That's why Lynda was so jumpy when she opened the door to us this morning,' said Bridget. 'She wasn't afraid for her husband's sake. She thought we'd come for her. And she wasn't lying when she said that Geoff had nothing to do with these murders. We arrested the wrong person.'

★

This time a marked police car led the way to Beaconsfield, its blue lights flashing, clearing a path down the fast lane of the M40 motorway. Jake followed close behind, with Bridget in the passenger seat. They were accompanied in the back seat of the car by a female liaison officer whose job it would be to stay with Lucy and Luke after their mother had been arrested. Geoff remained in police custody for the present, while Bridget decided what to do with him. At this stage it wasn't clear whether he had merely been an accomplice to murder, or had actually committed the murder of David Smith himself. It would take some time to disentangle the web of lies and to clear a path to the truth.

But one fact remained certain in Bridget's mind. Geoff Henderson had not killed Camilla Townsend, but had lied to protect the real murderer. And the conclusion she had drawn was the only one possible. That it was Lynda who had murdered Camilla, in a fit of jealous rage.

The two cars pulled up in front of the gates leading to the Henderson's home, their blue lights still flashing. *Now the neighbours really will have something to talk about,* thought Bridget. Geoff's grey BMW was still parked on the driveway, and the lights in the house were all on, so it looked as if Lynda was still at home. Was she waiting anxiously for a phone call from her husband? Did she know that he'd intended to make a full confession for the crime or crimes that she'd committed? Bridget guessed that the couple had already discussed what they'd do if the police came calling. The fact that a steak knife had been used to stab David Smith had not been released to the press, so Geoff could only have known that detail if Lynda had told him, or if he had committed the murder himself.

Bridget strode up the driveway and rang the doorbell. The two burly officers who accompanied her were quite capable of forcing entry if necessary, but she fully expected Lynda to just open the door. Judging from the woman's behaviour so far, she would be loathe to give the neighbours anything more to gossip about.

'Inspector Hart,' said Lynda when the door opened. 'You're back again.' She looked over Bridget's shoulder and took in the sight of Jake and the uniformed officers. 'My husband isn't with you?'

'No,' said Bridget. 'I'm afraid that he will have to remain in custody for the time being.'

Lynda took the news in her stride, as if she'd been

expecting it. 'And now you'd like to speak to me. Well, you'd better come inside. It's very cold standing here, and there's no need for everyone to know our business, is there?' She cast a last glance out into the street, then ducked inside.

Bridget followed her into the kitchen along with Jake, while the liaison officer and the uniformed men waited in the hallway.

The chocolate cake that had been baking earlier now stood on a plate on the kitchen worktop and Lynda was in the process of covering it in a thick layer of chocolate icing. She calmly returned to her task, spreading the rich, dark topping with a palette knife.

Lucy and Luke sat at the kitchen table with empty plates before them. Their faces were clouded with anxiety, and it was obvious that they were fully aware that their father was in police custody. Luke in particular looked strained, and Bridget wondered what Lynda had told them.

'Mrs Henderson, perhaps the children should go into the lounge while we talk?' The last thing Bridget wanted to do was arrest their mother in front of them. This was going to be hard enough for them to deal with. They didn't have to see her being led away.

Lynda rounded on Bridget. 'They stay here,' she snapped in a voice that brooked no argument. 'Besides,' she continued, softening her voice, 'I promised them a slice of chocolate cake. It's their favourite. They like it just the way I bake it. Don't you, Lucy? Luke?' She smiled at her son and daughter who regarded her as if they hardly knew who she was.

'What's going on, Mum?' asked Luke. 'Where's Dad? Why are the police here?'

So Lynda clearly hadn't explained anything to them. Perhaps she was still in denial, pretending that nothing was wrong. For a woman like Lynda Henderson, who had dedicated her life to the pursuit of domestic perfection, the shock of what was now unfolding might simply be too much for her to deal with. The chocolate cake was a last desperate attempt to shore up the foundations of her world before it all came tumbling down.

She smoothed the last of the icing over the cake with a final flourish of her knife, and gave a self-satisfied smile. 'The police have come to arrest me,' she said, as if she were addressing two much younger children. Perhaps in her mind they were still small, still dependent on their mother. Bridget recalled how Chloe had been at a young age: affectionate, doting, attentive. She sometimes wished that she could wind back the clock to those happy days herself. But children grew up. They became independent. They drifted away from their parents.

'You see,' continued Lynda, 'once upon a time, when your father and I were students at Oxford, your father became besotted with another girl. She was a very silly girl: an actress. She was no good for your father, but he was too young and foolish to realise his mistake. He'd got it into his head that he belonged with these actors and actresses and their silly, self-indulgent world. But he didn't. He belonged with me.' She lifted the plate bearing the cake and brought it over to the kitchen table, where Luke and Lucy were transfixed with horror.

'And so I saved him from the mistake he was about to make. I killed that girl, and I rescued him from that world and gave him a nice, sensible life. I did it for love, you see. Your father needed to settle down and get a proper job. And that's what he did, and that's why we've all enjoyed such a happy life together.' She began to cut the cake.

Luke and Lucy had both turned pale at this revelation, so calmly delivered. Luke looked like he was about to be sick.

Bridget moved forward to intervene. 'Mrs Henderson, for your children's sake I really think it would be better if you would just come with us now and...'

The knife in Lynda's hand flashed bright. 'No!' she shrieked. 'You stay right where you are. You can wait five minutes for me to give my children this one last treat. You can't steal this moment away from me.'

Bridget stopped in her tracks, eyeing the knife nervously. Out of the corner of her eye she saw Jake circling around the table to position himself next to the children. The burly officers in the hallway had moved into the kitchen. Bridget waved them back, indicating that they should wait by the kitchen door. There was no point forcing a confrontation. Not when that knife was in Lynda's hand.

Lynda plunged the long blade of the knife into the soft cake with a decisive, firm stroke so that the iced sponge yielded with barely an indentation. Was that how she'd attacked Camilla Townsend? With a single-mindedness of purpose that left no room for mercy? Her eyes were fixed on the cake, not giving Bridget a glance.

When Lynda spoke again, her happy, mumsy voice was back as if nothing had happened. 'I just want to give my children one last slice of chocolate cake before I go away. One last act of a mother's love. Surely you can understand that, Inspector? After all, don't you have a daughter of your own? Wouldn't you want her to have fond memories of you if you had to go away and leave them?' She cut three generous slices of cake and lifted them onto the plates in front of Luke and Lucy, keeping one for herself. She didn't offer any to Bridget.

'I'm really not very hungry, Mum,' said Luke.

Lynda raised the knife again and her eyes flashed. 'Eat it!' she commanded. 'I've spent half my life looking after you and your sister. The least you can do is eat the food I make for you and be grateful. That's all I ever wanted, was to be appreciated.'

'Okay, Mum,' said Luke soothingly. 'Chill, yeah? We'll eat it.' He lifted the cake to his mouth and took a bite. Lucy followed.

'What about David Smith?' asked Bridget, unable to keep her curiosity at bay now that Lynda was in full confession mode. 'Did you kill him too?'

'Of course,' she said. 'I could tell that he'd recognised

Geoff. He didn't know me, but I knew who he was. And when I saw him walk after Geoff, I knew exactly what his intention was. He was going to accuse Geoff of murdering that actress. All this time, he'd had no reason to think that Geoff might have had anything to do with her death. Nobody did, not even the police. Geoff has never been in any kind of trouble. But I could see what Smith was planning. It was written all over his face.'

'He looked like he'd seen a ghost,' said Bridget.

'I daresay,' said Lynda, taking a bite out of the cake.

'Mum, this cake tastes odd,' said Lucy, chewing on her mouthful. 'I don't like it.'

'Don't talk with your mouth full,' snapped Lynda. 'There's nothing wrong with it. I made it especially for you. Now eat it.'

Bridget suddenly realised the danger.

'Stop!' She ran forward and knocked Lucy's plate from her hand. The china shattered on the floor, scattering splodges of chocolate cake in all directions. 'Don't touch any more,' she shouted at the children. 'Spit it out!'

Lucy drew back in alarm, turning wide eyes on Bridget.

Maybe she had gone mad. Maybe she'd completely overreacted and frightened the child for no good reason. But Bridget had just had a vision of another family that had appeared outwardly perfect but which was rotten to the core – or at least the parents were. On 1 May 1945, the day after Adolf Hitler killed himself, Joseph and Magda Goebbels had calmly poisoned their six children with cyanide before committing suicide themselves. Hitler's propaganda minister might have deserved his end, and no doubt his wife had too, but not their innocent children. The story served to bring home the fanaticism of the most devoted Nazis. And Lynda Henderson was nothing if not a fanatic.

She glared at Bridget with a look of pure bile on her face, then lunged forward with the knife.

Jake grabbed hold of her from behind and held her while one of the constables dashed forward and disarmed her. The second officer closed a pair of handcuffs over her struggling wrists.

'No!' she wailed.

'Gather that cake as evidence,' Bridget ordered Jake. 'But handle it carefully. I want it analysed in the lab for any kind of toxin. And we'd better get these children to a doctor, just in case.'

Then she turned to Lynda. 'Lynda Henderson, I am arresting you on suspicion of the murder of Camilla Townsend and David Smith.' She recited the words of the caution on auto-pilot. The whole business had left her badly shaken. But it was over now.

Lynda offered no resistance as she was led away.

By now Luke was on his feet with one protective arm around his sister. He walked her to the front door, looking more confident and grown up than Bridget had ever seen him. As his mother was bundled into the back of the police car he called after her, 'You really are the worst mother possible. We deserved better. And so did Dad.'

CHAPTER 32

A few loose ends remained in the case, but routine police work quickly cleared them up.

The toxicology report found that the cake Lynda had attempted to feed to Luke and Lucy had been poisoned with sleeping pills. A search of the house had revealed several empty packets of Valium in the kitchen waste, which Geoff Henderson confirmed belonged to his wife. According to the lab report, the tablets had been ground into a fine powder and mixed into the icing of the cake. The sugar in the icing had served to disguise their flavour, but hadn't been enough to completely conceal the bitter aftertaste that Lucy had noticed.

Thank goodness the girl had mentioned it. Bridget dreaded to think what might have happened if the children had eaten it without complaint. Each slice of cake had contained more than twice the lethal dose of sleeping pills.

After Geoff Henderson learned of his wife's arrest, and in particular the way she had tried to poison herself and the children, he quickly changed his story, eager to put as much distance between himself and her as possible. He was released from custody after further questioning, although Grayson was still considering bringing charges against him for giving false information.

Bridget hoped he wouldn't. The children needed their father now more than ever.

Geoff's original confession had been accurate in all but one respect. In each case, the hand that plunged the knife into the victim's body had been Lynda's, not his. He hadn't even been present when Camilla Townsend had been stabbed to death. He had left her immediately after the party, after she'd refused his advances. It was Lynda who had followed her all the way to Lathbury Road, killed her, and concealed her body beneath the floor of the old house. She had confessed her crime to Geoff the following day, but hadn't given him a detailed account of how it was done. Hence the discrepancy between his story and the facts.

But there were no further anomalies. The double investigation had been concluded, and the culprit charged on two accounts of murder. Bridget was satisfied; Grayson was pleased.

Camilla's parents had finally been reunited with their daughter, following the positive identification of her skeleton from dental records. Now her remains could be returned to her home town for burial. Bridget had met with them, and had been impressed by their dignity, and their stoicism. They had waited more than twenty-five years for their daughter to come home.

Luke Henderson had announced his intention not to return to Oxford when the new term began.

'It's strange,' he told Bridget. 'Before this happened, I was desperately unhappy, but I couldn't see any way out. Mum and Dad had always put so much pressure on me to live the life that they wanted me to have, it was making me depressed. I knew that I didn't want to become like Dad, working behind a desk for long hours, doing the office politics, constantly pushing towards the next promotion, the next pay rise, the next rung on the ladder. But I didn't have the courage to say no to them. It was easier just to go along with their plans, no matter how miserable it made me. That's why I got into drugs, I suppose. It was a way to escape reality for a while and make everything bearable. But that was wrong.'

'So what will you do now?' asked Bridget.

A smile lit up his face, the first time she'd seen him look genuinely animated. 'The problem was that although I knew what I didn't want – a steady job, a mortgage, a pension – I wasn't sure what I actually did want. But hearing how Dad was so into the theatre when he was my age was a real eye-opener. I'd never imagined him doing anything like that. He'd always been the grey, boring accountant. So it's kind of given me permission to follow my dreams.'

'You're not going into the theatre, are you?' asked Bridget.

He laughed. 'No. That was Dad's dream, but it's not mine. I discovered what I really enjoyed when I had to stay on at college at the end of term. It was supposed to be hard labour, working outdoors on the college grounds, but in fact I loved it. So I'm going to go to the local college of further education and train to be a groundsman. With any luck, I'll be able to get an apprenticeship with New College. After all, I know the head groundsman now.'

'It's a bit of a change from a Law degree,' remarked Bridget. 'What does your father think about your plans?'

'Well, after all that's happened, he hardly has a right to object, does he?'

'I suppose not.'

'But in fact he thinks it's a great idea. He can see the value in training for a job and getting paid while I study, instead of just clocking up a huge student debt for a career I don't even intend to follow. As an accountant, he approves. In fact, me and Dad are getting on better than we have done for years. It's weird to say this, but Mum trying to kill us all and then getting arrested for murder has finally brought the family together.'

'I'm glad to hear it,' said Bridget. 'And I wish you all

the best.'

Jake and Ffion were also getting on much better than they had been in recent months, and Bridget was relieved. She wouldn't need to broach the awkward subject of asking one of them to transfer to another department. The danger of losing one of her best detectives had been averted.

But reflecting on the matter had led her to an awkward conclusion. Although she was fully aware that the rift between them had been due to their romantic break-up, she wondered if their difficulties might have been lessened if she'd taken a more proactive interest in their welfare. She'd never been very comfortable handling sensitive issues with her juniors, but she wanted them to know how much she appreciated them, and she was determined to do better in that regard in the future.

She would make it one of her New Year's resolutions to be a better boss – as well as to be a better mother, sister, daughter, and lover. What else was on her list? Oh yes, to cook healthier meals, to lose fourteen pounds in weight, to read more books, to keep to regular appointments at the hairdresser's and to swim twice a week. The same list as last year.

But she'd begin with trying to be a better boss.

She decided to start with Jake.

He was just putting the phone down when she arrived at his desk. He seemed pleased by whatever he'd just heard. 'That was Harvard,' he told her.

'The faculty dean?'

'Yes. He wanted to give me the latest news. It seems that Trevor Mansfield is in the clear. Following the Christmas holiday, the student who had made a complaint against him decided to withdraw her allegations. As a result, the university is dropping its investigation into his conduct and is going to reinstate him in time for the beginning of the new term. So he'll be returning to his teaching post in the New Year.'

'I'm pleased to hear that,' said Bridget. Despite all her

suspicions, she'd always felt a certain sympathy for the mild-mannered lecturer, and had been relieved when he'd been cleared of the two murders. Now he and his mother would be able to emerge from beneath the long shadow cast by past events and move on with their lives, their consciences clear. Cheryl, too, would be able to return to Cambridge, Massachusetts, with her husband's reputation restored.

'Now,' continued Bridget, 'you ought to take some time off. I ruined your Christmas break by calling you back to Oxford. Why don't you go back to Leeds and spend some time with your family?'

'Actually, ma'am, I don't think I really need to get away. I've done Christmas, and I'm keen to move on. Perhaps I'll save my days off for the summer. I was thinking I might go abroad next year. I've never really travelled much. In the past I've always gone back up north when I've had time off. But the world's a big place, isn't it?'

'It certainly is,' said Bridget.

She moved on to Ffion, who seemed equally upbeat. 'Got any plans for the New Year? I'm afraid that your Christmas got ruined this year.'

'Oh, I don't know,' said Ffion. 'Digging up a skeleton in a haunted house was a pretty cool way of spending my day off.'

Bridget raised an inquisitive eyebrow, trying to work out if Ffion was being serious or joking, but the DC's expression gave nothing away. 'But you won't be working on New Year's Day. I'm going to insist on that.'

'No need to insist,' said Ffion. 'I've already booked a few days off. There's something I want to do.'

It was tempting to ask what, but Bridget knew where to draw the line between being a proactive boss and becoming a nosey parker. She left Ffion to her work.

Back at her own desk, she allowed herself a moment to reflect on what would happen to the other people caught up in the case.

Hopefully Julia Carstairs was fully reconciled with Liz and Deborah, and they had managed to salvage something of their interrupted holiday.

No doubt Guy Goodwin was already back in the theatre, yelling at his cast, his dark eyes flashing. Perhaps his starring actress had recovered her voice and was back on stage. That would certainly help to lower the temperature during rehearsals. Bridget might make a point of getting hold of some tickets for the show herself. It would be a welcome treat for her, Chloe and Jonathan, and she was due some time off after working so hard over Christmas. But somehow she didn't think that Guy would be offering her complimentary tickets. If she did go to a show, she'd be careful to keep well out of his way.

Her one cause for sadness was the untimely demise of David Smith, aka Gordon Goole. She'd taken a shine to the tour guide and his theatrical manner. He had been an unwitting victim in this whole sorry episode. How ironic that he had finally worked out who had murdered Camilla, only seconds before that person had turned her knife against him. He had never had the satisfaction of seeing justice served. But if there was any compensation to this tragic story, it was that his death had been the catalyst for finally solving the mystery of Camilla's disappearance, and bringing her killer to trial. If the ghost of Gordon Goole lived on, Bridget hoped that his spirit would not be vengeful and unquiet, but might instead have found some peace.

CHAPTER 33

It was New Year's Eve, and Ffion was heading away from Oxford, along the M4, the motorway that provided the main link between London and South Wales. The traffic was busy as always at this time of year, and there had already been a couple of hold ups and delays. But her Kawasaki Ninja was the perfect vehicle for such moments. Ffion weaved the bike through the gaps between lanes, passing frustrated drivers to left and right.

It was growing dark by the time she reached the Prince of Wales Bridge, or as everyone called it, the Severn Bridge. The long suspension bridge that crossed the River Severn marked the border between Wales and England. It had been a long time since she'd crossed it. Now, as she drove over the wide river estuary, and felt the cold wind blow in from the sea, she realised that her return to her home country was long overdue.

It was Siân's persistence that had finally persuaded her to make the journey. When her sister made up her mind about something, she was a force to be reckoned with, and she had determined that Ffion would come back to Wales for the New Year's celebrations, come what may. Ffion had resisted at first, but her recalcitrance had proved futile.

'You have to come,' Siân had insisted. 'I've already told Owen and Arwen, and if you don't show up they'll be dreadfully disappointed.'

'That's emotional blackmail,' said Ffion, but after observing what a truly dysfunctional family looked like, in the form of the Hendersons, she had realised that perhaps hers wasn't quite as bad as she'd thought.

The bike pushed on into South Wales, past Newport and Cardiff, before turning off the motorway and up into the Rhondda Valley. It was fully dark now, and the ranks of green mountains that lined the route rose dark and massive around her. But she knew this place like the back of her hand. Eventually she turned off the main road and into Clydach Vale, and began to wind her way up the narrow valley.

The twinkling lights of miners' cottages beckoned up ahead. No miners lived here anymore, of course. The collieries were all closed. The valley had long since moved on from its industrial past. Ffion, too, having resolved her differences with Jake, was in the mood for resolution. Perhaps people did deserve a second chance.

She slowed as she entered the village, passing row upon row of identical terraced houses, their front doors giving directly onto the street. Many were brightly lit with Christmas lights and decorations, and a warm glow seeped out from behind closed curtains. She was nearly home.

The house was at the far end of the village. Beyond it the road came abruptly to an end, the green grass of the mountainside rising directly upwards from the street. A house like every other in the village.

And yet it was different.

There was just enough space for her to leave the Kawasaki on the pavement. She switched off the headlamp and reached into her pocket. The key to the front door was still on her key ring, unused for years. But when she slid it into the lock it turned just as easily as it always had. She pushed the door open and stepped into the warmth of the house.

'Hello, Mam, hello, Dad!' she called. 'It's me, Ffion. I'm home.'

★

Bridget's alarm went off at nine am, ringing loudly in her ears. She'd stayed up late the night before with Jonathan, welcoming in the New Year at the local pub in Wolvercote. At midnight, the entire pub had disgorged its occupants, and they had joined together on the village green to sing Auld Lang Syne.

Chloe had returned shortly afterwards, dropped off by Alfie in his car. 'Don't worry, Mum,' Chloe had reassured her. 'Alfie didn't have anything to drink. I was perfectly safe.'

Now a hangover was beginning to brew in Bridget's head, but she pushed the duvet away and slid out of bed. It was New Year's Day, a time for new beginnings, and a time for making promises. Bridget had already made one promise, and she intended to keep it.

'I'll see you later,' she told a still-sleepy Jonathan.

Miraculously, Chloe was already in the kitchen by the time Bridget arrived downstairs. She was nibbling on a slice of toast, her phone in one hand, thumbing idly at the keyboard. She put it down when Bridget appeared. 'Ready to go, Mum?'

Bridget considered the possibility of having breakfast, but quickly dismissed it. Her stomach wasn't yet in a fit state to receive food, and if she was going to shed those pounds, then it was best to start the year as she meant to go on. 'I'm ready,' she said. 'Let's go.'

During the small hours a thin covering of snow had fallen, and the grass and rooftops of Wolvercote were iced white. The roads were clear, however, and largely empty of traffic this early on the first morning of the year. It didn't take long for them to reach Vanessa's.

Her sister opened the door to her, all ready to go.

Bridget's parents were waiting patiently in the front room, sitting together on the sofa, already dressed for winter in hat, scarf and gloves.

They drove in Vanessa's Range Rover, Bridget's father in the front passenger seat, Bridget sitting in the back with her mother and Chloe. James remained behind to look after the children. Soon they were in Woodstock, the town where Bridget and Vanessa had grown up. The town that their parents had fled after Abigail's death, but where Abigail herself now rested.

The church of St Mary Magdalene looked as charming as a picture postcard, dusted with snow, its square tower as solid and immutable in real life as it was in Bridget's memory. Yellow stone glimmered softly against the metal grey of the sky. In a tree a blackbird began to sing as they walked the short distance together into the churchyard behind the building.

A smooth blanket of white covered the space between the headstones, smothering all signs of life. Yet Bridget knew that already the first primroses were in bloom, encased within tiny crystals of ice. Soon snowdrops and crocuses would emerge, and a carpet of colour would roll across the ground where snow now lay. A robin sang, perched in a holly tree, watching as they made their way between the stones. The bright red berries matched the bird's red breast, making a striking contrast against the green, white and grey backdrop.

When they reached Abigail's grave, Bridget dropped back, allowing her parents to take the lead. She bowed her head in silence as they stood, hand in hand, reading the familiar inscription on the headstone. Chloe stepped forward and kneeled beside the grave, laying a small posy of winter flowering jasmine next to the headstone. The bright yellow flowers seemed almost to glow in the pale January light.

Then Bridget's mother offered her hand, and Bridget took it, gripping it tightly, glove to glove. Chloe took her other hand and Vanessa linked arms with their father.

They stood together, in mute contemplation. No words were necessary. The family was united in understanding, and a shared sense of loss.

The barrier that had divided them for so long had finally been breached.

Afterwards, Bridget saw that Chloe's eyes were shining with tears. 'I wish I'd known Aunt Abigail,' she said. 'And I wish that I'd got to know Grandma and Grandpa better when I was growing up.'

'I think,' said Bridget, 'that you'll be seeing more of them in the future. In fact, I promise that we'll make an effort to visit them soon.'

'I'd like that.'

'And while we're on the topic of reconciliation,' she continued, 'I'm sorry that I was so angry with you when I found out that you had a boyfriend. I shouldn't have made such a fuss. It just came as a shock, that's all. But I'm sure that if you've chosen him, then he's a very nice boy.'

'He is, Mum. You'd like him.'

'Well, in that case I think that it's about time that you introduced him to me properly.'

Her suggestion was met by an awkward silence. Then Chloe said, 'All right. I'll bring him round some time.'

'That would be nice.'

'But Mum,' said Chloe, 'just promise me one thing.'

'What's that?'

'Try not to be too embarrassing.'

'I'll do my best.'

Bridget was making a lot of promises at the moment, both to herself and to others. This latest one, however, might prove to be the trickiest to keep.

Back at Vanessa's, Jonathan had arrived, and he and James had rustled up a baked salmon for lunch, adhering to Vanessa's strict instructions. Bridget's hangover had cleared in the sharp cold air and she was more than ready for a hearty meal. The salmon was accompanied by a crisp, dry white, and followed by sticky toffee pudding. Bridget poured hot custard over hers, and set to work devouring it.

Calories? They surely didn't count on New Year's Day itself. There would plenty of time for sticking to resolutions in the future. Right now, life was good, and Bridget intended to make the most of it.

PREFACE TO MURDER
(BRIDGET HART #6)

A dangerous book. A hidden secret. A deadly betrayal.

The Oxford Literary Festival is in full swing, but Detective Inspector Bridget Hart isn't there to learn about books. Instead she's been given the task of protecting Diane Gilbert, a controversial author who has received a death threat. Diane doesn't seem to think she needs Bridget's protection, but when the worst happens, Bridget's role switches to running a murder enquiry.

The only clues Bridget has to go on relate to Diane's new book which examines the murky world of international arms deals. Under pressure to identify the killer, Bridget finds herself drawn into the clandestine world of foreign governments and the British Security Service. She'll need all her wiles and the full cooperation of her team to follow the twisting trail of evidence to its logical conclusion.

Set amongst the dreaming spires of Oxford University, the Bridget Hart series is perfect for fans of Elly Griffiths, JR Ellis, Faith Martin and classic British murder mysteries.

 Scan the QR code to see a list of retailers.

THANK YOU FOR READING

We hope you enjoyed this book. If you did, then we would be very grateful if you would please take a moment to leave a review online. Thank you.

BOOKS IN THE
BRIDGET HART SERIES:

Aspire to Die (978-1-914537-00-4)
Killing by Numbers (978-1-914537-02-8)
Do No Evil (978-1-914537-04-2)
In Love and Murder (978-1-914537-06-6)
A Darkly Shining Star (978-1-914537-08-0)
Preface to Murder (978-1-914537-10-3)
Toll for the Dead - Due Oct 2021

PSYCHOLOGICAL THRILLERS

The Red Room

ABOUT THE AUTHOR

M S Morris is the pseudonym for the writing partnership of Margarita and Steve Morris. They both studied at Oxford University, where they first met in 1990. Together they write psychological thrillers and crime novels. They are married and live in Oxfordshire.

Find out more at msmorrisbooks.com where you can join our mailing list.

Manufactured by Amazon.ca
Bolton, ON